Lies, Spies and Nuclear RISE

Lies, Spies and Nuclear RISE

—a novel

Juggi Bhasin

Vitasta

Published by
Renu Kaul Verma
Vitasta Publishing Pvt Ltd
4348/4C, Ansari Road, Daryaganj
New Delhi - 110002
info@vitastapublishing.com

ISBN: 978-81-988295-4-2

First Edition 2025

MRP ₹ 495

Layout by Shubhpreet Kaur
Cover Design by Smriti Maheshwari
Printed by Vikas Computer and Printers, New Delhi

To the people who matter the most in my life—my wife, Sonu; my son, Karan; and the newest member of our small family, my daughter-in-law, Kshamta.

Contents

Chapter 1

Priya Kaul woke up feeling she was burning in a desert—her lips cracked, throat parched and her tongue uselessly licking serrations on her lips hoping for some moist traction. There was none. Her fingertips were ice-cold, and she could make no sense of where she was. She felt suspended like water drops on a leaf, poised to fall, yet unable to do so, stuck at the tipping edge. A sense of control had defined her life. So far. Maybe now she had lost it. Could she have lost the use of her limbs? Or, a stroke or a heart attack was wasting her?

She was Priya Kaul. For the people of India, she was a goddess incarnate. A woman who lived life on her own terms in a world of men. The look of her arched eyebrows expressing displeasure, a stretch of her saree *pallu* firmly around her head; even her deadpan looks behind black, oversized sunglasses were enough to send a chill through the most indomitable of spirits. It is said that even the

United States President, supposedly the most powerful man on the planet, was subjected to that unique, Priya Kaul-belt-treatment in a closed door meeting with her. And what was his fault? He had the audacity to threaten and dominate her with humiliating demands.

But now at 3 in the night in her home, she was in a paroxysm of night terror. The vestiges of her ruthless dominating self becoming a distant memory. And yet, purely from that old reflex she managed to throw the covers off the bed. And struggled to get to the door.

The gilded mirror was next to the door. The curtains were slightly parted, and moonlight coming in through the French windows illuminated the mirror. She looked at the mirror and saw an old woman, face drawn, eyes hollowed out. She screamed from the depths of her soul and sank to her knees shivering.

It was her. *She* was the face in the mirror. This is what she had been reduced to. An old, terrified, out of control woman living life on the edge.

She crawled on all fours to the bed switch and switched on the table lamp. She slumped near the bed, her head staring vacuously at the ceiling. She lay in that posture for a while and then she willed herself to get up and walk out the door.

She was Priya Kaul. She was feared and respected by all. There were no other words to describe her. And yet, she was at the far end of the world, lost, confused, and fearful like she had never been before.

The house lay in semi-darkness. Corner table lamps dimly lit up the rectangular drawing room, throwing funnel-shaped shadows on the walls. She stumbled on her way to the small refrigerator next to the dining table. She opened the Frigidaire and took out a vodka bottle tucked in between a row of cold water bottles.

Bottle in hand, she looked for a glass from the crockery shelf and a chair at the dining table. She sat for the next half an hour downing three stiff vodka shots. She began to feel more composed and in control of her emotions. She was thinking properly. It was not some crippling heart attack that had unsettled her. She could no longer manage the stress and strain of her eventful life. Good news was at a premium. Bad news never came in driblets.

She got on a line, euphemistically called RAX (restricted automatic exchange) by the Intelligence Bureau. There was a click and her man for all seasons, of night and day—Narang, answered.

'Madam.'

She heard his flat tone, the unchanging acknowledgement, and once again felt hopeful and connected to the world. Despite her panicked state, she thought of Narang. He never changed. He had the unique gift of always remaining the same. His reassuring voice came on the phone, and she felt better. It was as if his existence was defined by waiting for the phone to ring from her end. Even at 3 in the night.

'Narang, I cannot sleep.'

'I am here, Madam. Tell me what you need?'

She thought for a moment and then asked him about the rally Tapash had held in Patna earlier that day. The conservative news agency PTI (Press Trust of India) had given a figure of 3 lakh people. That many people had turned up to listen to Tapash to rant and rave against her. But the government held a significant stake in the news agency. She knew from experience that the numbers had been sanitised. But Narang would know. He always knew. He always had his ear to the ground. She asked him for the real number.

Narang hesitated for a second. Then he replied in his flat monotone.

'It would be closer to twice that number, Madam.'

Her breath was taken away. She was finally beginning to understand what lay at the bottom of her fears. She pressed on.

'What else? Where is it all leading to?'

Narang again hesitated. Then he answered pithily.

'Total revolution. He's given a call for that. An uprising of students all over the country against your government. And he no longer plans to be confined to Bihar. He's coming to Delhi. He plans a massive rally at Ramlila Maidan….'

Priya Kaul switched off. So, the enemy was at the gates.

Oddly, she was beginning to feel calm, more controlled, like her own self. She was an old woman in the mirror, but there was still enough fight left in her. She thought of herself as a plane hurtling to the ground heading for a crash. And then, the plane miraculously kissed the surface, and the wings lifted with new, inexplicable force to meet the sky. That was her of late. Touch and go, touch, and go.

And then, the calm of the night outside shattered. Something had happened. There was a crashing noise at the gates, a car horn blared incessantly, the searchlights came on and the guard dogs barked uncontrollably.

The powerful searchlights on the terrace picked up an ambassador sedan that had crashed into the gate at the driveway. The car headlight was broken, and the bonnet of the sedan was crumpled up from the impact. The engine was still running as Prahlad emerged from the driver's seat sodden with drink. The door to the sedan opened from the other side and a girl in a mini, the cut of her dress just above the knees, with cultivated long hair, emerged and ran towards Prahlad to steady him.

Priya Kaul squinted in the night light. A girl in a mini at the Prime Minister's residence. That must be a first. She had heard of the mini. Wasn't it a piece of clothing worn by the bohemian film and modelling crowd in that Bombay suburb of Bandra?

The girl in the mini steadied her drunk son, their arms laced into each other. The security staff were slinking in the corners, keeping a safe distance after reading the stay-away expression on the Prime Minister's face.

The girl walked across the porch, half dragging, half escorting Prahlad. He was blabbering incoherently. Priya Kaul noticed a half smile, a condescending look lurking on the girl's face. A flash of anger seized Priya at the spectacle unfolding before her.

The girl came up and announced.

'Prahlad had too much to drink today. He's not like this usually.'

'I will take it from here,' the Prime Minister replied curtly as she took possession of her son.

The sweep of the searchlight moving left to right lit up the girl momentarily and Priya Kaul shuddered when she recognised her. Wasn't the girl a well known model who draped towels, skimpy skirts or other similar wear, for the back covers of gossip and film magazines?

What had Prahlad got himself into?

Priya Kaul saw in her mind her plane crashing into a wasteland, breaking up into two and then going up in a ball of flames. It was then she knew she had finally reached the bottom of her fears. Chaos was spreading in her world, within and without.

★★★

Chapter 2

The new storm troopers of the party were shouting slogans in support of their leader Prahlad Kaul outside the gates of the Prime Minister's residence. These new entrants in the party had no patience for the subtle back room power games of the old elite in the party. The methods of the new lot were completely different. They were loud, abrasive and impatient to achieve results, even if it meant indulging in violence. The new lot was drawn from all walks of life—from slums, lower middle-income backgrounds, failed college student activists and even the dissatisfied sons and daughters of the current political dispensation and elite. They all found a common cause in Prahlad's leadership who, ironically, was the most entitled of the lot.

Seated at the dining table inside the most important house in the country, Prahlad liberally applied butter to toast. He thoughtfully crunched a piece of toast and took a sip of orange juice. At the other end of the table, Priya Kaul drank her morning coffee, dressed for the day. She carefully observed her son. Bespectacled, with long sideburns and thinning hair, he could easily pass off as a conscientious lecturer aspiring for a college job. She knew better though. A core of ruthlessness resided in him. He had a wild strain in him that was frightening at one level. Her family line was known for polite, gentlemanly behaviour. When she burst upon the political scene, she surprised everyone with her bold and tough decision-making. It had certainly been a first. But her son put all that in the shade. His trademark callous behavior and contempt for social niceties, rules and order was well known to everyone. Who did he take after? Silence reigned at the dinner table. She opened a conversation. 'What happened last night?'

'I don't care to talk about it,' he snapped.

His opening move. She knew the flow of the conversation. It had been like this for months, ever since he had assumed the role of the youth wing of her party. He was always short with her. She tried again.

'No need to be angry. You are my son. If I won't be worried about your safety who will be? It is not a pretty sight when the future leader of the country drives home drunk, nearly crashing a car, arm in arm with some…cheap model!'

He sharply looked up.

'Watch your words, mother! That cheap-looking model could just become your daughter-in-law very soon.' Priya almost spilled her coffee.

'Are you crazy?'

Prahlad Kaul pushed his plate with some deliberation and got up.

'I have said it before, and I will say it again. You are growing old, mother. Your decision-making is clouded. You really need to start thinking how to ease me in your chair.'

Priya could not keep the tightness out of her voice.

'I do whatever I do for you. That is my goal also. But we are not a bloody feudal monarchy that I can give you the baton so easily. Make your role as the head of the youth wing of the party count. Then, we shall see. Till then I have a country to run.'

'And I have a party to change in my own image,' he replied ruthlessly. He walked away to the patio, and his followers, some of whom had spilled on to the green lawn outside, raised a din in his support.

He suddenly turned and shouted across the hall.

'Weren't you supposed to go to Moscow tonight?'

She looked up and nodded wearily.

'Okay, then let me give you my shopping list. Ask Narang to pick up two cases of Stoli vodka for me. And a Matryoshka doll for Kamini. That's the girl you saw last night. Kamini likes kinky things. And nothing kinkier than a Matryoshka doll.'

He went out, and Priya closed her eyes and slumped in her chair. Her life was in a loop. No exit.

There was still some of the day left before she boarded her flight for Moscow late in the evening. Narang was already in the house, in his one-room anteoffice, preparing her schedule for the day. He could as well be a piece of comfortable furniture in her life. If he fell ill, even for a day, she would be out of sorts.

She opened her eyes and Narang materialised with a sheaf of papers in his hands.

'Madam....'

She shook her head silencing him and issued new orders.

'I won't be going to the office. Cancel my meetings for the day. Call Rhino. Tell him to meet me on the lawn in an hour. And Narang, could you pack it for me? I just don't have energy. *Kanjeevarams* and *Banarasi* silks for the official talks, the banquet, and then the evening out at the Bolshoi. The lingerie is in the third drawer in the walk-in closet. Not the usual place though. And pack in some extra layers and woolies. I don't want to freeze to death in Moscow.'

Narang, her man for all seasons and occasions, nodded and disappeared to do her bidding. She closed her eyes wearily for a short shut-eye.

The man in a dark grey suit, next to the Safdarjung runway, stamped his feet and rubbed his hands vigorously to keep the cold away. He watched nervously as the Cessna 150, a two-seater aircraft, plunged towards the ground from a height, then sharply banked to the left, went up again and did two rolls against a backdrop of a bright blue, cold sky. The man felt almost compelled to take out his cigarette pack and light one up. What if his boss crashed the Cessna performing his daredevilry stunts? The Cessna was not a theme park ride for boisterous children. And certainly not a suitable ride for a seventy-two-year-old geriatric, a legend in his lifetime as a spymaster.

The man in the plane was Sudhir Raina, also known as Rhino, the boss of all intelligence agencies in the country. He was known as a man of taciturn nature and measured speech. He had survived smallpox in his childhood and his expressionless, pockmarked face and probing eyes never gave anything away. The man was a chain-smoker. Throughout his career, he had been saddled with various adjectives and expressions. The most common being 'the power behind the throne' and the 'keeper of the Ice Maiden's secrets'. The same man was the second most powerful person in the country after Priya Kaul.

Only Rhino really knew who he truly was. A child out to play in the blue skies with his inseparable toy, the Cessna 150. He was fiercely loyal and protective of Priya Kaul. He could walk on water for her.

The wheels of the Cessna finally touched the tarmac, and the man in the grey suit edged closer. Seeing him approach, Rhino knew urgent summons had come from the Prime Minister.

A little later, Rhino stepped on the lawns of 7, Race Course Road and greeted her in Kashmiri.

'Tsawutukh chukh, Priya?' (How are you?)

'Have been better,' she replied tiredly.

In the unwritten rules of engagement, Rhino was allowed an initial note of affection. After all, both were Kashmiri Brahmins; their families had known each other from Ganderbal in Kashmir, and Rhino, many years her senior, had watched her grow up over the years as a woman of substance.

They settled down in cane chairs and Priya came to the point.

'Rhino, I feel cornered in. I feel a weakness coming over me. It is new and not a very nice feeling. I cannot sleep at nights.'

Rhino's brow creased.

'Yes, Prime Minister,' he joined in. 'I have also noticed, of late you have been…kind of…unsettled. Anything particular on your mind?'

'Everything, Rhino. I am coming unstuck. I called you to give me the true picture. Give me the lay of the land.'

Rhino drew her a picture in measured tones. A true picture with no padded-up narration. The economy was tanking and prices were soaring; socialist policies and unreasonable labour laws made the situation terrible. The military was short of critical equipment; the citizenry at large was running out of patience. Student unrest could just not be contained. But she knew all that. She wanted more. She pressed him for something more that had escaped their attention.

Rhino replied.

'I have done an extensive sweep of your cabinet colleagues and their close friends. Nothing out of the ordinary there.'

Her expression changed. Her eyes had a haunted look.

'You disappoint me, Rhino. Do you not know how some of them plot and plan behind my back? They pretend to be my colleagues; they swear undying loyalty to me but some of them sheath knives to be taken out at the right time. The real question is: which one of them is it? The country's parameters could not have gone down so drastically without reason. I know they are in cahoots with the CIA (Central Intelligence Agency). The American President, Fielding, cannot stand the sight of me. Even as we speak, he could be plotting an assassination attempt against me....'

Rhino hesitated before responding.

'That may or may not be true. The United States President is beset with problems of his own. The Vietnam War is sapping American resolve, and a phone tapping scandal is seriously troubling Fielding. Maybe there are other reasons for the downturn?'

Priya Kaul looked animated.

'Are you becoming a fool in old age, Rhino? Have you

taken your eyes off the ball? Should I start looking for another intelligence chief who looks after my interests? I know all about your daily morning Cessna joyrides and endless supply of imported Chesterfield cigarettes. You want that fancy lifestyle to disappear?'

The imperial arch of her eyebrows was back again, and Rhino knew the meeting was over.

He politely got up to take his leave, but Priya Kaul stopped him in his tracks.

'One more thing. If you choose to stay, get me intel on this girl called Kamini. The one my son is dating. As soon as possible.'

★★★

Chapter 3

A snowstorm at night-time in Moscow changed Priya Kaul's plans. Sheremetyevo airport had shut down. Her delayed flight would not land until well past noon the next day. By the time her aircraft took off from Delhi, en route to Moscow, the sun was out in that city even when it was bone-chilling cold. The snow around the main runway had been cleared away in anticipation of Priya Kaul's visit. The Air India special plane piloted by Indian Air Force pilots, approached the main runway, and Priya noticed something unusual about the reception ceremony awaiting her on the ground. Priya was no stranger to Moscow. It was one of her favorite cities to visit. She was well versed with the official reception during state visits. But as her plane dipped its wings, it was clear to her that the red carpet laid out in her honour was longer than usual. The Gvardiya tri-services guard of honour standing in the cold near the tarmac looked fit and certainly elite.

And the entire area was crammed with children wearing traditional Sarafan and Poneva with striped shirts, and waving India-Soviet Union flags; their faces lit up. A stunning beauty stood a little apart, holding a basket of Khleb-sol, a kind of bread and salt offering.

Priya's spirits soared as she saw the reception entourage whiz past her as her plane kissed the tarmac. Something was up. She was being given more than special treatment. Almost on cue, Narang, who sat behind her, came up and whispered in her ear.

'The pilot has just informed me that Chairman Fyodor Miroslav will personally receive you at the airport. It is a rare honour, Madam. He seldom does that.'

Priya Kaul permitted herself a rare smile. Maybe things were not so bad. Maybe the answers to her existential dilemma lay in Moscow.

On the ground, Miroslav greeted her with repeated bear hugs and kisses on her cheeks. He whispered conspiratorially in her ear.

'You grow more beautiful every time I see you, Priya.'

'And you are such a flirt,' responded Priya, suppressing a laugh.

With the official ceremonies over, Chairman Miroslav insisted that Priya take a ride with him in his personal ZIL limousine. It was the longest, the most expensive and the best protected car in Moscow. As the car sped through the streets of Moscow, both sides of the road were lined with citizenry and children waving India-Soviet Union flags. The limousine finally arrived at the Rossiya Hotel, reputedly the largest hotel in the world. An entire wing on the third floor had been reserved for the Indian delegation. The Presidential suite had been decked up for Priya's comfort. It had a bird's eye view of the oddly-shaped, turgid towers of the Kremlin as the hotel was barely a few hundred meters away from the outer perimeter of the fortified Kremlin palace. Chairman Miroslav saw her to the gate and affectionately kissed her again.

'I am looking forward to hosting you to a special programme at the Bolshoi in the evening, dear Priya.'

Priya Kaul felt like a young girl out on her first date. Moscow and the right kind of people in the city had this effect on her.

'Oh, I so look forward to that, Miro. Thank you for all the courtesies you have extended to me and my team. You honour my country by doing that.'

'Dear Priya,' replied Miroslav sagely, 'it's always the man or the woman at the top who makes us do what we do. Countries come after. Never forget that.'

Miroslav's words stayed with Priya as she relaxed in her Presidential suite, while Narang unpacked for her. He then took out a wine bottle from the bar and prepared a drink for her. Her routine of having a pre-evening drink or two never wavered. The morning, full of work and all kinds of challenges, excited her. But an evening, full of emotional uncertainty ever since Prahlad had come of age, unsettled her. She needed her drink to get through that. But today a strange excitement was coursing through her. And the taste of Bacchus only enhanced it. She sipped her drink and stretched languidly in an armchair.

She asked Narang, 'Do you think Miroslav has a crush on me?'

Narang blushed, if such an appearance or emotion could be attributed to a middle-aged, stodgy, keeper-of-secrets man.

'It's not apt for me to answer this question of yours, Madam,' Narang replied officiously.

Priya smiled knowingly, but persisted.

'Oh, come on, Narang. There are no secrets between us. For God's sake, you even arrange my lingerie. I am a single woman, a widow of vintage times as it were, the Prime Minister, but still a woman and not a demigod as some might think I am. I do like being appreciated once in a while and knowing that I am still desired. You can tell me all that. Speak your mind, man. I won't fire you for your impertinence, if that is what you are afraid of!'

Narang stood as a model of penitence. Hands covering his crotch, head bowed, a deep blush spreading across his face end to end.

'Madam, who would not have a liking for you? You are the most charismatic person—man or woman that walked this planet. Chairman Miroslav would not be an exception if he is charmed by you. I have no doubts about that. But I also feel he is looking for something else. Today's reception was quite out of the ordinary, a bit out of the usual, staid Soviet character.'

Priya sobered up a bit as Narang's keen observation stayed with her. But she still did not want to return to her earlier depressive state. If she could, then she would prolong her stay in the afterglow of being wanted, to be a person of desire. She looked forward to her evening programme.

If there was ever a bigger flirt than Miroslav, of all the heads of State, then surely it would be Chairman Khaled Hamadan of the PLO (Palestine Liberation Organisation). Never mind the fact that Khaled headed a stateless state which was always looking for support and aid from its many sponsors and benefactors, especially the Soviet Union.

Khaled was a charmer and, as his detractors would say, a terrorist in that order. During his many meetings with Priya, he would fondly embrace her with 'sisterly' hugs and warm kisses on the cheek. Priya often wondered about the intensity of the passion Khaled displayed for her publicly. But she liked it because she believed in Khaled's cause. He could be overbearing, always talking excitedly and incessantly, but the breadth and tenor of his passionate views stayed with people. It was a coincidence that Khaled was in Moscow during Priya's official visit, and he insisted on a private meeting with her. They met in a room next to the grand St George Hall in the Kremlin. An official photographer and a news team from Indian state television Doordarshan recorded the meeting. Narang noticed that the lead cameraman was enthusiastically recording all the flourishes and embraces between Priya and Hamadan.

Narang silently crept up behind the cameraman and fiercely poked him in the ribs.

'I know your lot. You will sell this footage to foreign networks for a few dollars. If that happens, I will put your arse on a hot plate and transfer you to the most underdeveloped place in the country. You will show me the entire footage, and I will whet it before it is telecast. Understood?'

The shaken-up cameraman nodded vigorously as Priya and Hamadan settled down for a discussion. They chatted as old friends, though Hamadan closed the conversation with a subtle, prescriptive warning for Priya. 'Miroslav can be a charmer extraordinaire. But, always remember, he is a Russian bear. Beware of his embrace. He will go to great lengths to secure the Soviet Union's interests. Tread carefully, Priya.'

By night, the Bolshoi cast its magic spell on Priya, transporting her to a different realm. On display for her benefit was a performance of the age-old Tchaikovsky classic *Swan Lake*. The lead role of Princess Odette was performed by Svetlana, the lead dancer in the Bolshoi theatre company. Priya and Chairman Miroslav shared the main box in the theatre, in a non-ticketed show held specially for the Indian delegation and members of Soviet Union's Politburo and party officials. A procession of liveried waiters served them the best pink champagne and crafted canapes. The enactment of the tragic tale, Svetlana's pirouettes and twirls and her interpretation of unfulfilled love affected Priya deeply. The aural and visual splendour of the performance stirred her. What were her troubles when compared to this ethereal display of beauty and poise? They were a speck, really insignificant in the higher idealism of life.

And then, out of nowhere, she suddenly remembered Khaled Hamadan's warning. She struggled to push that note of discordance from her mind. She whispered in the dark, 'Svetlana is so captivating. She does not seem human.'

Miroslav smiled wolfishly and gave his interpretation, 'Indeed, dear Priya. But credit must also be given to her mentor. In life, there is a performer and then there is a mentor. One cannot succeed without the other.' Priya weighed up the significance of what Miroslav had just told her. The Hamadan warning was flashing in her mind. Best to ignore it, she thought. She wanted to play along with the metaphor suggested by Miroslav. 'And you would be her mentor I assume, Miro. You mentor her all nights or only once a while?'

Chairman Miroslav burst out laughing. They clinked glasses and drank some more champagne.

'How well you know me, Priya. But on a more serious note, how does it go with the Americans? Are they still meddling in your affairs? Can I be of help in any way?'

The point of her visit was suddenly clear in Priya's mind. Something was in the offing. Maybe it could help in settling her unsettled state of mind. She had to know.

'Miro, the Americans are always interfering. But I know how to keep them at bay. But is there something you wish to say to me? It's not like you to beat around the bush.'

Miroslav edged closer and placed his hands on Priya's. 'Dear Priya, I wish to make the relationship between our countries special, one that will be be remembered by generations. What I am about to say is for your ears only. We have developed a special variant of the MiG series combat aircraft. It is the MiG 25 Foxbat. It is state of the art; the West is guessing about its lethality and, I can tell you, they are terrified of its potential. I offer you this plane, Priya. We will sell it to you at very reasonable discounted prices. Later, we can even set up a joint assembly plant of the aircraft in India. America has no answer to this plane. It will eliminate the American threat to you for all times to come.'

A stab of fear coursed through Priya. She felt at a loss to understand her own emotions. She should have been overjoyed at the offer. But she knew there was a catch, a bloody spanner in the works which would be coming.

Miroslav edged even closer, if that was possible. He

was whispering in her ear, 'In return, we ask for a very small favour. Lease the Lakshadweep archipelago to us for the next twenty years. We need a naval presence in that area to counter the American Armada dominating the Indian Ocean. We kill two birds with that move, Priya—we check American hegemonistic aspirations and protect you from predatory American moves in the high seas.'

Priya's heart sank. So, there it was. An offer that was really no offer. No matter her standing in the country, she would not survive a day politically if she mortgaged a portion of the country to a foreign power even though friendly. She closed her eyes, and the entire fantasy of her trip to Moscow became clearer. The answer to her troubles did not lie in Moscow or her meetings with Chairman Miroslav. She had been fooling herself thinking something would turn up in Moscow to eliminate her problems. She felt a headache. Maybe she had drunk too much champagne. Svetlana's last act was beginning to get on her nerves.

***

Chatper 4

How do you deliver a message of hope when you are feeling hopeless within? It was an existential question. And it was dogging Priya as she stared at the group of a dozen men, her core senior cabinet, in a wood-panelled room in South Block. She looked at their faces. They were eager to hang on to every word she spoke, chiming in with praise for her, then applaud and serenade her for a successful visit to the Soviet Union. Well, that's what she had gone there for, after all, wasn't it? And that was why this meeting had been called in the first place. The choreography of beaming faces, impassioned words in praise for her, the full-throated orchestration of the slogan—'Priya is India and India is Priya'—they knew that script by heart, rehearsed and rendered so many times.

But the meeting did not run like a script. It was far from it. For starters, Madam's mind was elsewhere. Her eyes were fixed to the ceiling, her eye twitched—a regular phenomenon of late—indicating she was preoccupied; her thin lips tightly pursed. She knew the visit had been a flatliner. Nothing was lost, yet nothing was gained. Miroslav had probably returned to this old routine—further dragging his countrymen in economic misery and screwing Bolshoi dancers at night. Back home, she was struggling to find a magic bullet for her problems. She debated in her mind whether she should ask them for ideas on an exit strategy to deal with the unrest developing in Bihar and spreading across the Hindi heartland. Ask them? At the moment, they seemed like helpless animals on a farm, expecting their next feed. And then, out of nowhere, Sardar Kuldeep Singh, her Foreign Minister, displayed his recently grown spine. He ventured into the unknown without a warning.

'Madam, did President Miroslav ask for a slice of Indian territory? There are rumours circulating to that effect. I thought I should ask….'

'You would do what?' countered Priya.

Sardar Kuldeep Singh shut up.

The Finance Minister, Venkatachaliah, perked up. 'Though unrelated to the subject of the meeting, the industrial output is at an all-time low, Madam. I thought you should know. There are reports that trade union leaders could call for a nationwide rail strike. If that happens, we are sunk.'

Priya had heard about dominoes falling, but before

her eyes, she could see her chess pieces—the ones she would toy with at will—attempting an uprising.

And then, the knife was put in her back. Her Defence Minister, Ram Charan, spoke up. He was supposed to be the ultimate loyalist, the most sensible man in the cabinet, the scheduled caste leader who was an asset as well as a trophy emblem of caste-free secular politics. Well, Ram Charan also joined the bandwagon.

'I have no money left in the kitty to purchase howitzers,' he declared. 'The border of Punjab and Rajasthan is very vulnerable. Despite the lashing we gave the Pakistanis not so long ago, the Americans continue to arm them. The situation is precarious, to say the least. Can we talk about that?'

What was going on? They were supposed to be here to discuss her visit to Russia and applaud her, and not raise serious questions about the state of the country. Were they all in the employment of the CIA? All out to sabotage her and stop her in her tracks? Bloody traitors, one and all! They no longer looked like helpless animals. Rather, they were animals in waiting to ambush her. The room seemed to darken for her.

Her face was a mask. Priya was not given to tongue-lashings. Her method was more old school, some would even call it imperious. She simply turned her head away and looked at the picture frame on the wall adjacent to her. It signalled to the men in the room that the meeting was over. Madam was displeased. They finally got the message and trooped out of the room. Only she and Narang were left. Narang sat in a corner, hunched over a file. He could read well what was going on in her mind. Perhaps the only one to know. He did not wait for fresh orders. He quietly got up and told the security outside the room that Madam was calling it a day and heading back home.

Priya's head throbbed as her entourage of cream-coloured Ambassadors sped down Raisina hill. Ahead protestors milled on the India Gate lawns—protestors who felt no fear in calling her names and even jeering at her.

Had everything gone berserk? How had the protestors managed to reach so close to her entourage? Was her security set–up completely compromised? Bloody CIA must have been throwing money-filled bags in the air expecting all and sundry to grab the shower of descending currency notes.

From the corner of her eye she saw a female protestor break the police cordon and run towards her vehicle. The next moment, she was at her car window; her face suffused with rage. She slammed a poster at the sedan window—a poster dipped in red paint. It read, 'Resign, bitch. Your time is up.'

★★★

Chapter 5

A welcoming house often rings with peals of laughter from family members, the prattle and shrieks of little children running around or perhaps even the dignified sound of silence of elders in the family reading a book or listening to the radio at low volume. 7, Race Course Road resounded with shrieks and wild calls of a different kind—one of amorous, sexual play. Prahlad was chasing Kamini around the dinner table. Prahlad, in starch white kurta pajama, frolicked a bit before he attended to the business of the day. Kamini, in a revealing nightdress, shrieked, egging Prahlad to run in circles around her.

Priya Kaul came out of her room wondering if the entire world had gone mad. She could not believe her eyes when she saw her son chasing the girl called Kamini, displaying debauchery in full view of the house staff.

'Prahlad!' she screamed.

Prahlad and Kamini continued their catch-the-nightie

game. Priya shouted again. The chase and grab play slowed down, and Kamini, flashing that same mocking smile, finally disappeared in the folds of the house.

Prahlad, a little out of breath, leaned against the dinner table, cleaned his spectacles with his kurta and gave his mother a piece of his mind. 'What a timing, mother! You came home early to play spoilsport? You are really doddering into old age, aren't you! Cannot tolerate your son enjoying himself, right? I wonder what will be next.'

Priya's face was a picture of despair.

'Prahlad, this is not an isolated house in the hills. People are always watching. They are everywhere....'

'So what?' shot back Prahlad. 'Are we answerable to them? Have we ever been? These people you talk about will decide how I will lead my life. The temerity of that thought!'

Priya Kaul knew she could not win an argument against him. Weirdly, a part of her was also terrified of him. She tried to change the indelicate subject that was pitting her against her son.

'On a different note, Narang tells me you will be launching a new initiative this afternoon. From the old Delhi area. You want to fill me in?'

Prahlad put on his spectacles and spoke in a whisper, 'Mother, you are always picking on me. But you will soon realise I am your true inheritor. I am starting a programme that will change the face of this country. One of the big problem of this country is its teeming masses. People are sprouting everywhere. Like cockroaches, they breed and grow, creep everywhere, consume and degrade all our resources. You think poverty can be removed by mouthing slogans, as you and your minions are adept at doing? One has to do something about these cockroaches to restore the balance. Nip and snip the evil in the bud....'

Fear, as a living entity, gnawed at Priya's belly. What was Prahlad attempting to do? What did he mean by nipping the problem in the bud? Was Prahlad's youth wing going down the path of the Nazi brown shirts and emulating its inglorious reign of terror? What was her son talking about? What was he transforming into? But a more troubling thought for her was: had she pushed him into becoming the kind of man even she was afraid of?

★★★

Chapter 6

The day began like any other day for Mohammed Nazir, owner of shop no 345 in the Ballimaran area of old Delhi. Mohammed opened the shutters of his stationery shop slowly, and with some loving care dusted the shelves stacked with notebooks, drawing paper, pens and coloured pencils. His job done, he poured himself cold water in a glass from a *surahi,* drank it and settled down waiting for school rush hour when students would turn up to buy his wares. He thought of Fatima and the last night. Fatima, his second wife, was so much younger than him. The precious memory of resting his head against her hip and then slowly moving down to kiss the soles of her hennaed feet. He smiled inwardly. Life was good.

The late afternoon mist had lifted, and a group of energetic young men, all dressed in white tight-fitting kurta pajamas, made their way in the airless *gali*, towards his shop. They beamed as they came up.

'Chacha,' spoke up the leader of the pack. 'You are a hard man to find. But find you we did. So, Chacha, put down your shutters for the afternoon and come with us to the camp. You are a prime candidate for the camp.'

'What camp?' answered Nazir irritated. 'I have a business to run.'

The leader of the group leaned forward. 'Come you will, Chacha. Orders from your local MLA Waziri. You know him well, don't you?'

Who did not know Waziri? The brash goonda leader of the area was known to be equally quick with fisticuffs as with his quicksilver tongue. So, these men were part of that brat pack. What had the sublime old political party mutated to in the present day and age? He felt sorry for Priya Kaul. She was a good soul though. Nothing could dissuade him from voting against her.

'Let's get on with it whatever it is,' he replied tersely. 'But I warn you. I have a business to run.'

After a short ride in an open Willys jeep, they entered a camp perimeter. Strays barked everywhere; eddies of dust swirled in the air, and men and women, who looked like medical personnel, moved back and forth in hospital green. A chill ran up Mohammed Nazir's spine. He heard groans from a nearby tent. The flap of the tent opened. A middle-aged man, much like him, emerged from the tent—buckling at the knees, the belt of his trouser open—weeping pitifully, held firmly by two burly attendants in hospital green.

The man caught Nazir's eye and wailed.

'Miya, meri mardangi ko kaat ke kude ke dabbe mae fekh diya!' (They have snipped my manhood away!).

And just like that Mohammed Nazir knew what it was all about. He turned to flee the horror zone and ran straight into the brat pack leader who straightened him by the collar. In the distance, a loudspeaker was blaring, *'Desh ka neta kaise ho? Prahlad Kaul jaisa ho!'* (Prahlad Kaul is the youth icon leader of the country!).

Through the wall of swirling dust, Prahlad Kaul emerged, standing atop an open jeep, smiling beatifically, his hands in a namaste posture.

The leader of the pack pushed Mohammed Nazir.

'You had your *darshan* of our beloved leader! Now to business!'

And then, the next few minutes were a blur to Nazir—a violent interregnum between a life he had known and dreamt so far and now a life snipped after.

He was dragged onto a rusted hospital trolley, caked with the blood of others, and forced to lie on it. Before he could comprehend what was happening, he was injected with a shot that immobilised him waist downwards. Two doctors, a man and a woman, bespectacled and masked, emerged and immediately went to work on him. He felt pinpricks around his testicles, and looked up in terror, but the two doctors were absorbed in their work, speaking a language that made no sense to him.

They tinkered with him, and, after a while, the more senior among them nodded appreciatively and both withdrew. The world stopped for him, and he was left alone briefly; the dust outside shone in a ray of sunlight that filtered in the camp tent through a tear in it.

The sensation slowly returned in the lower part of his body. Somebody came to help him get off the trolley and sit in a chair. A steaming cup of coffee, overdosed with sugar, was thrust into his hands. Another person came and inserted a fifty-rupee note into his shirt pocket.

After a while, he emerged from the tent, the loosened cord in his pajama trailing on the ground. He walked like the man with the weight of buckled knees. In the distance, the sky was rent by the call of the Muezzin. A life changed forever thereafter.

★★★

Chapter 7

Priya Kaul went ballistic on the telephone with Prahlad.

'Prahlad, have you gone crazy? I am flooded with calls of atrocities in these camps…how could you…what…. No, I will not shut up…. What, you dare me to…. No, I won't keep my voice down…. Prahlad…Prahlad…. What's going on with you….'

Shrunk in a corner, Narang slowly shook his head. Priya'a face was wet with tears. She slowly put back the receiver in its cradle. Her hands shook.

'Narang, try and get me on the line with Rajan. At this time of the day, he should be in the dormitory. Maybe he could speak some sense to his younger brother.'

Narang quickly got up and obliged. Luckily, the caretaker of Jesus College, Oxford, was on the rounds when the phone rang. The urgency of speaking to the Indian Prime Minister's other son was conveyed. The caretaker thought about it and obliged.

Rajan, at that moment, was admiring his tie knot in the wall mirror of his hostel room, humming a popular Cliff Richard number *We don't talk anymore*. He saluted his good-looking self in the mirror and proceeded to tie his shoelaces. The prospect of meeting Christine Ricci in a pub down the hostel road excited him. There was the anticipation of holding hands with her, perhaps even stealing a kiss in the smoke-filled bar if she permitted. And, of course, there would be the added thrill of listening wide-eyed to her over the top, impassioned, hard left views on world politics. After all, Christine was a child of her generation—a world of socialistic advancement rolled up in a stick of marijuana. Christine filled his senses.

There was a sharp knock outside his door. He opened it and the caretaker poked in his head.

'Your mum's on the line, matey. Make it quick though. You know we don't encourage this sort of a thing at this hour. But she's the frigging Prime Minister of your sweat-soaked country, so there you have it!'

Rajan's mood darkened. He went downstairs and picked up the receiver. He had a sense what it would be about. He listened to perhaps the most powerful woman in the world—breaking down at the other end, giving him an overview of things with Prahlad and desperately asking him to intervene.

He replied politely, but firmly.

'Mother, you know my views on this subject. I don't

interfere in Prahlad's life. Honestly, I detest both Prahlad and your…eh… style of politics…it is best if you keep me out of it. So, there you have it then…sorry to put it so bluntly, but seriously, I can't see how I can be of any help. Prahlad has been on this trajectory for a long time, and you only have encouraged him. Some would even call it reap the whirlwind syndrome…well, that's more than what I want to say on this matter…. Look, I have an appointment and am in a hurry…so speak with you another time, mother….'

At the other end, Priya sat on a chair, staring vacuously into space. She had been to the manner born but had always fought her battles like a commoner. She had been airdropped in the top chair by her father, but the battles that she had to endure along the way was the stuff of legends. And it was always the enemy within—the group of ministers in her earlier term who had unfurled the flag of rebellion against her. She had to politically shred them with great skill and cunning. And now her son was fast becoming the enemy within? She could not help but think. Did her children *really* care for her? Prahlad had become so unapproachable, so alien. And Rajan never had any time for her concerns. These were the cuts that hurt her the most. It would be so easy to drift into nothingness and leave all this behind. So easy.

There was a picture of her father on the wall opposite her. Perhaps it was taken in the last few years of his life. He looked worn out and defeated, lying in an armchair—the breath of life going out of him—with a drooping cigarette in his fingers, staring unfocused into space. She had to pinch herself to believe she was developing the same habit.

Why the hell was a picture of defeat adorning the walls of her house? She felt an anger stirring in her. To hell with it all! She was not going down. She was not her father, and perhaps her children were not her. Maybe it was just that.

She looked at Narang resolutely, the old steel rising in her voice.

'Get a car for me, Narang. You and I will be taking a trip. We will travel deep into the interiors of Bihar, to Darbhanga. Tell Swamiji I am on my way. I want his undivided attention for the next couple of days.'

★★★

Chapter 8

A woman and a servile-looking man stood near a makeshift runway in the middle of nowhere. All alone, with just two suitcases near them. Nothing else. Swamiji's instructions had been clear: no security detail, no one should be seen around the runway when he made his appearance in the sky. Narang had been given some leeway, though. After all, it was not a Prime Ministerial visit. It was the visit of a woman who had come searching for some answers. When you come looking for something, then the rules of the giver or the interpreter must be observed. Such was the case here.

Priya Kaul's neck craned up to the sky. The heat was sweltering, and sweat hung onto her like a cloak. And then, in the sweltering heat, Swami Dharmachari's aircraft, a Cessna 4-seater, appeared as a speck in the sky with the sun behind. The speck grew larger, and soon it was visible that Swamiji was piloting the aircraft. The abilities and intrigue of this man was boundless. Even from that height,

Priya felt Swamiji's eyes bore into her, piercing through her and into her soul.

The plane soon descended onto the makeshift tarmac, and Swamiji stepped out to greet the most powerful woman in the world who, now, looked quite distracted. The sight of the man emerging from the plane sent a quiver through Priya. It had always been this way.

Swamiji was of an indeterminable age. He was as sprightly and energetic as a youngster, even though he had come in the world many moons ago. His leonine, jet black hair locks graced his shoulder blades; the curvature of his muscular upper frame rippled as he descended the short stairway. He sported a wildly growing beard and a white muslin dress—best described as a cross between a toga and a woman's saree. The draping of the 'Swami gown'—as the owner of the yellow gossip, politico rag *Plitz* often described it—was artful. In his weekly Yoga show, telecast over state television, India quite clearly saw Swamiji's hirsute chest and ripping shoulder blades, yet the folds of his gown hid his private parts well. However, the irascible editor of the *Plitz* claimed the Swami never wore any undergarments, perhaps to encourage the circulation of his rag.

The Swami was a world-renowned practitioner of Yoga and wellness. But his most striking feature was his eyes. The dimwits called them the 'eyes of Rasputin', but the more enlightened called them 'wells of desire and longing that you would want to jump into'. Such was the aura of the man who emerged from the plane.

Priya Kaul prostrated on the ground and kissed the Swami's feet.

Swami Dharmachari smiled and, helping Priya to her feet, embraced her. He kissed her on the forehead and whispered, 'Your place is not at my feet, but close to my heart. Know that, child. You don't look your usual self. Though far from you at my ashram, I have felt your pain. Loneliness and confusion in life draws out the lifeblood. But no harm done. I promise to help you restore the order of things. For the next two days, you and I will undertake a journey of the mind and the soul. Come, child…let me take you far away from your worries…'

Swami Dharmachari grasped Priya's hand and guided her up the stairway. Tears welled in her eyes. She felt a deep sleep overwhelming her.

Time slowed down for Priya as she sat next to Swamiji in the Cessna, her eyes heavy lidded, head resting against his strong shoulders. He skilfully piloted the plane up in the vast, sun-drenched expanse. Sitting in the cramped cargo hold on the floor, Narang smiled. A streak of hope was spreading in the sky.

The remains of the day and the time thereafter remains a bit sketchy. There is no clear documentation of what happened next. Years later, when the world had changed completely and an era had passed, Narang—old, doddering and six months away from his demise—opened his sealed lips which he had sworn not to open ever. He wrote his memoirs of the time he had spent serving Madam. The sceptics argued the tell–tale, or the tall tales, memoir was quasi-fiction, written to make money to pay for his medical bills. Narang, of course, died an impoverished, lonely, forgotten man.

Two instances written in the memoir from that eventful day stand out. The Swami took Priya deep into the jungles, to his Ashram. The last leg of the journey to the Ashram makes for an interesting reading. Priya passed out as soon as the plane landed on a dirty makeshift runway. The Swami then lifted up Priya, lost to the world, and carried her well over a mile, to his hide-out. Narang, sweating profusely, lugged two suitcases behind the Swami and his boss.

On reaching the Ashram, the Swami took Priya to the 'Awakening room'. If Narang's accounts are to be believed, the Swami revived her with sweetened lime water, and made her sit cross-legged on a raised platform. He pressed his forefinger at the base of her spine and ran it up to her neck. She woke up with a start, her eyes opening wide and spinning with demonic energy. The Swami had awakened the *Kundalini* (feminine divine energy) of the most powerful woman in the world.

These accounts could be exaggerated, but other Ashramites from the era bear testimony to another occurrence which is probably closer to the truth. Priya Kaul was seen doing *seva* in the Ashram next day, looking completely relaxed and freshened as if awakened after a long, deep, and satisfying sleep.

To summarise an account from Narang's memoirs, this is what happened next. After her Kundalini's awakening, Priya was bursting with explosive energy. Swami Dharmachari had to physically restrain her from hurting herself and others around her. And then, as suddenly as the awakening had occured, she fell asleep, and slept for over twelve hours.

The last bit of his account after that is blurry, even borderline sacrilegious. Well, take your pick if you want to believe it. So, Priya woke up, and the Swami took her to the cleansing chamber for the final rituals. It is said that he again made her sit cross-legged on a *thara* (stone pedestal), dressed in a simple, handspun cotton saree, sans a blouse. He poured warm water over her and cleaned her face and body with a red-coloured Ayurvedic paste. Then, he poured warm water over her again, scrubbing away her physical and metaphysical impurities. She sat still and content; a beatific smile lit her face as the water streamed through her hair, armpits, pores and crevices. She felt the nihilism of her existence wash away with the rust-coloured water streaming down. She again felt an explosion of energy that vibrated in her like a tuning fork. But this time it was more controlled, nuanced and subtle. She suddenly felt hungry as if she had been starving for a long time. And she felt the need to talk, to have a conversation with the Swami. Of the way ahead.

★★★

Chapter 9

Relaxed, refreshed and free of mental detritus, Priya sat cross-legged in front of the Swami in the practical chamber. Looking sharp and eager, she was ready for a conversation with the Swami.

Swami Dharmachari sat in the same posture opposite Priya, his eyes looking into hers. He spoke slowly with emphasis, 'Child,' said the Swami, 'there is a concept of reality and illusion. If we can grasp this concept fully then we have found the solution to many of our problems.'

'Can you explain how this might have a bearing on my problems?'

The Swami momentarily kept quiet. Even though he was the giver and she the receiver, even though she prostrated herself at his feet and he lovingly bathed and cleansed her of impurities, he knew she was still unknown and unpredictable. She was known to ambush when one least expected it. No peer, minister or even a sage could claim immunity from her astonishing and forceful decision-making. Certainly not him whose ashram, Cessna joyrides, and free flow of funds was completely dependent on the generosity of the Prime Minister.

He needs to tread a fine line and yet show the value of his advice to Priya.

He spoke with a degree of caution.

'I can sense, child, that you are worried about Prahlad and Rajan.'

There was a moment of silence. Then, she slowly nodded, giving him the go-ahead.

'Every parent,' spoke the Swami, 'is under the illusion that they can shape their child's path in the world. It is their ultimate ego trip. They think the child can be the spitting image of themselves. That would be a mistake. Even if a doctor's son becomes a doctor, it is not to fulfil their parent's ambition, but because the child perceives the value of their choice. It is as true for a doctor as it is for a criminal, or anyone else. Human beings think and make choices for themselves. It is an illusion we make it for them.'

'What's your point, Swamiji?'

'Let your children be. Perhaps, at this point they don't see the value of what you have in mind for them, perhaps they are resentful of some childhood hurt, or perhaps they enjoy putting you on the edge. There could be a million reasons. Let it go, and then it might come back. Life is a loop, not a straight line.'

Priya was not fully convinced. Yet, she saw the merit of what the Swami had just told her. She asked him another important question that haunted her, 'I am besieged by enemies who plan and contrive to bring me down. I know my popularity is also dwindling. How do I recover lost ground? How do I become Priya Kaul again?'

He replied, 'You and I are both creatures of the real world, child. I can create the illusion of a person levitating by the power of Yoga. You can pretend to remove poverty from the country by a simple slogan. Both are untrue. Every process takes time. Poverty might be removed from India in the future. Another Yoga guru might make people genuinely levitate decades later. Not now. That is the illusion. But the reality is: people are impatient. They want immediate results, and so they suffer. That is why you are becoming unpopular.

'To counter that we must create the illusion of reality. How to do that? There is a way I can suggest. Give people something that will distract them from their real problems. Give them a euphoria that takes them into a different consciousness. It cannot be a mere slogan, an inauguration or a scheme. It must release a kind of kinetic energy, powerful enough to lift people up from their miserable state and empower them. This burst of energy will achieve two objectives. It will take their minds off from their pressing needs for a long time. Secondly, it will reinvent you as a goddess of *shakti*, of power, on earth. This will cloak you in an invincible aura; nothing will permeate this shield. You will have a trouble-free reign thereafter.'

Priya Kaul's eyes opened up, showing her pupils. It was as if she had attained enlightenment.

'Understood, my Swami,' she simply said. 'Now bless me for the task.'

Swami Dharmachari touched her forehead with his index finger. Her body quivered immediately, and a procession of images flashed before her eyes. It was like watching the avant-garde, eclectic work of the celebrated documentary film-maker S Sukhdev in a private theatre all alone. Hundreds and thousands of disjointed, provocative images flashed before her eyes. And then they all disappeared slowly, and only atomic symbols lazily floated in her consciousness.

She knew she had found her answer.

★★★

Chapter 10

Dr Venkat Iyer sensed the picture postcard beauty of Leh crumbling before his eyes. He was feeling more than light-headed. His head was spinning as if he had been lifted off his feet by an unknown force. The benign ulcer lodged deep in his gut was also acting up. A thought crossed his mind: maybe this is how it would end for him. And, if that happened, what would he leave behind? A small pension to keep his wife and daughter going in his absence. Two snapshots flashed onto his mind. He could clearly see his wife where she always was, in the kitchen, her back turned to him, grinding the *dosa* batter. He would miss that if he exited the world. But what would be really unbearable for him was not seeing his daughter Tara ever again. Tara, autistic since birth, was always reticent with her emotions. The only time she would respond would be when he returned home late night from work, tired out of his mind. Yes, he would terribly miss that look on her face if he went away.

A farrago of images blitzed his mind. He heard the strange, urgent sounds of something clattering on wheels near him and felt someone steadying him as he passed out.

He woke up after a while, breathing in an oxygen mask, looking at Priya Kaul. She was holding his hand. She gently scolded him, 'We nearly lost you there, Venkat. All because you were too proud to tell me you were feeling uneasy ever since we stepped off the flight. We are in Leh, at the Thiksay monastery, at an elevation of 12,000 feet. If you need oxygen support, which most people from the plains do in these parts, you ask for it. If something had happened to you…the thought of it…the most intelligent and valuable man in the country gone; my point man looking after the country's nuclear programme…' She shuddered.

Venkat Iyer smiled weakly. What could he say? He was keeping pace with his boss—the country's Prime Minister, a woman he respected and admired, and for whom he could do anything. Could he not even keep pace with her atop the monastery? The wind whistled in their ears, the air rarefied, the sky so blue, the knife-edged mountains encircling them and the flood plains of the mighty Indus River spread out below like a grey, wrinkly sheet on both sides. His boss, that incomparable woman, was bouncing with energy atop the monastery almost like someone who has been possessed. And he could not even keep pace with her?

Another two faces popped up in his vision—Rhino and the chief medical officer of the district. The doctor examined him again, took off his mask and nodded, giving his approval to Priya, 'He's much better now, Madam. Good thing is we had the oxygen cylinder in a rolling cart on the rooftop. That helped, of course. He can sit up, but no sudden movements please.'

Rhino gently eased Venkat up on the stretcher in a sitting position. He asked him, 'Think you can walk a few steps, Venki? It's almost time for the discussion.'

Venkat, with new-found energy, could not let the observation pass. 'For god's sake, Rhino, I am not a cripple! I don't eat *wazwan mutton rogan josh* like you for my energy, but my *sambhar-medu vada* also packs in quite a punch!'

There were a few titters in the entourage, and Venkat was helped onto his feet. Soon, Priya was left on the rooftop with her two trusted loyalists. They slowly made their way to the west wing of the vast terrace, the wind howled in their ears like a fiend dancing around them with a scythe.

A light shone in Priya's eyes. 'Gentlemen, absorb the incredible, untouched beauty of this place before we talk,' she instructed them. 'It will help clarify the mind.'

They kept quiet and soaked in the stunning majesty of the rugged landscape stretching for miles. If there was a God above, then perhaps the distance to reach him from the rooftop would be short.

Priya turned her back to the mountain range and addressed the two men, 'We are at the edge of the world—on its rooftop, in perhaps one of the most forlorn, desolate and stark places in the world. We can shout out to the heavens from here; they might listen to us. You two—Venkat and Rhino—are the men I trust the most in this world. I say this to both of you, perhaps for the first, and certainly for the last time in my life. I find it hard to trust people. It has always been like this. I stopped believing and trusting people after my father died a defeated and bitter man. I have asked you to accompany me on this trip for a specific reason.'

Suddenly, she stopped speaking and looked pensive. She turned her back to them. *Silence*. Venkat could have sworn that her eyes had watered, perhaps remembering her late father. Understandably, she did not want them to see her frail and choking with emotion. She took her time in collecting herself. Then, facing them, she resumed, 'China is next door, and if one travels in a straight line for 250 kilometres from this point, there is Skardu in Pakistan. And, several thousand miles away, there is America. Gentlemen, I asked you to accompany me on this trip because I need your help in sending a message. A message to these three countries; a message to my beloved countrymen. I want it to be a message that will be remembered by the entire world long after I am dead and gone. A message that will never be forgotten.'

The wind had picked up, howling and whistling now; even Rhino, unflappable most of the time, felt chilled to the bone. He could sense what she was getting at. The audacity of her idea and thought! A silver bullet to end all her problems! Brilliant! But, it could not be done. No way! Had Venki figured out what she was driving at?

Priya continued, 'The irony of this morning does not escape me. As I was walking up the stairs of the monastery, it struck me that this is the abode of the Buddha, and the message of peace nestles deep in the bosom of this monastery. And, what I propose…' She again stopped speaking to take her time, her face now intense. She shot a piercing look directed at Rhino.

'You are a chain smoker, Rhino, right? What do you use, a cigarette lighter or matchsticks, to light up your cigarette?'

Rhino looked embarrassed. What had got into her today? She was toying with them.

'I…I….I...' Rhino was stammering.

'Speak up, man!' she cut in sharply. 'Stop acting coy like a girl. I know you smoke. How do you light up your cigarettes?'

'Matchsticks,' he finally answered.

'Wonderful,' she countered. 'Now give us a demonstration. Light up a matchstick for us. Cup your hands. Show us how to do it. Venkat, come closer. I want you to closely observe the lighting up of a matchstick.'

Venkat thought even she might be feeling light-headed on the rooftop. Her behaviour was bizarre, to say the least. But he did as was told.

They stood closely in a ring, spreading out the flaps of their thick coats to shield Rhino from the strong wind. Rhino fumbled with the matchsticks till he finally got one right. The flame shot up in his cupped hands. Priya looked other-worldly. Her eyes were now fixated on Venkat.

'What just happened, Venkat? Tell me.'

The top scientist of the country frowned. 'Rhino lit a matchstick; that is what happened,' replied the puzzled scientist.

'Wrong,' Priya cut in. 'You tell us, Rhino. From the look on your face, I know you have figured it out. Smart man. Tell us, Rhino.'

Rhino, back to being his unflappable self, replied deadpan. 'There was a release of kinetic energy when the matchstick was lit. That is what happened.'

Priya distanced herself from the ring, the steel in her voice rising. 'Correct. Release of energy. That is what happened. Now, both of you listen to me very carefully. Venkat Iyer, you will build a nuclear device for me, and we will carry out India's first ever nuclear test which will release an unimaginable energy. A world-class device and explosion that will make the world sit up and take notice of us. You have six months to build this device and carry out the test. Rhino, you will supervise the entire operation.

You will ensure it succeeds at any cost. That, gentleman, is my brief for both of you this morning.'

Dr Venkat Iyer could not believe what he had just heard. His heart pounded, and he feared an attack coming on. He drew in deep breaths.

Rhino was certain that it was the last day of his career. Surely it had to be. He spoke in his usual deadpan tone, 'Prime Minister, I have known you all my life. I can no longer keep the truth from you. The thing is, I lied to you sometime back when you asked me about the extent of CIA infiltration in the cabinet. I lied to save you the worry. The fact is, and I have known it for quite some time, the CIA has infiltrated all important institutions in our country. Many bureaucrats and journalists are on its payroll. They most certainly have assets in the cabinet also. I am trying to weed them out, but I have not been entirely successful.'

Rhino's hand instinctively reached in his coat pocket where his resignation letter should have been. Priya unexpectedly smiled. 'You think I don't know that, Rhino? But, thank you for being honest. I might be a paranoid woman, but my paranoia is my defence shield, it helps me survive, maybe not sleep well at night. Yes, I know all about the CIA problem.'

'No, you don't, Madam,' resisted Rhino. 'US President Fielding is under a lot of pressure on the surveillance tape issue in Washington. He is looking for a distraction. If the US finds out that we are going in for a nuclear test, they will bomb us back to the stone-age. Nothing can save us then, not even the Russians.'

Priya looked at Venkat. 'Ignore what he says, Venkat. You tell me. Can you pack enough plutonium in your device and give me a bomb in six months' time? Yes, or no?'

Without thinking it through and purely out of reflex and loyalty, Dr Venkat Iyer answered, 'We can try…well, yes, we can get you the bomb, Madam. Yes, I think so.' Priya looked at Rhino triumphantly.

'There. It is settled, Rhino. The Americans will bomb us only if they know about our plans. And this is where you have no choice. Stop fishing in your coat pocket for a resignation letter. I am not letting you go. You, Rhino, will conduct the ultimate deception operation the world has ever seen. You will conceal our intent from the world at whatever cost. I want my bomb, gentlemen, and I will have it.'

★★★

Chapter 11

Harry Smith (Freckles) was oddly thinking of his name when his flight, a Pan Am shuttle, out of London, touched down at Delhi's Palam airport. Harry Smith, or for that matter a John Smith, was not a pedigreed name. It was as common as a McDonald's outlet in mid-west America. Who were the John Smiths or the Harry Smiths of the world? They were not Ivy League for sure. They were the faceless face in the crowd, always merging with the local colour. He could mingle anywhere and with anyone; if anyone remembered him after a meeting, it was for his shock of red hair, and freckles under his humourless eyes. Plain-looking, ordinary, American Joe really.

He was comfortable with all that. He stood out in contrast to his colleagues and peers at the company headquartered at Langley—spooks like him who dressed like bankers. They would come to office in bow ties, while he was always dressed in khakis and cargo trousers. But the real difference between them and him was that almost all of them came from a background—either family money, or Ivy League. He had none of that. He was a bastard, quite literally. Social services had found him in a bin in a seedy corner of Harlem, New York. His point of origin was known to everyone at the Agency. There were rumours that his Harlem birthing was perhaps a rare, but not unheard-of, union between a redhead white, hippy woman and a black, heroin-addicted man. There was no stopping the rumour mill, really.

Coming from such a culturally diversified background, it was a mystery how Harry Smith found employment at the Agency. Not only that—he was ahead of the curve of most others of his batch. He was the section chief in charge of the entire Indian subcontinent. There were rumours that he reported directly to the CIA director. Even President Fielding knew his name. He would be consulted on all matters related to India-Pakistan.

Freckles rose in the Agency at a time when the field agent had come into his own and was perceived to be more valuable than the bow tie, striped suit thinkers and strategists clogging the Agency. Freckles was a man of the bazaar and shady side streets lurking with danger. He thrived in such locations, be it in Beirut, Damascus or even West Berlin. He knew how to put together a team, work against all odds and get a result. The Agency recognised his talents, and handed him the job of section chief of the

South Asia division when the best of talents in the Agency ignored that part of the world for being insignificant in value and rooted for western Europe and central America.

But Freckles accepted the position with alacrity. He knew that this part of the world would be the place to be in the future.

The seat belt sign went off in the plane and Freckles unbuckled himself. The air hostess, a platinum blonde wearing a blue suit, walked up to him with some pills in her hand.

'Malaria pills,' she offered. 'Had a spare pack. Thought you might need it.'

'No, thanks,' Freckles smiled. 'I am a gin, tonic and quinine man, and that should take care of that.'

She smiled and hesitated.

'You would be staying at the Ashok, right? Everyone does. Only watering place in town. I am on the second floor. Give me a buzz if you feel lonely.'

'Sure,' Freckles responded positively. 'I will keep the offer in mind.'

The stairway had come up, and a blast of hot, humid air hit him as he went down the stairway. There was a strange fetid smell hanging in the air. As he walked towards Immigration, he saw knots of people gathered around a broken-down toilet. The chatter and noise in the Immigration hall was unbelievable.

The ride to the American Embassy in the

Chanakyapuri area confirmed the scepticism expressed by many observers of Delhi and India. The Third World cloak of ordinariness and poverty was not exactly a lie. But, there were exceptions. The neatly trimmed lawns, and wide streets of the Chanakyapuri area for instance. For all the socialist chatter about India, it was clear that life here was as uneven and unfair as in any corner of the Middle East or Africa.

Inside the vast confines of the American Embassy, Harry was ushered to Ambassador Samuel Douglas Jr. A jug of lemonade with clinking ice cubes rested on a side table next to the Ambassador. Samuel kept sipping lemonade from a glass and wiped the sweat off his forehead.

'So, Harry, what perfidious sin have you committed that they have sent you to this cursed hole?'

Harry replied unsmilingly, 'I opted for the posting. I am lucky to be on this beat. So much to learn. Delhi appears a fascinating place.'

'Ah, an Indophile!' laughed Samuel. 'You are not the only one. They call it the magic of this place. Even the sanest minds turn out here. For the life of me, I can't see what they see in this country. Can't wait to finish my posting and say good riddance to this scrapyard. Oh, my wife is also one of those Indophiles. She sets off for the Janpath area every day, to shop and chat and God knows do what. Care for something stronger than a lemonade?'

Harry shook his head. He carefully observed the

Ambassador. The glass of lemonade nestled on his potbelly. An unlit cigar rested in the ashtray. His cheeks were inflamed. Perhaps he had ventured out in the heat. Harry hated this lot—privileged, probably owning houses along the Potomac, in all likely, friends of Fielding bravely taking up the job for a three-year term to oblige their friend. However, half of their time was spent in Washington anyway.

Harry decided to pry open the can. 'You heard anything out of the ordinary Ambassador? Any suggestions, any hints, some intelligence that has come your way?'

Samuel shook his head. 'Priya has too much on her plate to be concerned about Pakistan. Only thing I am hearing is, she might not last even the next six months. The Indians are too busy fighting among themselves to give a thought to Pakistan. You can tell that to your director and even Fielding, I dare say. I know you are their blue-eyed boy.'

Freckles controlled his irritation. It was idiots like these who had lost Vietnam for them. He gently questioned the Ambassador in his best flat monotone, 'A local is looking after surveillance?'

'Yeah, real colourful character. He should get in today to be paid his weekly, what do they call it? Ah, the *hafta*! His weekly bribe! You will understand why we indulge with that. You want to meet him?'

Freckles did not answer. He stared impassively at the

Ambassador. Samuel, for a man of his girth, suddenly sat up alert in his chair.

'Listen, blue-eyed boy, let's cut out the horse shit. I know you have been sent here with an agenda. Don't take me for an idiot. I know that. So, here's the deal. You can revamp the intelligence set-up here as you wish. You need not get any clearance from me if you want to visit Islamabad or Kabul. You have the run of the place. The resources at the Embassy are at your disposal. Only, get me out of this place…this blasted country. Fielding no longer takes my calls. Maybe he's too caught up in his tapes mess, or he's dumped me here and forgotten. A simple trade off, eh? I know you have leverage in Washington.'

Freckles kept quiet as he observed the Ambassador crumbling before him. He quietly responded, 'If that is all, I shall be on my way, Ambassador. Good day to you.'

Freckles was on his way out when the Ambassador called after him. A voice in despair.

'It can get lonely at the Ashok. It's nothing but a government dump of a hotel. I can organise something for you for the nights. Give me a buzz.'

Freckles stepped out in the heat, breathing freely. He waved off the driver and decided to walk the short walk from the US Embassy to the Ashok hotel. By the time he arrived at the hotel, bag in tow, his shirt clung to him drenched in sweat.

He completed the registration formalities, signing in

as a trade representative of a manufacturing company. He collected his room key and walked past the Frontier restaurant to take the elevator to a room upstairs. The stewardess on the plane sat in the restaurant bar sporting a gin and tonic. Their eyes met, and she smiled at him. He ignored her and pressed the elevator button. His days and nights would be occupied by an excitement of a different kind.

★★★

Chapter 12

'Care for something stronger?' Rhino held a glass of half-filled scotch against the light. A lit cigarette rested comfortably, almost fashionably, between his colourless lips. A thread of smoke trailed up to the ceiling. Dr Venkat Iyer looked with some envy at the older man. What would he not do to have the constitution of this man? This man, in his early seventies, is eating, drinking and smoking—imbibing the worst dietary choices and still remaining as fit as a horse. And here his peptic ulcer was killing him. Venkat held up a glass of water against the light. 'The ulcer does not allow it, Rhino. How I wish!'

Rhino nodded in agreement and drew a chair closer to their worktable. It was well past midnight, and both men were ensconced in Rhino's Sujan Singh Park flat, near Khan market. There were papers strewn on the table, names crossed or ticked on them.

Rhino summed up the work effort. 'We have been at

it for three days. We have pared the list from 300 to 150. What would be the final number?'

Venkat frowned, hesitant to commit himself to an answer. He wanted the luxury of tinkering with a large team, but he understood Rhino's compulsions. A large, floating base of personnel working on the bomb was not possible.

'70-75 scientists, max,' offered Venkat.

Rhino crushed his cigarette and let out a whistling sound.

'That's a lot. A logistical nightmare. Not so much for you, but for me. I had hoped for a very small team.'

Venkat pushed back his chair.

'I understand, you need to whet these people. But this is a bare minimum number. If I can ask, Rhino, what is it you fear the most?'

Rhino was loath to reply. He was a reticent man by instinct. He had never laid out things in black and white for friend or foe. He would always leave room for surprise, a new gambit or a shocking turn at any stage in the game. But he would have to trust his comrade in arms in this endeavour. He gave his reasons clinically.

'Venkat, practically every institution in the country is like a sieve at present, including your BARC (Bhabha Atomic Research Centre). You have no idea what people can do for a wad of greenback. We might loath the Americans, but we love their currency. Now, there is a peculiar problem with BARC. The very nature of your work entails that your people must work closely with the western nations, especially the Canadians and the Dutch. These powers co-operate with you assuming that you are building up your nuclear capability for peaceful purposes and for future energy requirements. If they get even a whiff that we are making a bomb, diverting plutonium from our reactors to make a mark in the world, all hell will break loose. They will not only rescind all agreements with BARC, but will also go the extra mile to backlist the entire scientific pool. They will impose severe sanctions on us.

'That means all our access to the latest technology, specialised research, and critical components and minerals will come to an end.

'You are, of course, aware of all this.

'What you are not aware of is that if their intelligence agencies get into the act, they will start luring the best talent in the country. Not only that, they will also offer free scholarships to teenage children of our scientists, specialised medical care for the seriously ill, and a host of other incentives. Then, our patriotic fervour and commitment might not be of much use against these powerful temptations.

'And lastly, they will rain vengeance on you. We are an economic basket case, as it is. That will ensure we are reduced to sub-Saharan levels.'

'Shit!' responded Venkat. 'So, what do we do?'

Rhino took out another stick and lit it. He relished

every word and said, 'We resist them. And when it comes to that, no one can match up to Priya. She can turn the globe on another axis if she makes up her mind. That is why, you and I do what we do.'

Venkat viewed his glass half-full. He quietly said, 'I am a scientist, Rhino. I deal with data and facts. That is all I know. You deal with the improbable. That is your job description, not mine. Tell me, how do I get my 75 men without opening a can of worms?'

Rhino blew a smoke ring in the confined space; it hung just above his head for a while before disappearing into ether.

'Venkat, my friend, blowing a smoke ring is akin to an art form perfected after hours and hours of practice.

'Now, listen to me carefully. There is always a before and an after of major world events. What we are attempting to do will be a spectacular world event. If we are caught before the event, we will end up paying a hefty price for it. Even Priya will not survive her job then. She will have to bow out of office. But, in case we succeed, we will end up being damaged, but not burnt. Simply because, after an event, the agitation of the human mind settles down. Take the case of Hiroshima and Nagasaki. If the Japanese knew they would be obliterated by a nuclear device before the bomb was dropped, they would have bitterly fought with the last man. But, the bomb was dropped and millions died, they accepted their fate and made peace with the same country which wiped out millions of their countrymen.

'Today, Japan cannot look beyond America. This is what I mean when I say the before and after of any event.'

Dr Venkat Iyer got up and put on his coat.

'It's late, and I must be on that early morning flight to Bombay. I guess, you have figured out the before and after of these 75 men already?'

Rhino replied deadpan, 'They will go through a scrutiny, a test that will be nothing short of an X-ray. We cannot afford to have even a single team member who is compromised by money, divided loyalty or even ambition. There will be a before in their selection, not an after. I am going to mount one of the most secretive, deceptive operation ever undertaken to choose these men. Prepare yourself, Venkat, for endless days of rigour. You could end up with, not one, but many ulcers in your gut.'

★★★

Chapter 13

Six months ago

A night in Bombay, a bird's-eye view of the city. Cooperage and Azad Maidan, Ballard estate at one corner and the Fort area and the docks on the other, all the way down to the row of shops in Colaba and diagonally across the Gateway of India—all the iconic landmarks of South Bombay were rain-soaked. The patter of rain on slick, tiled roads was continuous. Earlier in the day, the monsoon had struck the city. The sea had breached the wall girdling the stretch from the Gateway, right up to Radio Club. More fury of a very active monsoon was expected tomorrow.

Next to the Radio Club, in a hotel named Bahadur, done up in art deco style, a man nicknamed Sunflower was doing best what he was infamous for. He was charming the pants off a young adult, Jyotika. They were at it in a room on the third floor. Sunflower strummed the guitar rendering a soulful version of the Beatles hit number *Norwegian wood*, as Jyotika took off her top, bell-bottoms and then undergarments, one after another. A poster of the hit movie *The Graduate* was pasted on the wall opposite her. In what could be best described as life imitating art, Sunflower fascinatingly watched, much like Dustin Hoffman from the movie, Jyotika raise her naked leg, just like Anne Bancroft did in the same movie.

Jyotika's bush was clearly visible, and Sunflower strummed the conclusion of the song with renewed energy. He looked at the invitation closely, as Jyotika said in her throaty voice, 'Now, you do the same for me. I want to see the real you. Take off your jeans and shirt.'

Sunflower put down the guitar and obliged. He took off his clothes but stopped at the underwear. Jyotika feasted her eyes on his magnificent body. His mane of hair fell on his shoulders, artfully arranged, a streak of colour running through it. Rippling musculature, crow lines around the eyes of a man in his early thirties—eyes with brown flecks that were piercing but soft, lost and innocent yet cunning.

Jyotika felt thrilled deep down. 'You have ivory skin. My, my…'

'Genetic disposition,' he offered. 'Sikh father, Italian mother. A one-night stand creation of my parents; screwing in passion in a hotel room in Milan. Just that one night. They split their ways in the morning, never to meet again. That's that then.'

'Poor baby,' she commented. 'I will love you more,

then. But first, you must take off that last remaining piece of cloth.'

Sunflower shook his head. 'No, we wait. I want to give you the complete experience. Just a little while longer.'

If one were to walk down from the building Bahadur, turn left and walk in a straight line, then they would land up at the majestic Taj Hotel at the end of the road. In an executive suite of the hotel, the jute king of Calcutta paced the room. He would frequently consult his watch. Sitting in a corner, Seth Khandelwal's fixer Chaubey observed his benefactor.

'*Sethji*, you need not worry. It will go as per plan. It's curtains for Sunflower. Take my word.'

Chaubey was referring to a plan which he had devised and set in motion with the blessings and financial muscle of Khandelwal backing it. Khandelwal had given his go-ahead for the plan having reached a point of despair on dealing with Sunflower. Or to be precise, he was in a corner, not knowing how to deal with his daughter Jyotika, one who had stripped for Sunflower minutes ago.

Barely twenty plus, Jyotika was the spoilt, headstrong, but independent minded daughter of the jute king. She had been married to an industrialist's son, almost by coercion, on the day she had turned eighteen. Sickened of her potbellied husband whose only passion in life was overseeing the packing of jute bundles in a factory, Jyotika revolted and fled her Calcutta home.

She landed in the dream city and took up lodgings in a chummery in the Colaba vicinity.

And there, in the by-lanes and rain slickened streets of Colaba, she met Sunflower. A girl, who had dreamed fantasy, courtesy Mills and Boons paperbacks, met this hard drinking, Schopenhauer and Freud-quoting man, intellectually refined yet debased, who strummed the guitar and screwed all and sundry, living life on the edge. The girl should have been attending thank-you dinners at homes of family and friends with her potbellied husband. Instead, she was spending days and nights with Sunflower, drinking beer at the Leopold café, the favourite hole in the wall in the city of the discarded yet bohemian detritus citizenry of the world. She saw a new world exploding before her eyes, revealing its fascinating, seamy, desirable and undesirable spillage.

To cut a long story short, Jyotika had never met a person with the personality and swagger of Sunflower. She was besotted with him. Meanwhile, Seth Khandelwal's man Friday and fixer, Chaubey, tracked her down to Colaba. Chaubey understood the contours of the problem. Jyotika could be coerced and brought back to Calcutta again. But it would not solve the problem. Sunflower was the problem. Jyotika was obsessed with him. She would escape again.

Chaubey then suggested to Sethji the diabolical. Desperate to claim his only child, Sethji agreed. The idea was to bump off Sunflower from the face of the earth in a fake encounter.

Cut to the present. Karandikar, a police officer attached to the Colaba police station, arrived with his team of three men at the building Bahadur in the pouring rain. A day before this, Chaubey had piled up wads of currency notes at the desk of the concerned officer. Karandikar's smile had broadened as the pile of notes grew in front of him.

The game plan was simple. Karandikar would arrive at the hotel, and break into the room precisely at the time when Jyotika and Sunflower were having coitus. How would Karandikar know about all that? The reception clerk had been bribed to report to the police team minute by minute movements of the two lovers. Karandikar would then burst into the room to arrest both Jyotika and Sunflower on charges of bigamy. The script to be followed would be—Sunflower would resist arrest and attempt to snatch the officer's firearm, and subsequently he would be shot in the melee.

Everybody would go back home happy after the staged killing. The officer and his men would pocket the money, and the jute king would reclaim his daughter who, after reflecting and having no other choice, would return to her marriage.

Of course, no tears would be shed for Sunflower, a low-life well known in Colaba for episodic debauchery and borderline criminality. Good riddance to disposable trash!

But, unfortunately for all characters in the play, the

mise en scène planned by Karandikar and Chaubey did not go as planned. The unexpected and untimely arrival of Ismail upset the game plan.

Ismail, a person of Moroccan origin and a part-time cook, used the spiral staircase at the back of the building to go up undetected. He came in through the window of the room as Jyotika stood naked in front of Sunflower, precisely 15 minutes before the police's arrival. His entry into the room was facilitated by Sunflower who opened the window for him. Jyotika screamed in shock at the unexpected arrival.

Sunflower went up to her and embraced her to calm her down.

'I only asked him to come. Look at him. Isn't he a magnificent specimen? I want this night to blow your mind with a kind of intense pleasure you wouldn't even have imagined existed in this world.'

Jyotika shuddered and shrank away from his embrace. Sunflower turned away his affections, redirecting them towards the Moroccan.

The two men had eyes only for each other. The Moroccan eased Sunflower of his remaining clothing. Sunflower helped Ismail strip his sweat-stained clothing.

The two men kissed passionately; ivory and black flesh intertwined and created contours that flowed within and without. Their muscles, bones and uneven breathing in unison. Jyotika watched them making love first in horror, and then fascination, as a burning, unquenchable desire grew in her.

Suddenly, Sunflower gently pushed the Moroccan away. He stood stark naked in front of her.

'Come to me, Jyotika. Now it will be the three of us. An unholy but pleasure-filled triangle. Life is all about geometric shapes. Let us complete ours. I promise, you will remember this night for the rest of your life. Give in to your deepest desires and fantasies, Jyotika, Joyeux coot, Mademoiselle!'

Sunflower spread out his arms inviting her. Jyotika, as if under spell, looked at him in complete confusion and wonderment. She violently shook, her hands covering her breasts. She could not believe it—perhaps a force of nature propelled her to take the first step and walk towards Sunflower.

Sunflower gently eased her hands away from her breasts. He kissed her on her dry, quivering lips, gently as a feather touch. No more than that at first. And then, Ismail gently kissed her naked back. She started to cry and laugh at the same time. Then, the three intertwined like a mythological plant—its creepers dancing in the air, flowing and curling in each other, a complex, intricate, intractable mesh of life and passion.

She felt wave after wave of sheer pleasure irradiating her, cascading, ebbing, and never ending in her deepest recesses. She was in the vortex, the circle of life in its very nuclei. Her senses were inflamed with unimagined joy. And then, in almost slow motion, the door of the room broke open, torn off at hinges and men with guns burst in, yelling sickening obscenities.

Who would control the narrative after that? Karandikar or Sunflower. Both men had less than three seconds, or perhaps none, to decide what to do next. Sunflower knew what it was all about; he could sense what Karandikar had in mind. The gun hand was taking its firing position. This meant he had to dodge a bullet in a millisecond.

Sunflower like a naked, Greek Olympian athlete of yore, turned and raced to the open window at incredible speed. He dived out of it, halfway in his run a bullet singing past his ear. He hurtled down the spiral staircase at the back of the building, breaking his fall two floors below while clinging to an iron railing.

He found himself looking through the open window of a hotel room below. A newly-married woman wearing her wedding *chura* (sacred bangles), lay on the naked torso of her young husband. Both were watching a new release *Raja Rani*, the lead actor, Rajesh Khanna, soulfully singing *Main ek chor tu meri rani* to Sharmila Tagore.

The woman screamed her guts out on seeing a naked man outside the room window hanging onto a railing and peeping in. Sunflower looked below and calculated the fall—he would survive it. He silently dropped another two floors, absorbing the pain that shot up his knees.

He quickly recovered and pounded down the road, disappearing in a by-lane.

Upstairs, Karandikar knew he had lost the plot. Nonetheless, he had to give it a try. He sent his three-man team to hunt down Sunflower, despite knowing that it was pointless. He pointed his service revolver at Jyotika and Ismail, and screamed orders at them. 'On the floor, you two! Lie on your stomach, hands behind your head and look up at me.'

Jyotika was screaming and crying at the same time. Ismail grimly looked at the broken door, calculating his chance to escape. Karandikar was consulting his watch.

After a while, the three-man team returned. The head constable whispered in the officer's ear. Karandikar could not hide his disappointment. He looked at the two naked individuals stretched on the floor in front of him. He took a decision.

He sheathed his weapon in his hip holster. Then he bent on his knee and took out an unregistered firearm from his ankle holster. Ismail immediately knew what would happen next; Jyotika did not. Karandikar shot both Jyotika and Ismail between the eyes in quick succession. Jyotika probably never comprehended how swiftly and ruthlessly her life had been snuffed out.

Then, Karandikar fired a couple of rounds on the ceiling and took another shot aimed at the *The Graduate* poster. Dustin Hoffman suddenly looked silly looking lustfully at Anne Bancroft, with a hole in his head.

Karandikar, then, wiped the firearm clean of all prints with a hanky and carefully placed the weapon next to Ismail.

The three-man team did not even blink at what their boss had done. They had been compensated for any eventuality. They knew what their boss was capable of. They understood the need to alter the story. That Sunflower had escaped and the plot had failed could not be told to the jute king. Men of such powerful disposition have a limited capacity to tolerate failure. They seek compensation for failure or incompetence. The bribe money would have to be returned, of course, but it would not stop there. The powerful jute king was quite capable of ending Karandikar's career. He could get him replaced, suspended or even dismissed from the lucrative Colaba police station.

Unless, of course, Karandikar altered the story, which he did. The new version would say that, before the police team arrived on the scene, the diabolical Sunflower—under the influence of drugs, probably heroin—had forced the innocent Jyotika and a foreign national, Ismail, strip and make love at gunpoint. The sadistic Sunflower did not stop at that. He played Russian roulette with them and fired a few rounds in the walls. Finally, he gave in to his perversity, shooting both the young girl and the cook in the head. Then, he wiped the unregistered firearm clean of all prints and placed it next to Ismail, before escaping through the window and backstairs.

It was end of the road for Sunflower in Bombay. Maybe he would be talked about for some time in the by-lanes of Colaba, and then the file on him would eventually be closed and the case forgotten. The place was a hot-spot, a kind of magnet, for all kinds of international characters on the loose—many of them on the run from the law. These were men and women living outside the pale of society, leading debauched, bohemian, and unconventional lives. Drug mules, smugglers, good-looking women of ill repute, hippies, the seekers of karma and forever peace, the addicted and the vicious, the drunkards and the druggies—they were all there in Colaba.

Death in the by-lanes of Colaba was not uncommon. It was a routine, everyday event. No one cared when the flotsam of society dwindled in numbers.

Sunflower was gone, and if he would be remembered at all, it would not be for the double murder he had supposedly committed. It would be for his unique name.

★★★

Chapter 14

Mother and son ate their breakfast in silence. Priya knew all too well that her relationship with the son she loved—almost to a distraction—was fractured. Surprisingly, an old habit had not changed—they would still have breakfast together every day. Even more surprisingly, it was Prahlad who would insist on it. There would be little conversation on the breakfast table, but the simple act of sitting across the table facing each other held out hope for Priya—that the thread binding them had grown tenuous, but had not snapped yet.

Priya attempted a conversation, flashing a broad smile. She was happy that her son was relishing the omelette. He looked preoccupied, but cheerful. Maybe there was still some hope. A return to the old ways, perhaps?

'It's a lovely day today. Quite surprising though. Where's your youthful brigade? They are not outside the lawns making a ruckus. They are taking a day off?'

Prahlad drank some orange juice before answering the gentle query with a deadpan face, 'They are not here, mother, because they are all at Kamini's farmhouse, finalising arrangements.'

'Arrangements? What arrangements?'

Prahlad put down his fork and knife.

'Mother, Kamini and I are getting married this Sunday at her dad's farmhouse. Perhaps, I should have told you earlier. Completely slipped my mind.'

Priya Kaul suddenly felt as if a tinnitus sound pierced her ear. It grew louder and intense, becoming so strong as if it would cleave her brain. She felt numbed and yet cold. She heard herself speaking, as if her voice was coming from afar.

'You are what? Getting married to that.... Have you gone crazy, Prahlad? Has that witch taken possession of your mind? How can you do this to me?'

Prahlad threw a napkin on his plate with disgust. He nosily got up in a rage. His finger shook as he pointed it accusingly at his mother.

'That is why I did not want to tell you, because I know you too well. All your life, you have tried to control me. Not even once you have considered what I think or feel, or what I want. It's always been about you. Well, I have news for you, mother. I have broken off the spell. I will be spending the rest of my life with Kamini. You can accept it or not. You can fry in your misery for all I care. We are going ahead with our marriage plans this Sunday. You can choose to attend it or skip it. Your choice. I won't be breaking a sweat over it either way!'

Prahlad stormed out of the dining room. The tinnitus noise she had experienced was subsiding. Her eyes stung with tears. Her body was wracked in sobs. Sitting on that dining table, she felt like the loneliest woman in the world. She was shut out, unable to get back in. It was lonely, frightening and hopeless—all at the same time.

Later, Priya collected herself to think straight on the new crisis in her life. She forced herself to evaluate her own feelings and actions on what had just happened. Maybe, there *was* a grain of truth in what Prahlad was saying. She could be resentful, commandeering and, perhaps, even biased at times. Maybe, Prahlad had been groaning under the weight of her frailties for a very long time. After all, what did she really want for him? The very best, to say the least. And maybe, she had misjudged Kamini? Could she pretend to be enthusiastic about her son's wedding? She should try, at least.

Priya Kaul steeled herself on the wedding day to keep matters civil. She would have to put on her best smile, of course. As her sedan came closer to the farmhouse, loud sounds of Punjabi-style revelry rent the air. She braced herself in her official car.

The next one hour swam in front of Priya as an unreal, disjointed, and incredible event—the kind she did not even know existed in everyday life. It was really a melange of unsettling images that stayed in her mind. Her *samdhi* (her son's father-in-law), a retired army officer, came swaying up to her and embraced her, or rather ambushed her, his cheeks flushed, and his breath reeking of whisky. And then, he had the audacity of twirling hundred-rupee notes atop her head and throwing them in a shower on the *dholwallahs* (drum beaters). There were fleeting images of Kamini smirking at her, perhaps silently laughing at her discomfiture. The ultimate insult came when she gifted the Atth (gold chain) tied to a Dejhor (ear pendulum-like jewellery) and fixed it to Kamini's ear with her own hands. Five minutes later, Kamini casually took off the family heirloom and tossed it over in the stubby hands of her mother, who immediately disposed of it in an opaque black ladies bag kept by her side. The sheer audacity of the invited guests—drinking straight from whisky bottles and even celebrating by firing in the air with unlicensed weapons in the presence of the Prime Minister. A chiaroscuro of unashamed vulgarity!

And then, the image that stayed with her—as if she was looking at herself from a distance. After the awe of the Prime Minister of the country attending a raucous Punjabi wedding had died down, she found herself sitting alone, unattended, in a section of empty chairs next to the marriage *mandap* (sacred marriage spot). Alone, watching her son and his new-found family and friends dance wildly in the distance after conclusion of the marriage vows, drunk out of their minds.

She looked at her son, not recognising who he was. She knew, then, she had lost him, perhaps irretrievably, forever.

★★★

Chapter 15

The iron cage elevator came to a stop on the fifth floor and Venkat Iyer, tired out of his mind, stumbled out, making his way to his apartment. The corridor leading to his apartment was in the dark, save a ceiling light that blinked furiously.

'What the hell?' thought the scientist. 'What had happened here?'

As he made his way to his corner apartment, he observed in the dim light a plastic sheet covering the length of the floor. The ceiling panels had been prised open leaving a jumble of wires hanging out precariously.

'Bloody maintenance,' he swore under his breath. 'They can never get anything right. What was so urgent that they had to rip up the entire corridor?'

Dr Iyer was about to press the apartment bell when he saw the watchhands on his wrist. It was close to midnight. Both Jayasudha and Tara would have gone off to sleep.

Best not to wake them up. He took out the spare key and inserted it in the keyhole. The front door swung open to a brightly lit household, up and about. Jayasudha sat on the dining table engrossed in the Tamil magazine *Kalki*. Tara sat cross-legged on the coir carpeted floor, assembling and dismantling building blocks.

'Both of you should have gone to sleep. Why wait for me?' he protested. Jayasudha smiled and got up to take care of his briefcase.

'Even if I wanted to sleep, she would not let me. You know that perfectly well. She waits for you. Always has, always will. Now, shall I warm up some sambhar? You must be starving.'

Dr Iyer loosened his tie, carefully observing his daughter engrossed in the building blocks.

'Don't bother, Jaya. I have had some snacks during the day. Don't really have an appetite.'

'*Aiyo*, Venkat,' responded Jayasudha. 'That is so careless of you. Those canteen snacks are not good for your gut. You know that, yet you always forget to take precautions. Let me at least make some cooling lemonade for you to ease your gut.'

'Okay,' he replied absentmindedly. 'I will spend some time playing with Tara.'

During their short interaction, Tara did not look at her father even once. She was intently looking at the building blocks. Dr Iyer went up to her and sat next to her quietly.

He picked up a building block to help her. She smacked his hand away. Again, back to the fierce concentration. He waited with bated breath. Then, she gently pinched his hand giving him the go-ahead. He fixed the building block in its proper slot. He put his arms around his daughter and kissed her on her forehead. She pushed him away. Demonstrative affection was not her cup of tea. He played building blocks with her for some time before she snuggled up to him in his lap and went off to sleep.

He waited a while, picked her up, put her to bed in the next room and gently closed the door after him. He went to his room, sat on his bed and took off his wristwatch. Jayasudha came up to him holding a glass of lemonade. As he took a sip, his whole body shook with sobs. As Jayasudha took the glass from him, he took off his spectacles and buried his head in her waist. She stroked his salt and pepper hair and whispered, 'It's okay, Venkat. It's okay. I understand.'

Tears streamed down his eyes as he looked up.

'She is so vulnerable, so innocent. And so, so… affectionate. I…wish I could do more for her. Look at the cruelty of fate. I am the topmost scientist in the country. I can break the atom to create unheard of energy. Yet, I cannot restore my daughter's health. There is no cure for her ailment, and there might never be. How cruel, cruel it is all then….'

Jayasudha sat by his side as he curled up and rested

his head in her lap. She continued to ruffle his hair and softly spoke into his ear, 'You are a good father and a caring husband, Venkat. That is all that matters. And we three love each other. Completely, unconditionally. Now and forever. That is enough for me. And, who knows? It might also be enough for Tara. Only she knows what she thinks in the deepest recesses of her mind. Maybe she is happy in her own world? Why should we presume otherwise?' Dr Iyer fell quiet, and they both held each other. The warmth of her embrace calmed his frayed nerves. He began to feel drowsy and drifted into sleep. Jayasudha softly spoke in his ear, 'I have never seen the kind of maintenance work they did today. They not only dismantled the corridor ceiling, but also inserted new wiring inside the apartment. The telephone connection will be restored tomorrow. Wish they would have given an advance notice before undertaking such repairs.'

Dr Venkat Iyer was suddenly wide awake. He immediately knew what was going on. All the telephone lines and light devices were being bugged. Not only him, but practically every scientist associated with the project was under surveillance. He might be close to Priya Kaul, but even he had not been spared—he was also under the scanner. That was classic Rhino. 'Believe no one, trust no one' was his guiding principle. Maybe even Rhino was under surveillance in some bizarre way.

He got up and put on his spectacles. Jayasudha,

looking worried, got up beside him.

'What is it, Venkat?'

Dr Iyer spelt it out clearly, 'Listen to me very carefully, Jaya. For the next six months, we will be on test. Under severe test, I should say. I am to undertake a project of the utmost national importance. I cannot utter a word about this project to you. They make fun of these terms now, but in this case, it is all true—this project is a top secret. I have been in charged with to execute this project…to make it successful. I will be grinding others to carry out the project. But, make no mistake about it. I will also be in the mixer; there is no escaping that. Now, my success completely depends on you. All three of us will come under intense pressure inexplicably. And, we will only get through it if you hold the line for all of us. I will be asking a lot from you, Jaya. I have no other choice.'

★★★

Chapter 16

The forty-seater, underground film screening theatre in Langley went dark. The projection beam brought to life the opening credits of the film *Ice station Zebra*. Two men sat in the theatre, but not next to each other. CIA Director, Joe Stanstedt, sat in the front row, dressed in his trademark tweed jacket and bow tie. Freckles sat in the last row watching the film. What was he doing in the auditorium watching an old film he was least interested in? He had been told to attend the movie screening. Rumour was rife that the CIA Director was obsessed with it, watching it hundreds of times. But, his thirst for watching it again and again was insatiable.

Freckles partly slept through the film, waking up only when the lights came on in the private cinema. A girl in a smart, blue uniform wheeled in a mobile tray laden with a whisky decanter and Coke cans. Stanstedt turned his attention to Freckles seated at the back and broadly smiled.

'Come up and sit next to me, young man.'

Freckles moved up the seating and the Director offered him whisky splashed on ice cubes.

Freckles politely refused.

'I don't drink, Sir.'

'Well, then maybe a Coke can? You surely can't refuse that.'

The two men settled in their seats and sipped their drinks. Director Stanstedt opened a conversation.

'You must have heard from the grapevine my obsession with the film. The rumours are true to an extent. I do feel the urge to see the film again and again. Howard Hughes, that crazy millionaire aviator, had a similar obsession. But, I am not nuts like him. Question is what drives me to watch the film again and again?'

The Director looked askance at Freckles giving him a chance to answer. Freckles kept quiet. The Director smiled and splashed some more whisky on ice cubes.

'Not much of a talker, are you? I am impressed. You are a listener and not a talker. You will go far. Anyway, the point of meeting here instead of an antiseptic office is this—I love the film because it is set in such a rugged, lonely and isolated place. And the most consequential decisions impacting national security are taken out there.'

The Director paused again, giving Freckles a chance to chip in. The tight-lipped spy stared back at the Director stone faced. Stanstedt continued.

'India is your beat. Honestly, no one cares about India. Many folks here confuse the country with the Red Indian nation. India is a basket case. Its neighbour Pakistan is way ahead on all parameters. Even some countries in Africa are doing better than India. And yet….'

Freckles stepped in and quietly replied, 'And yet, like the Arctic in the film, India in the future will be a place of potential. All sorts of possibilities will emerge in that country—possibilities that will impact the whole world.'

The Director stopped smiling and picked up a file kept on the seat next to him. He leafed through Freckles' confidential file and looked grimly at this man posted in India.

'You are an orphan, right? You must be resenting everyone in this building who are to the manner born. That is but a natural reaction. If I were in your shoes, I would also be resentful. Incidentally, I am also to the manner born. And, I would advise you to work twice as hard, maybe take twice the risk, to reach anywhere in the hierarchical ladder. That is the truth. Accept it.

'Now, let me expand the term "twice as hard". We have picked up intelligence that the Soviets could be planning something big in Afghanistan. Their formations are amassing and a massive build up is taking place. If the Reds move into Afghanistan, an important geo-strategic part of the world would be lost to us. So, we have a huge threat, but we also have an opportunity that comes once in a lifetime.'

The Director paused, holding up his glass in the air.

He swirled the fast-melting ice cubes and watched in fascination the ice disappear in the bourbon.

'Freckles, we will not do anything to stop the Soviet march into Afghanistan. We want them to go in. But, once they are in, we will close Afghanistan around them like a trap. We will bleed them dry for months, maybe years. How do we do that? We will fund and build up a resistance force of Afghan guerrilla fighters that will drain the lifeblood from the Soviets. It has already been suggested to call these guerrillas Mujahideen. These guerrillas fight for their faith and community (ummah). Our friends in the Pakistani agency ISI will be their handlers. But, of course, we will control the entire chessboard, from opening moves to checkmate.'

The Director gulped down his whisky and turned his full attention to Freckles. A manic zeal lit his beady eyes.

'Do you understand what all this means? Think of the possibilities. Knowing the Soviets, and their ego and pride, they will not be in a hurry to withdraw quickly then. We will bleed them continuously like a serrated knife placed on a chicken's neck, slicing through millimetre by millimetres, taking our sweet time to chop the neck off. The slow bleed over time will reduce Soviet power to a hollow shell. Their military will be winnowed and denuded, and their economy will be devastated. Who knows, maybe it could even lead to a breakup of the Soviet empire? That's how the chess board will be laid. And, this is where you come in.'

Freckles suddenly understood the man demanding his attention. He understood what the man represented. It would be old school, entitlement to the good life, privileged and to the manner born, American capitalism and power at its most bloody, rapacious, and powerful best or worst. At various time in history, such men were termed as profiteers or, at other times, patriots upholding their country's interests. It would depend on what was your inclination in world affairs. The only thing true of such men was that they would go to any extent to secure what they really wanted.

The Director's remark, 'This is where you come in' burnt like an ember in Freckles. The bizarre setting of attending a private movie screening and drinking whisky on the rocks faded away from Freckles consciousness. Suddenly, he was alert, and hungry; he already saw in his mind the chess pieces move zig-zag in a cutting-edge game. He wanted all that was being offered to him. But, for that he would have to be stone-faced, and clinical, showing no emotion. Appearances mattered. He knew, that was the test.

The Director absorbed Freckles' reaction and continued, 'You, Freckles, will be the first-ever agent, my point man, who will set this gameplay in motion. There will be hundreds of other agents involved, but they will all come in later. You will lay the groundwork. Your job is to get the Pakistanis interested in our offer and take charge of the Afghan resistance—this means that you will liaison with the ISI to get the ball rolling. That will be your test.

Dealing with the ISI is not for the chicken-hearted. They are the kind of people who will take our dollars, gladly accept the arms and ammunition we provide them with, and yet stab us in the back.

'And, know this, Freckles, without the Pakistanis on board, there will be no Mujahideen in Afghanistan. If that doesn't happen, the Soviets will win and disengage that part of the world from us.

'And, the key to keeping the Pakistanis interested in this gameplay is India…' Freckles, of course, knew why India would be the key to the puzzle. But he pretended to go along, listening to his super boss in full flow.

'India, Sir?' he politely enquired.

The Director made himself another drink.

'India is the key because Pakistan is obsessed with India. They fear they can give their utmost to the Afghan operation only if they don't have to keep looking over their shoulder, worrying that India might come up from behind and attack them someday. So, the moot question is what we do with India.'

'Sir?'

The Director let out a low laugh.

'That is what we are known for, isn't it, Freckles? We do things to other countries. We amputate them, and make them hobble to our advantage.'

Freckles studied his senior counterpart with intense concentration. This was going beyond what he had expected. And the Director told him so.

'We kill many, many birds with one stone—released from the CIA catapult. Fielding hates Priya Kaul; she has humiliated him in the past. How can we forget the Bay of Bengal humiliation? She outshines our President with her articulation and personality on the world stage. He wants her gone. So, make that happen, Freckles. We have an opportunity now—she is at her weakest. The Opposition is mounting intolerable pressure on her government. Make inroads in the Opposition ranks. Precipitate a regime change, at least, spread chaos in that country. Force their military to remain occupied with the internal affairs and not bother with Pakistan. Clear the decks for our Pakistani friends so that we can play the great game in Afghanistan.'

There was complete silence in the theatre. The Director edged closer to the Chosen One.

'Freckles, you were born a bastard. I don't mean that in a pejorative sense. I mean it as a strength. I can sense the fire burning fiercely in you. A bastard always has a point to prove in a world of the entitled, to the manner born. So, prove your point. Make this happen. In return, I promise you to take you to the very top.'

The Director got up and painfully walked to the door on arthritic legs. He paused his hand on the doorknob.

'What kind of a name is Freckles anyway?'

★★★

Chapter 17

Freckles was back in Delhi, sitting in the office of the US Ambassador to India, Samuel Douglas Jr. The senior diplomat sat on his chair, facing Freckles shifting weight uneasily. An unexplained tension hung in the air. Freckles was absorbed in a file proffered by the Ambassador. Freckles did not look particularly happy with what he read in the file. He looked up sharply. 'Best we call him in and quiz him. That would set my mind to rest.'

The Ambassador toyed with a paper cutter kept on the desk. He did not seem pleased by Freckles assertion which appeared like an intemperate order. Moreover, the Ambassador was fond of Shanti Bhushan. After all, he only had recruited the man and trained him before deploying him for operations. He was comfortable with whatever the man stood for.

Samuel Douglas scowled and pushed buttons on the intercom, instructing his personal assistant to send in the man in question.

Shanti Bhushan, rotund and bowed, walked in with hands folded in a namaskar, smiling beatifically. Freckles looked at him carefully. The man did not look or behave like an asset—he looked more like a caricature from some bygone era, the kind who scrapes and bows to white people. Freckles was least interested in cultural bipolarity games. He simply wanted to get the job done. The job description demanded a man on the CIA payroll in Delhi, a local to keep surveillance on senior bureaucrats, politicians and journos. Shanti Bhushan did not look that man, maybe, his appearance was deceptive.

Freckles knew he had to assess him. He quizzed Shanti Bhushan about his work profile, and soon realised that he was more of a liability than an asset. His modus operandi, if one could call it, was bribing clerks and stenos in offices and bumbling his way in the corridors of power. Freckles doubted that even a mid-level government officer or bureaucrat would allow such a person to walk in their office and open a negotiation. Another few minutes of quizzing convinced Freckles that the Intelligence Bureau (IB) in Delhi was aware of the man's activities, and tolerated him because he was ordinary and incompetent. Maybe, they wanted him to stay in circulation to keep tabs on the American Embassy.

Was that the case, or was it something else?

Freckles no longer cared to quiz the greasy-looking

man. It was useless, a lost cause. Shanti Bhushan got up and bowed before the Ambassador. Samuel Douglas smiled, opened a drawer in his desk, pulled out a thick wad of Indian currency notes, and tossed it to Shanti Bhushan like a bone to a dog.

'Great job, Shanti, tailing the Chief Secretary the other day. Send me a report of all his watering holes. Keep it up!'

Freckles noticed the exchange of looks between the Ambassador and the asset—a brief look of understanding, comfort, and easiness. That very instant, Freckles knew. He had his answer. He understood why incompetence was at a premium at the Embassy.

The Ambassador was on the take. The Ambassador was disbursing large sums of unaccounted money for surveillance operations, the value of which was close to zilch. And, he probably had a cut in the outflow. The quality of intelligence collected in New Delhi was close to a big, fat zero simply because the Ambassador, close to retirement, was lining up his coffers. Freckles knew his feelings for the Ambassador were not exactly polite.

Cold-faced, Freckles summed up the meeting after Shanti Bhushan had left the room.

'I can now see, Sir, why you indulge this man. It is crystal clear to me that the network here is nothing but a complete set-up—a scam no less. I am sorry, Sir, I will have to send a report to the higher-ups…'

Samuel Douglas' face purpled with exertion and rage,

'Why, you pimply-faced, little brat! The temerity of you to make such an accusation! I will have your balls tied to a string wire…'

The door to the Ambassador's room suddenly opened by the unannounced arrival of Justine, the Ambassador's wife. She walked in the room and threw a clutch of shopping bags on the sofa. She looked hot and flustered. Freckles checked himself, got up and did a quick curtsy, offering his hand.

'Delighted to make your acquaintance, Ma'am. I don't think we have met,' Freckles said.

Justine, somewhat calmer, managed a smile and shook Freckles hand.

'Ah, you must be the super spook Washington has sent to transform our lives. The man with a great name, Freckles! Welcome friend!'

The volatility in the room subsided at Justine's colourful description of him. Freckles smiled.

He noticed that though she was around fifty, or thereabouts, she wore her years lightly. She was tall and angular, and browned by the Indian sun; her light-grey eyes sparkled intelligently, almost playfully. She wore an Indian-styled, ethnic kurta-churidar. It was well known in Embassy circles that she was an Indophile, and would be found loitering around the Janpath area market in Delhi on most afternoons.

Justine flopped on the sofa and said her piece to the

Ambassador, 'Darling, can you imagine they are closing the café Bankura at the cottage emporium for renovations! I had plans to host a lunch party for renowned practitioners of the sarod instrument. Now those plans will have to be shelved. I am in such despair!'

The Ambassador welcomed the relief provided by his India-loving wife. He was squirming under the steely gaze of Freckles who knew in an instant that he ran a sham operation. He knew he had no choice, but to pass the baton to the ruthless, young and impatient spy. Maybe, he could still hold on to his job for some more time.

He smiled for the benefit of his wife.

'It's okay, dear, we can host your friends at the Embassy. The staff will even plan for a…what do you call it…a sarod recital on the premises…how about that?'

Justine let out whoops of delight, gathered her bags and streamed out of the room. Freckles waited for her to exit the room and then slowly got up clutching his satchel. He paused near the door.

'I am sorry, Sir, for the rudeness. Whatever you might have done, or not done, your wife enjoys an excellent reputation in Washington. I am prepared to let sleeping dogs lie. But, know this—all these malpractices end right now. I am taking over the entire intelligence operation. There has been a power shift here—you are free to verify that. I have an agenda, and nothing on the earth, least of all you, can stop me from realising that.'

Freckles walked out slowly and waited at the door for a few seconds. He strained himself, and heard the voice of a man sounding contrite.

'Thanks for the reprieve, son. Maybe there's been some bad decision-making here. Shit like this happens in such out-of-sight, out-of-mind places. Have it your way, young man.'

Close to 10 pm that night, Shanti Bhushan, after a satisfying meal of chicken curry and rice, stepped out of his house for a short walk to have a popular late-night digestive known as *paan* (a betel leaf wrapped up with areca nut, slaked lime, fennel seeds and cardamom). Shanti Bhushan lit a cigarette and hummed a popular tune as he slowly made his way to the local *paan wallah* shop around the corner. Life was good. Money was flowing in, and his stars were aligned. He was feeding bullshit to the ignorant Americans which no one bothered to verify. Such an easy, simple and lucrative job.

A black Ambassador, with tinted windows and faulty headlights, suddenly shot out from a side street at incredible speed, heading straight for him. The last sound Shanti Bhushan ever heard in his life was the roar of a powerful Ambassador car as it rushed towards him. Next, he sailed in the air, his body torn and bloody. He was transported to his childhood, to the annual Dusshera village fair. He was on the top of a Ferris wheel, staring down. Load-shedding had cut off the electricity and the

Ferris wheel had stopped rotating. He was stuck at the top. 'Bloody electricity cuts!' he cursed under his breath. It could be an all-night affair before he and the others on the wheel could be rescued. How he longed to escape this country and run off to America!

Life had come full circle. He was back on top, where he had been stuck a long time ago. But this time around, he was not coming down.

★★★

Chapter 18

'Call me Mr F,' spoke the freckled, intense-looking young man. The older man sitting opposite the American in an eatery in Patna did not look convinced.

'Your full name and designation, please.'

'Why?' contested the young man.

'Because it matters in India. We don't deal with riff-raff. I just hope I am not wasting my time talking to a hippie. There are so many of them in India, looking for God knows what.'

Freckles suppressed a smile. The man was right, of course. Only low-budget American tourists, some of them euphemistically called hippies, bothered to come to India. He had managed a meeting with the right-hand man of the Opposition leader, Tapash. It was said Alvin Mahuto was the brains trust of the Opposition movement, with the singular goal to unseat Priya Kaul. This man would be key to what he was planning next. He could not let this meeting fail. Reluctantly, he took out a card from his trouser pocket and placed it before Alvin.

The swarthy-looking older man carefully looked at the card. 'Central Intelligence Agency' was embossed on the card, along with the company logo. The name 'Harry Smith (Freckles)' stared back at Alvin from the bottom. And so did the designation, 'Bureau Chief'.

Alvin frowned, not looking convinced at all.

'Bureau Chief…what is that? What do you do?'

Freckles was genuinely stumped momentarily. He stammered, 'I…I guess, I am the man who connects the dots…'

Alvin Mahuto's face became a contemptuous mask. He flicked the card to the ground. 'You are wasting my time, Mr F.'

Freckles held up his hand, 'Don't go. Give me a minute to explain. I think we got off on the wrong footing here.'

Freckles looked around in the eatery which doubled up as a recreation centre for retirees in the evening. Someone had left behind a cheap pack of cards resting on the sugary rings of tea glasses on a table. Freckles borrowed the pack of cards and proceeded to build an inverted V-shaped house of cards with vacant spaces in between. Task completed, he scribbled a number on a paper napkin and slid it in the vacant space.

Quite intrigued, Alvin collected the napkin and looked at the number. Freckles lowered his head and looked at Alvin cold-faced.

'I am the moneybags man in the CIA. I am quite prepared to help your cause financially. You can add some zeros to the number, and we will give you the cash every second week of the month.'

It was now Alvin Mahuto's turn to lower his head.

'What do you seek in return? Do you want to bring Coca Cola back in India?'

'I don't care about aerated drinks—they are bad for health. I want something that would benefit both of us. We both want Priya Kaul to go. Our President cannot stand her. You must be aware of that. We are prepared to fund your agitation to unseat the Prime Minister. Bring about, what we call, a "regime change". Now, can you get me a meeting with Tapash?'

Alvin Mahuto did not respond immediately. He was breathing heavily, a crick developing in his neck. But, he kept his head lowered. He carefully chose his words,

'A meeting with Tapash is out of the question. He would never deal with the CIA or, for that matter, the Americans. He's a hard core socialist. He has opposed America all his life. He is an inspirational figure. His job is to inspire people; my job is to fuel the agitation. We keep separate compartments. You deal with me—this means you must trust me if this has to work.'

Alvin Mahuto scribbled on a paper napkin and pushed it towards Freckles. 'Those are the details of a bank account outside this country. You make an initial transfer of cash. Then, we will take it up from there.'

Business concluded, both men got up and rubbed their necks. Freckles looked at his house of cards on the table. He drew in a deep breath and exhaled forcefully. The stack of cards crumpled like matchsticks. Freckles coldly looked at Alvin.

'So easy to blow it away, isn't it? Now, just imagine if Priya Kaul was sitting in the middle of this house. What would happen to her?'

★★★

Chapter 19

The man at the window, ensconced in a fourth-floor hotel room overlooking the city square, looked through a telephoto lens. He made a few adjustments to his camera settings, and the images of the Bath village square sharpened perceptibly. It was not tourist season, and a blustery wind swept across the square. Few tourists milled about the main courtyard, and that suited the man at the window just fine. His camera picked up two tourist buses that alighted not too far away from the main courtyard. A bunch of Indians disembarked from the buses and slowly made their way to the main square.

The group of Indians could have been an advertisement of India's diversity—varying in shapes, sizes and features, skin colour palettes and even attire. There were those clad in tweeds and the traditional monkey cap to ward off the cold. But some of the more adventurous opted for the in-fashion striped, long sleeve, T shirts and short, rimmed

Fedora hats. But, practically all of them had Kodak cameras slung across their neck. After all, the wonderful healing Roman spas at Bath had to be captured on film.

The man at the window took a break from his surveillance and made some corrections on a piece of paper pinned on the noticeboard above his study desk. Then, he reached for the phone and dialled a number at the Indian High Commission in London. A matronly, greying blonde, with hair tied severely in a bun, picked up the receiver at the other end.

'Yes?' she asked curtly.

The voice at the other end was equally terse.

'They have arrived. Best you be on your way. And organise the van from Soho.'

The stodgy woman put down the receiver and picked up her bag. Lots to be done before she made the journey to Bath.

The group of Indian senior scientists working at BARC coalesced around Dr Venkat Iyer, their group leader. He had surprised them last week by proposing a four-day trip to London and Bath. His reason was simple—they had all put in hard work, especially at the CIRUS (Canada India Reactor Utility Services) reactor, and the senior leaders in the country were happy with the broad-basing and development of indigenous nuclear technologies for peaceful purposes. So, to that end, a four-day junket was suggested.

It was no secret that the country was going through tough times. The economic indices were majorly down. That might be true, but who could resist the prospect of an all-paid trip to the United Kingdom? Despite the condescending attitude and racist behaviour of many Britishers, London was still the preferred destination. A trip to London meant boasting rights for the missus amongst her relatives and friends that the government had chosen her husband for an all-paid trip to the United Kingdom. It could also mean the purchase of a Philips electric iron for the missus, Lindt chocolate bars for the kids and maybe, just maybe, an imported Grundig television set for the family. Now, if that miracle and purchase happened, then the entire family could watch the Sunday movie on Doordarshan, and listen to the film songs package called *Chitrahaar* on Wednesdays, on the imported screen of a Grundig TV!

Dr Iyer addressed the group of scientists in the town square.

'Friends, a few words before we enjoy what all Bath has to offer. You have earned this trip, and you deserve it. We have had a good two days in London, and we should repeat the same in Bath. Unlike London, I will not be a nanny on this trip. You are free to form your own groups, explore the place and shop as you will. All meals and our lodging expenses are, of course, taken care of. Just remember to assemble tomorrow at this square at 3 pm for the return trip. Any questions, anyone?'

The large group of nearly a hundred scientists broke off in splinter groups, while a few ventured out on their own. Many of them headed to a nearby hotel to check out their rooms. The famed Roman baths were, of course, on everyone's must-visit list. Others ambled off, walking along the cobbled streets to grab a pint of Guinness in the various pubs and dives dotting the meandering streets. A few with a sweet-tooth walked to a nearby café to grab a bite of the famous English scones, washed down with tea imported from the sloping hills of Darjeeling. And some others sat on the benches in the town square, talking obsessively of their projects and research.

By 9 pm, most of the scientists had checked in their hotel rooms tired, but happy, with the exertions of the day. Many called it a night and went to sleep almost immediately, while others out of habit struggled with a few pages of light reading before hitting the sack.

Close to midnight, some of the scientists in their rooms woke up to the sound of soft but persistent knocking on their doors. Turning the lights on, bewildered scientists opened their doors. Though the hallway was dark, the profile of the person knocking on the door was clearly visible. And, the profiles of all the girls at the doors of the scientists were almost identical—a blue-eyed blonde seductively positioned at the door. Most of the girls wore short tartan skirts with halter neck tops showing deep cleavage, with an all-knowing, come-explore smile pasted on their faces.

Their entry line in the room was a script whispered softly, 'I am here to provide service, Sir. To relax you. It's all been taken care of, Sir. I will be completely discreet about this. There will be no tales told of this night to anyone. May I come in?'

Most of the scientists rejected the advances of the audacious girls. Whether they did so out of the conviction of their moral fibre, or whether the images of their wives back home preparing sambhar in the kitchen swam before their eyes at that very moment—or perhaps it was the thought that, at the end of the day, they were government servants who could be sacked for such indiscretions—their exact motives remain unclear to this day. But yes, most rejected a night of temptation.

Yet, some did succumb to the pleasures of the flesh—a few not many.

But surprisingly, not even one of them mentioned these strange intrusions in the night to their colleagues, or took up the matter with the boss. It was the age-old truism that whether they had indulged themselves or not, they all felt guilty by association.

And a guilty man quickly learns to keep his mouth shut.

★★★

Chapter 20

This series of odd unexplained incidents did not end that night. They continued for much of the next morning. A matronly white woman, with hair severely swept back in a bun, was seen conversing with scientists, either in pairs or when they were roaming around alone. She appeared to have an uncanny ability of being in different places at the same time.

The gist of her conversations with the scientists was on the following lines.

'I would like to take a moment of your time, Sir. I have a proposition for you. The agency I work for is aware that you are a person of exceptional brilliance. It is our assessment that your talents are wasted in your given role and in the country of your birth. Come, and join us. You will be paid in dollars and pound sterling, ten times more than your current compensation. You will be posted at a nuclear facility in a western European capital, or somewhere in the United States. You will work amongst people who will be appreciative of your talent.

'Your family, Sir, will also be taken well care of. We will ensure that your children, especially those of college-going age, smoothly enter into prestigious colleges, like Oxford and Cambridge, or the Ivy League colleges in America.'

After her proposal, the matronly lady proceeded to take out a manila envelope from her oversized purse.

With great deliberation, she looked at the stunned scientists in the eye and tried to close the deal.

'Sir, there are £ 500 in the envelope. Even if you reject our offer, please accept this small token of appreciation. It could come in handy picking up items and gifts from the duty-free. Take your time, and let us know whenever you are ready to crossover. Contact details are given in the envelope. Good day to you, Sir.'

Noting how many scientists accepted the envelope is pointless. What is more significant is that these strange encounters rattled the group of scientists no end.

At 3 pm, the entire group assembled in the town square to board their buses. A dozen odd scientists went missing from the group. Yet, no one was prepared to talk of the strange occurrence. The mood of the group had considerably darkened, a sense of dark foreboding gripped everyone.

The two tourist buses left Bath soon after, hitting the high road to London. They soon approached the town of Salisbury. In the distance, military trucks stood idling, with troops lolling around them. They continued onwards, passing vast, lush, deserted cornfields stretching out on both sides of the road. Dusk was rapidly falling, and the light was growing weak.

A red Volkswagen Beetle entered from a side country road, tailing the two buses speeding along the road. Many of the scientists in the second bus looked at the tailing car with a degree of apprehension. The matronly woman, who had been surreptitiously meeting the scientists, was driving the car. A man sat at the back of the car, his face shielded by the rim of his Homburg hat.

And then, without a warning, the two buses halted at the side of the road. The Beetle also stopped, some distance away from the buses.

Dr Venkat Iyer was first off from the lead bus. He signalled to his fellow scientists to embark and gather around him in the middle of a cornfield.

The sullen group of scientists obliged, but a senior colleague could not bear it any longer.

'What the hell is going on, Venkat? I feel the need to speak freely, even if others choose to remain silent. Ever since we have come to Bath, all kinds of visitations and debaucheries have been occurring...'

Dr Iyer held up his hand, counselling silence. The matronly woman emerged from the Beetle and walked towards the group, holding two large wicker baskets. The group viewed in shocked silence when the woman came up to them and put down the baskets. She proceeded to take out cheese and cucumber sandwiches, and offered it to the group. Then, she took out a thermos flask and poured tea in styrofoam cups.

'Thank you, Mrs Chevalier, for your service,' intervened Dr Iyer. 'I will take it up from here. You should be on your way. It would be getting quite late for you.'

The middle-aged woman curtly nodded, closed the wicker baskets and walked back to the Beetle. The man in the back seat of the Beetle emerged and walked towards the assembled scientists in the field. It was spymaster Rhino.

Practically all the scientists started to speak at the same time. There was anger and frustration in their voices. Dr Iyer again advised restraint.

'I understand you have many questions. But, let me speak first. And then, Rhino. You do know him, don't you, or, at the very least, know about him. For the uninitiated, he is the Intelligence Chief of the country.'

But, the dam had broken—the scientists were unchecked and unrestrained. Angry voices rent the air. Rhino moved in the middle of the melee and whiplashed his voice with venom.

'Shut up, everyone, immediately! We are not in a school play! This is a very serious situation. It is an issue of national security. You will all listen to me very carefully, and then, if there is a need, I will take questions after that.

But before I do that, listen to what Dr Iyer has to say.'

There was pin-drop silence after that. Rhino took out a cigarette and lit it. Dr Iyer took over.

'First of all, my deepest apologies for what I have put all of you through. It is in a sense inexcusable. We all go back a long time. You are not only my work colleagues, many of you are also my dear friends. I know that I have played with your emotions and feelings, and, if I may say so, with your loyalties…especially to the organisation we all work for and the country. So sorry for all this. But it was unavoidable. We were running a test. And, I am happy to report that most of us passed that test. However, a few failed it, and that accounts for their absence. They have been put on the first flight back to the country. They will, of course, be reprimanded and suspended from duty. And, probably, isolated from the rest for some time.'

A senior scientist spoke up, 'Have you taken leave of your senses, Venkat? What is the meaning of this? What stupid test are you talking about?'

Rhino crushed his cigarette under his boot and took over.

'Fair question, Sir. And the answer to that is, we are on the cusp of implementing a project that will make world headlines. This group standing in this cornfield will carry out that project. Under no circumstances can details of that project be leaked to the outside world. And the men and women implementing that project must have an extraordinary moral fibre and an unmatched sense of loyalty to our country. Mrs Chevalier, with whom some of you were acquainted some time back, works at the High Commission in London. She is one of us. She has done yeoman service for the country many times. I am sorry for the cheap tactics of sending those girls from Soho to tempt some of you to make a mistake. And all those offers of working at nuclear facilities in western capitals were, of course, bogus. We were testing your resolve to withstand the lure of temptation. I make no apologies for all this though. Extraordinary times call for extraordinary measures.'

The peevish senior scientist again spoke up, 'What is this extraordinary project you keep talking about?'

Rhino looked at the man in the eye and spoke slowly and deliberately.

'Gentlemen, all of you, under the able leadership of Dr Iyer, will build a nuclear device that will be tested soon. You have been given six months to assemble this device. If even a word of this project gets out, we, as a nation, will come under the heel of western powers. That cannot be allowed under any circumstances.

'Now, here's the deal, gentlemen. You are the handpicked group that will carry out this task. You will be subjected to inhuman pressure for the next six months. Your phones are already tapped, and each member of your family is under round-the-clock surveillance. Forget about a life outside your workplace and this peer group.

The stakes are extraordinary for this project. If any one of you leaks this project, or slips up, or ends up getting compromised, you might just get shot. I hope I have made myself clear to all of you.'

★★★

Chapter 21

The undercarriage of the Pakistani Datsun 4 by 4 military vehicle rattled violently as the driver gunned the engine with more power to help him negotiate a road gouged with endless pits. The pit path snaked its way across a pebbled, arid landscape. The sun mercilessly beat down on the Datsun. The driver was doing his best to prevent the vehicle from flying off its wheels and turning turtle. After every minor victory at keeping the vehicle going he would turn to his co-passenger seated beside him and smile broadly, showing yellowed, stained teeth.

Freckles fiercely clutched the support loop above him for his dear life. The whites of his knuckles showed as his stomach churned relentlessly, vomit rising in his throat, itching for a release. His army-issued Ray-bans were smudged with sweat beads freely pouring down his face. The pain ride through the stony desert was an experience worse than mounting and riding a mechanical Rodeo bull in Texas. Welcome to Pakistan!

Just when he thought he could take it no longer, he saw deliverance at a distance. A tent, known as a *shamiana* in those parts, had been erected in the distance. An array of senior army officers sat in the tent. As the Datsun edged closer to the shamiana, he wondered if he was hallucinating in the heat. Strapping, liveried army waiters were serving beverages to the military top brass. They were all sweating in the intense heat, but swilling drinks at the same time. He took off his Ray-bans and watched in disbelief as the army chief, whom he recognised from a photo, helped himself to some scotch in a cut glass offered by a waiter. The waiter brought a large soda flask with siphon and pressed the snorter to dilute the whisky. The smell of sizzling chicken tikkas wafted out of the tent. It was all so surreal and beyond belief.

Freckles found himself shaking hands with the army chief and the ISI chief of Pakistan. He was the guest of honour at their little function organised in the middle of nowhere, surely at a great cost. All for his benefit. With not a blade of grass visible for miles around, the cost of lugging the entire infrastructure for the event must have been enormous.

Freckles gathered his wits and asked his hosts, 'Eh, General Khan…could not help, but wonder, why organise this welcome here…of all the places…'

The beefy looking Generals all started laughing.

Someone backslapped him as if he was their buddy from a long time ago.

The army chief's ruddy face broke into a smile.

'Well, Mr, what was your name, Mr Freckles, we are all Khans here! As to your second concern, this little function was organised here to make a point. I will tell you about that a little later. But, first things first. Some Macallan 18 to slake your thirst? It takes some doing coming all this way.'

'I don't drink,' replied Freckles with a hint of irritation.

The top general looked surprised. 'Oh…That is so sad. Well, maybe a chilled Coke can, then?'

Freckles rolled his eyes. How could the same shit keep happening to him again and again?

Freckles settled for mineral water, and indicated to the army chief that he was ready to talk. The General, chewing a mouthful of chicken tikka, vigorously nodded and smiled at the senior officers surrounding them. They got the message and left. The army chief, the ISI chief and Freckles sat down for a private discussion.

Freckles drew a rough map of the region on the uneven earth with the opposite end of a fork. He tapped the country contiguous to Pakistan. The General chimed in.

'Afghanistan? Well, what of it?'

'General, is it true that the Afghani is a ferocious fighter? No one can subjugate him. They march to their own drumbeat?'

An expression of disdain crossed the army chief's face.

'I would beg to disagree, Mr Freckles. It is we, Punjabis, who are the best fighters. But yes, I would concede that the Pashtun can be quite a handful. And you are wrong in saying they march only to their own drumbeat—they march when we tell them to march.'

Freckles nodded in satisfaction.

'Wonderful, General, to know that. And, that is why I have come to you. Something of huge significance is about to break out in Afghanistan. And, we need your help to get on top of things in that part of the world.'

Freckles then outlined the plan and vision of his boss. The General's face masked the emotions he felt as Freckles rolled out the contours of the plan. He was icy calm. He knew the world would be at his feet soon, if he played his cards right. He gave nothing away when he responded to the young intelligence officer from the CIA.

'My young friend, do you understand what you are asking of me? You are asking me to turn my face away from India and instead look at Afghanistan, and stare at the mighty Soviet Union in the eye? Do you think creating and training an army of resistance fighters, you call the Mujahideen, is a child's play? Do you think this is a week or a month's job? This enterprise could take years and years to fructify. It will pivot this entire region in a completely different direction.'

Freckles leaned back, closely watching the General.

'I could not agree more with you, General. And, Sir, know this. You would be helping the cause of democracy...'

The General's face became flushed as if he had been slapped. His face looked murderous.

'*Behanchod*, how dare you insult my intelligence!' The General's outburst was best lost in translation. He simmered down and Freckles realised he had made a faux pas. Both men gave each other some space and then the General spoke up.

'Mr Freckles, not for the sake of democracy, but for practicality, I want to show you something, follow me, please.'

As the three men trudged out in the heat, Freckles noticed that the ISI chief had passed on a thick glove to the army chief who slipped it on. The sun was relentlessly beating down on the three men, and Freckles felt a bit dizzy. Both the army and the ISI chief were looking up in the sky. The ISI chief took out a strange whistle and blew on it. Both men looked up. Through the torpor of the shimmering heat haze, an object appeared in the sky. The object, a large bird, plunged from the sky, diving at an incredible speed in, what is known as, a stoop manoeuvre, much like the Stuka dive bombers of Second World War vintage.

Freckles was stunned as, within seconds, the large bird with razor sharp talons flew past him, settling down on the gloved hand of the army chief. The brown-eyed Falcon made eye contact with its benefactor and then flew the distance and swooped on a bowl kept nearby filled with duck meat.

A shiver ran up Freckles spine. The army chief gave Freckles his undivided attention.

'My American friend, this is a Saker Falcon. It is not a bird found in these parts; it is a migratory bird that appears this time of the year. It is one of the finest predators known to man. And, it is a very unpredictable bird—it attacks all kinds of animals, including man. It has been known to tear out men's eyes and rip their throats with its talons. But, I control it…with meat. Am I making sense to you, Mr Freckles?'

The three men returned to the tent. Freckles recovered from his sub-continental shock. He understood how the game was played in this part of the world.

The three men settled in chairs forming a semi-circle. Freckles took out a cheque book from his jacket and pulled out two cheques. $ 10,000 for the army chief and $ 5,000 for the ISI chief. He handed over the cheques to the two men who quickly pocketed them. Freckles explained himself.

'This is just a *nazarana* (douceur), as you call it in your country. I will be depositing regular cheques in your personal accounts from now on, rest assured. I also understand you would be looking for an arms package for your country on very easy terms. Given. But, you must help us build and arm the Mujahideen.'

The army chief leaned forward, his ruddy face aflame in the heat.

'Mr Freckles, both of us might be corrupt bastards, but we are also patriots. What you ask of us is a full-time job. We can only do it if we are assured about India. We want to be sure, that mad woman, Priya Kaul, is not planning an armed strike on Pakistan. Check, and verify. That's what I am going to do before we agree on this deal.'

'Can I be of help in any way?'

'No, Mr Freckles. Try and understand the complexity of the problem in this part of the world. We are aware that Priya Kaul is besieged now. We also know she might try something stupid to distract attention from her internal mess. So, we will verify the situation on the ground on the India-Pakistan front, before we give you iron-clad guarantees. Till then, thanks, but no thanks, for the "nazarana".'

Freckles looked out of the tent. The predatory bird had had its fill of the meat, and was climbing the sky. Whoever had said that people of the sub-continent were emotional, and maybe even fools, had got it completely wrong. They were even more ruthless and transactional than many of the sharks he knew in Washington.

★★★

Chapter 22

Perhaps this was love, if such a thing even existed. Sue was unsure, as she stroked the face of the man lying on top of her. Her fingers traced the shape of his strong jawline, playing with the greying hairs of his clipped beard. She rubbed his ear and looked into his eyes. His face was suffused with some emotions for her—it had to be love surely. But then how could she know? She had never experienced it. Her parents had separated when she was not even ten years old. She had been raised by her grandmother who was preoccupied with her own health issues and had neither the sense nor the time for good parenting. And then came along her brute of a husband, a wife-beating alcoholic. Her marriage had collapsed within less than a year. Going through one disaster to another, she kept her sanity and hopes alive for a better tomorrow, thanks to her job.

It was a decent job, not high profile, yet important in its own way. She was a stenographer in the Home Secretary's office, but not the only one, there were two others. But, they were younger and committed to their work only up to a point. After 6 pm, a drink at the bar and a night out with the boyfriend took precedence over matters of state.

Growing up, Sue Higgins understood all that even though she did not know the first thing about love and passion. She would help the girls by taking on their work after 6 pm. This meant taking shorthand notes of top secret letters dictated by the Home Secretary and typing them out. It became the norm, and not the exception, that Miss Sue Higgins would be found in office late at nights, typing out letters, attending to the file cabinet, and finishing the work of others.

Everyone in office knew she had no one to go back home to. So, they piled her with requests and the usual, 'Can you do me a favour, dear Sue?'. She always obliged because, in the absence of a real family, all the people in the office became one.

Sometimes, when there would be no one in office around midnight, she would pack up after complete exhaustion, go to the toilet and find herself looking back at her own reflection in the mirror. The first of the crow lines appearing on her face even as an abdominal bulge announced arrival, ruining her flat stomach. She would close her eyes and drift away in thoughts. All this was expected; would it not be? She was not a seedling, but a woman close to forty. She would let her mind drift, eyes closed and involuntarily run her fingers over her breasts, circling her nipples. How nice it would have been if she had someone to do that for her?

And suddenly, she would shake out of it, open her eyes and smile at herself in the mirror. Silly girl! Love, passion, tenderness? Those terms were a writer's imagination in a Mills and Boons paperback.

She would then put out the toilet lights and trudge out of the office building in Westminster, taking the last tube from Marsham Street to her one-room Chiswick apartment. Almost alone in the train carriage at that time of the night, she would keep thinking of adopting a cat to be her companion. That was the extent of her ambition.

And then, out of nowhere, Dr Aziz entered her life. The enigmatic Dr Aziz had moved upstairs only a few months back. They would cross path in the mornings when she would be rushing out to catch the tube. Or late evenings, when, somehow, he was always around the doorway, checking his mailbox or taking out garbage bags. There would be an exchange of polite greeting and nothing more. A month later, she discovered he was a consulting doctor in a polyclinic outside London. It never occurred to her to ask him what he was doing in a place quite far away from his work centre. Two months down the line, one day, she suddenly asked him if he would join her for tea in her apartment. He appeared to think about the invite, but then agreed. She knew he was from the sub-continent, probably Pakistan, but his gait and demeanour were quite different from the stereotype. And what was the stereotype? The men from that part of the world were thin and scrawny, walking around with heads bowed as if they were ashamed of something. It was a racist stereotype, she knew, but matters of race, equality and even human rights were of no concern to her.

Dr Aziz was tall, quite tall, very well-built, athletic maybe, and a man of sharp features with remarkably enigmatic eyes. They were kind and genial, but sometimes they appeared to have that wait-and-watch look of a hawk. She could not quite place him. Anyway, she quickly categorised him with her own stereotype—tall, very dark and very handsome.

The tea meeting piqued her interest in him. He spoke slowly, carefully and there was something intense and deliberate in the way he would move and conduct himself. He was a good listener too. In the very first meeting, she poured out her heart to him. She felt quite comfortable around him. Had their tea meeting ended with him stealing an embrace and a kiss from her, she would not refuse. But it ended with him doing a curtsy in, what could be best described as, an old fashioned way before leaving for his apartment upstairs.

She soon became obsessed with him. Tall, very dark, very handsome, and a gentleman to boot.

The intimacy between Dr Aziz and Sue developed

slowly over a period of a few weeks. And then one night, when it was cold, and dark and damp, he took her. He quite literally tore her clothes off her, and made love to her ferociously, almost like an animal on a rampage, entering and breaking repeatedly. In just one night, he made her addicted to pleasure of a kind that did not even exist in the realms of her imagination.

She soon discovered two sides to him. Though the courteous, self-effacing Dr Aziz was still there, it was receding. It was being replaced by a man in a hurry to try out the most difficult positions and outrageous corners for love-making. One day when both of them returned late at night, they made love in the doorway of the apartment complex—he lifted her skirt up, parted her legs and straddled her. It was almost as if he was challenging the world to discover their public trysts of love-making.

And then, he proposed making love in her office after everyone had left. She had refused initially, the very idea was preposterous. What if they were caught? She would surely lose her job. They could both end up in prison. Yet, he persisted with his demand. He used an old trick that men use in the sub-continent to persuade women—he started to sulk and avoid her. The interplay of his indiscreet and compelling urge to flirt with danger along with a complete indifference to her, left her hurt, bothered, confused and even angry.

One day when she could bear it no longer, she yielded

to his demands. She did not want this relationship to end. She was prepared to walk on the edge to hold on to him.

A little before midnight, she contrived and smuggled him in. And he proved that it was worth all the risk she had taken. He made love to her on her work desk like a ravaging beast, an animal that wounds you but spares you. She felt clawed, bruised, and stretched no end. Her body was on fire, and she was exhausted out of her mind. She sank into a deep, sound sleep, and she must have slept for a while because when she woke up on the table he was sitting naked on the room sofa, eerily composed, watching her. He had a go at her again.

Finally, he finished with her around 1.30 am. She felt reborn, deliriously satisfied. They both stumbled out of the building.

It became a pattern repeated several times in the weeks to follow. But recently, as she microwaved a lunch packet on a Sunday afternoon, her mind took her back to all the steamy encounters in her office. A terrifying thought struck her. The intense love-making would almost always lull her to sleep in contention.

Her periods of sleep would range from a few minutes to sometimes as much as 20-30 minutes. And all of this happened in a room stacked with top secret files and important letters of Her Majesty's government.

Doubt began to plague her. She thought it through, and her rational side told her that she was being paranoid.

The man was not Russian or some Soviet spy. For God's sake, he was from the sub-continent. Those people were meek and diligent, minding their own business, did they not? Forget the thought of being a spy. They would be eternally grateful to even get the chance to visit London. To even think that he was manipulating her was a laugh and a hoot.

Nevertheless, she cooled off her amorous liaison with him for a while. The secretive encounters in her office stopped. But after a while, she started missing their bouts of intense love-making. The longing to be taken by him came in waves. Finally, she decided she wanted him back in her life.

Cut to the present. She lay under him quite satisfied, but something was amiss as she stroked his greying beard. She sensed something was off. The room was dark and involuntarily her hand reached for the bed switch. The table lamp by her bedside came on. She looked in his face and screamed from the depths of her soul.

The warmth in his caring, brown eyes which had drawn her to him stared at her from only one eye. The other eye looking intently at her was coal black. His hands were moving involuntarily by her side searching for his contact lens which had fallen off. It was not simply a misplaced lens. She knew it was as if the mask he had been wearing all along had come off. She was looking into the full face of his ruthless hideousness. It was the face of a killer. She just knew it in her bones. She fiercely struggled against him, trying to free herself from his grip. But his leaden weight immobilised her.

He smiled, gently stroked her lips, and re-arranged a wisp of hair fallen on her forehead. She could not even croak a word. Her throat was dry, and a sense of fatalism was settling in her. She knew it would be over in the next few seconds.

He jerked her head the opposite side with a swift and professional dexterity; the snapping sound of her broken neck sounding like a shot in the still room. She died instantly, the shock in her eyes a signature of her sudden death. He kept straddling her for a while before getting off her reluctantly. He sat by the bedside, holding her hand, murmuring to himself.

'Tenth, or was it eleventh?'

Finally, he got up and forced himself to do the makeover. He shaved his beard in the bathroom sink and flushed down his greying beard. Ditto for his contacts and the toupee he was wearing. He looked at himself in the mirror.

The self-effacing Dr Aziz had disappeared, and a different-looking man stared back in the mirror in the yellowed light. This man had the watchful eyes and visage of a predator, a predator whose code name was Viper.

Viper dusted every object in the apartment clean of his fingerprints. Then he sat down on Sue's work desk and wrote a one-line note: 'Sick of everything. I am tired, lonely and old. Best for me to exit this life.' He had studied her handwriting over the past few weeks and was confident he could nearly replicate it.

He left the note on her desk, returned to the bedroom, and dragged her limp body from the bed all the way to the drawing room.

The wood stove in the room had made the entire apartment quite cosy. He opened the hatch and felt the heat from the stove on his face. He dragged Sue up to the stove and inserted her head in the stove. The smell of burning flesh immediately filled the room.

He would have to be quick and stealthy now. He put on dark tortoise sunglasses and straightened up the lapels of his thick coat to shield his face. Then, he very quietly and deliberately went out of the apartment and closed the door. A man in no hurry. He made sure no one was loitering near the banister winding down to the ground floor. He exited the building with his head down.

He walked the street and crossed it to the other side. He walked into a convenience and spent some time browsing through a rack of daily newspapers and magazines. He selected a small bottle of mineral water and went up to the bored-looking Asian man sitting behind the counter punching digits on a calculator. He took out £ 5 to pay for the bottle. Without looking at him, the man accepted the payment, returned his change and slipped a taped envelope along with it.

He exited the convenience and briskly walked down the road. A police car with flashing siren shot past him and pulled up near Sue's apartment block. He ducked into a side street and walked to the underground station. He threw the bottled water in a trash can, and carefully opened the envelope, taking a minute to go through its contents.

There was a diplomatic passport and a PIA (Pakistan International Airline) economy class air ticket in the envelope. He looked at his wristwatch. Less than three hours to go before he caught his flight back home. He would have to hurry.

There was a sticky note pasted at the back of his passport.

It read: 'Spend a day with your family. You will be infiltrated across the border at 0300 hours next day. Infiltration team will brief you on the mission objective.'

Viper tore the note into bits and swallowed it. He took the escalator to go down the station and catch a train to Heathrow airport.

★★★

Chapter 23

The downpour had stopped some time back. The road curving away from the Babina cantonment area was slick—with rain and something else. Dozens of snakes were slithering on the road. The snake infestation in Babina was known to one and all. The locals in the area were used to them. But even they would carefully watch out for the poisonous ones mingling with the less lethal lot.

A tall, well-built man walked down the road that led to a low income housing colony on the outskirts of the cantonment. In the distance, the man clearly saw the gun turrets of Vijayanta tanks in battle formation, packed cheek by jowl in a largish compound. The man turned and calmly continued on the road, walking over the snakes, not in the least afraid of them. A closer look would suggest he was not from these parts. There was a mix of disdain and ruthlessness in his eyes. Perhaps, as he walked the road, Viper wondered where he had inherited his cold-bloodiness from. And yet, unlike many others of his ilk, Viper was perfectly self-aware, knowing well why there was so much of a violent streak in him. He could almost feel a bond with the creatures slithering across the road, and it was not just because his code name matched with theirs.

Viper consulted his wristwatch and slowed down. The house he was visiting was in the distance. Purely by instinct, he broke his stride and took a moment to observe the house from the distance. By instinct and habit, he was not on time to meet his contact in Babina. He had arrived almost half an hour earlier. The meeting with Bhanu Lal, the man in the house, was significant. Bhanu was among a string of assets the ISI had established around sensitive military installations in India. For instance, Babina headquartered the 31st Armoured Corps of the Indian Army. The ready-to-move-out Centurion and Vijayanta tanks were placed here. Settlements had come up around most of these cantonments and forward posts. The denizens of these settlements made a living by supplying fresh fruits and vegetables, and day-to-day commodities, and offering minor services to the cantonment.

The job of assets like Bhanu was to supply information of any new equipment purchases or the increasing or decreasing troop strength in these cantonments. The surveillance operations carried on by this string of low-level, traitor-spies was invaluable. The ISI chief had stressed this point to Viper. The brief of the ISI chief to Viper had been to carry out a risk assessment of the enemy's offensive capabilities as soon as possible. Viper would have to squeeze his assets for all the information they could provide. It also meant that he had a mandate to strengthen the assets that did well and eliminate those that had been compromised or posed a threat to the overall mission objective.

Viper loitered under a tree a bit longer and took in all that he needed to know. Then, he walked to the front door of the house and knocked.

Bhanu Lal opened the door. He looked visibly surprised, maybe a little flustered.

'You are early, *Sahab*? Everything alright?'

Viper carefully eyed the man. Behind Bhanu, he could see his family, his wife, a five-year-old child and a middle-aged woman. They hastily retreated further back in the house. Viper was curt and to the point.

'Why should it not be alright? You knew I was coming. Were you expecting someone else?'

Bhanu Lal quickly recovered and put on a false smile.

'Apologies for the indiscretion, Sahab. I was just making conversation. Let's go up to the terrace. We can converse in peace there. Shall I ask the missus to make some tea?'

'No need,' replied Viper. 'Lead the way up.'

Up on the terrace, Viper again assessed the surroundings. The tank formations in a large enclosure were clearly visible from the elevation. Sugarcane fields dotted rest of the acreage spreading for miles around. A cluster of dark clouds was quickly gathering above. It could rain any moment.

'Your report then,' he demanded. 'And make it quick.'

Bhanu Lal gave his assessment. The gist of his surveillance report being that the situation was status quo. There had been no signs of any new, extraordinary activity or a movement of troops and equipment.

Bhanu Lal finished with his report, but Viper's eyes still burned in him. A sweat had broken out at the back of his neck. He silently prayed for this nightmare to be over soon. And then Viper softly whispered.

'Bhanu, you are lying.'

Bhanu Lal's body shook. He could not stop the trembling, his hands folded.

'No, Sahab. I am not lying. Every word of what I say is the truth. The situation is the same as it was six months back when you came visiting. Believe me.'

'I don't believe you,' hissed Viper. 'New equipment has been purchased, Bhanu. There is a brand new Lambretta scooter outside your house. There is even a thresher machine in the courtyard. The women inside are wearing new clothes. It looks like Diwali has come early to your house. Someone has been lining up your pockets. Right, Bhanu?'

Bhanu Lal's eyes wildly flickered. He desperately

tried to look at the road adjacent to his house and made an abortive attempt to flee. Viper moved incredibly fast and caught him and pinned his arms behind him. Then, in one swift movement, he dislocated one arm from the socket joint, immobilising Bhanu. The man screamed in pain. Viper went for his throat and choked him with inhuman strength, cutting off all sound and air supply. The world dimmed for Bhanu. He could feel as if everything inside him, rising from his throat right up to his brain, was imploding.

Viper asked a final question.

'How long, Bhanu, how long have you been double-crossing me, you traitorous bastard?'

In his dying moments, Bhanu understood he had to tell his executioner the truth if his family were to escape the wrath of Viper. He struggled to speak.

'The Military police and IB team will be here in less than ten minutes…'

With incredible force, Viper swivelled Bhanu's neck the opposite way, breaking it like a twig snapping under the heel of a boot.

Even before the inert body hit the ground, Viper bounded down the iron staircase. The women in the house saw the man with a face full of wrath charging toward them. They screamed for their lives in pure terror. Viper dealt with the remaining family in the most horrific manner. He forced the three surviving members of the

Bhanu family in the kitchen. Then, he took out the rubber tubing that connected the gas cylinder to the gas stove. The two women threw themselves at him, clawing him, spitting at him, and beating him with their fists knowing death had arrived. It was outside the kitchen, seeking a way in. The five-year-old girl child stood in a corner, mute, frozen, unable to comprehend what was going on.

Viper brutally forced them back in the kitchen and shut the door from outside. The pungent gas was fast filling up the kitchen. The women were screaming their guts out, banging against the shut door.

Viper opened the 2X2 feet window outside the kitchen. He met the frenzied looks of the struggling women. The eyes of the five-year-old girl, rooted to a spot, had considerably widened. The women rushed to the window to escape their fate. Viper withdrew to a safe distance, took out a cigarette and lit it calmly. He looked at his wristwatch and smoked for a while, enjoying the cigarette even as the screams of the women inside the kitchen reached a din. Then, he finally stubbed out his cigarette and stood facing the women. He smiled at them one last time and took out the lighter again. He tossed the lit lighter in through the small window.

The kitchen exploded and chunks of cement and human parts flew in all directions and rained all around. In the distance, he heard the wailing of a police siren. It was a surreal sight as flames and the exploding gas lit up the house and a hail of rain descended from above, dousing the fire.

Viper quickly walked away from the house to a nearby sugarcane field. In a minute he would be lost within it. The rain was now descending in sheets. Somewhere in the distance, lightning struck a tree, and sparks danced around a fallen branch.

Bhanu and his family had ceased to exist in Viper's consciousness. As he made his way through the sugarcane field, only one image stayed in his mind. His *apa*, Shazia, screaming her lungs out, her hair wildly flying in all directions as a ring of fire closed around her. And he, a five-year-old boy, standing in a corner, watching his elder sister and the mayhem erupting around them with wide-eyed wonder. It was an image that stayed with him for a long time as he left the Jhansi-Babina belt and made his way to Jodhpur, his next stop to meet his next asset.

★★★

Chapter 24

Kamini raced the Beetle across the field to meet the flying object coming straight for the windshield of her car. She clearly saw Prahlad's face in the cockpit of the glider—expressive like the face of a child let loose in a candy store with no one to stop him, a look that would stay with her forever, till the end of days. He was smiling fiendishly, carrying out one of his outrageous stunts in the glider. He had terrorised her to drive the Beetle full throttle, straight in the path of a glider he was attempting to land. Flying object in a collision with a speeding car in a field.

He wore outsized goggles as a red ascot jauntily tied around his neck fluttered in the stiff breeze. And that devilish, I-don't-give-a-damn look riveted her, terrified her.

'Don't break your damn neck, you fool,' she silently prayed. 'If you die what will happen to me? They will put me on the stake.'

And in the next moment, the underbelly of the glider

barely kissed the roof of the Beetle, and her heart was in her mouth. She need not look back to verify if he had crashed or had touched down safely. She knew the answer. And she knew it would always be the same for her.

He was a man addicted to walking on the edge. He would always be. That was him. Nothing and no one could change that. And even she wasn't far behind. She also had her pet obsessions, some would even say kinky disorders. They were a pair. That is why they got along so well. A couple of wildings let loose in the world.

He ran across the field to sweep her up in his arms. In the distance, she could clearly see he had landed badly in the field. One of the wings of the glider had broken off and was flung some distance away. But he was safe. The man in the goggles and the red ascot looked like a blur approaching her.

She felt a heat stir up in her. He would want his prize. He lived for moments like these. She knew him so well. In anticipation, she unzipped her maxi and let it slide down. No words were exchanged as he held her against the bonnet of the Beetle, in the posture and will of old conquerors.

Later, when they lay semi-nude in the field, entwined in each other arms, she gently slapped him across the cheek.

'What if you had died?' she asked him not in mock jest.

He shook his head with seriousness.

'I could not have. I am the heir apparent. I was born to rule this country. Maybe when I am old, very old, then maybe, yes, but not now...no...it's not possible...'

She lay back, listening to his stories of conquest, and then, he whispered in her ear,

'Don't get mad at me, but I have agreed that we will spend the weekend with Mom. I think this estrangement thing with her is getting quite serious. We must stop it. See it this way. I am the heir apparent. But, it is also true she is pissed off with me. She looks after my inheritance after all...that is this country...so, I don't want to fuck up till the time I inherit it. We need to build some bridges with her to regain trust...bide our time...'

She slapped him harder this time to shut him up. She quickly thought it through. She did not say another word but wormed herself deeply in his arms. The subtle changes in her postures told him her heart was against the proposal, but she would go along with him.

That same night, Priya Kaul slept peacefully for a change. Just when she had thought the situation with Prahlad had crossed the point of no return, he called up and conversed with her. He wanted to build bridges back to her. He and Kamini would come over and spend the weekend with her. A sliver of hope at last.

She woke up in the morning, freshened up in the attached bathroom and even applied some lipstick. Prahlad was a great believer in a healthy breakfast, seeing it as the most important meal of the day. She looked forward to sitting on the dining table with him. Just like old times.

She walked into the living area, and Prahlad was at the dining table, relishing an omelette. But something looked different. It took her a while to figure out what had changed. The dining table was re-arranged wrongly. Prahlad sat at the head of the re-arranged table looking out of the bay windows. And something strange was happening in the green lawn outside. Kamini, in shorts and a Woodstock T shirt, was playing with dogs. Priya frowned and looked closely. Not even pedigreed dogs, but strays. Where had she got them from?

Her good mood faded away, and she sat down stiffly at the table. She hated the positioning of the dining table. It had been re-arranged for people inside the dining room to look outside and even those outside the lawn could get a view in. There was no such thing as privacy.

Prahlad droned on about the political threat from Tapash, and questioned her what she was planning to do about it. But, his attention was fixated on the lawn and Kamini's antics with the strays.

And then, even before Priya could make sense of the altered mise en scène, Kamini burst in the dining room with the strays. The strays immediately owned the space. They leapt around with gay abandon, barking continually and one of them made a beeline for Priya and leapt at her.

Horrified at the canine invasion, Priya shrieked in disbelief.

'Get this filthy creature off me! At once!'

But both Prahlad and Kamini were not in a mood to oblige. Prahlad seemed genuinely amused by the intrusion, and Kamini was simply being Kamini. The adventurous explorations of strays mattered more to her than the niceties of an old woman, albeit the Prime Minister of the country.

And then one of the strays knocked over the food plate of Priya Kaul and slobbered over the fried egg and toast, spreading the mess on the floor. It was then that Priya Kaul lost it.

She banged her fists on the table like a maddened person and screamed.

'Get out! Get out! All of you! How dare you do this to me! I am the Prime Minister of this country and not a beggar on the street you can treat with contempt!'

She collapsed in a chair, engulfed with wracking sobs.

There was complete silence. The unconcerned strays polished off the remains of the breakfast and wandered off in the house looking for more. A mask of fury changed Prahlad's face. His words whiplashed the tense silence in the room.

'You are right, Mother. Beg you will! You will beg for my love, but you won't get it! Look at you! An intolerable, old, cantankerous woman, totally cut off from the times. Adopting a stray is a sign of maturity and good citizenry, but no, you prefer to stay walled up in your hideous, make-believe world! You won't breathe fresh air and fresh ideas, and you won't even let anyone do that! I thought I was doing you a favour by reaching out to you, but you have proved again that it is all a wasted effort! Well, Mother, I won't forget and forgive how you have insulted my wife in this house! We are leaving, Mother. Go back to your dark hole!'

Priya Kaul looked up piteously, her face streaming with tears. She saw a sight she would never forget for the rest of her life. Her son, the one she loved the most in the world, was looking at her with the wrath of the world on his face. And her daughter-in-law was standing next to him, erect, arms akimbo, with a smirking smile across her face.

It was a look she would keep with her for the rest of her life.

★★★

Chapter 25

Priya Kaul returned to office the same morning after Prahlad and Kamini packed their bags and left. That was the only option available to her to escape the 'hideousness' of her existence, as her son had put it. There is only so much pain a human being can endure. After reaching a point, one must establish contact with other human beings to either unload on them or stifle them.

Priya Kaul's high point of anger and despair and hopelessness manifested when she became deadly quiet, communicating only in terse one-liners and commands. It was well known to everyone. The moment she walked into office, everyone knew and trembled with the apprehension that 'Madam was in the mood'.

It started with a meeting with senior cabinet colleagues. Witnesses in the secretariat pool outside her office swore that so many of the senior ministers, even veteran warhorses, were summoned and exited her office in tears after receiving tongue-lashings. After that, it was the turn of the bureaucracy. They were not merely given a dressing down. Many of the top bureaucrats were put to the stake. It is said that, on that day, a record number of bureaucrats were either given marching orders or transferred to the most inhospitable spots in the country.

Priya Kaul's man Friday, Narang, could be seen escorting all the worthies to her office and doing the same job, and they left shaken and stirred as it were. All this carried on till late into the night. Finally, close to 10 pm, it was Rhino's turn to come face-to-face with Priya Kaul.

The veteran spymaster settled in a chair, and Priya Kaul was quick off the mat.

'Where are we with the bomb?'

Rhino took a moment before answering, it was difficult for him to read her mood. He could clearly see she was not in the zone. Something very deeply had upset her. He replied matter of factly, 'We are on track. But there are serious challenges coming our way…'

'Will you give it to me in the time frame I have asked for?'

How should he reply to such a question? If only he could explain what was happening behind the scenes. The shock of the selection procedure and rejection of others had affected the productivity of some scientists. The inhuman hours they were all spending in CIRUS to meet the timeline was playing with their physical and mental wellbeing. To top it all, the cloak-and-dagger games with the inspection teams of the IAEA (International Atomic Energy Agency) was taking a toll on everyone.

And, if the scientists were feeling the pressure, could their families be insulated? Would they also not absorb the pressure? Besides, the pressure was relentless—the secrecy of the operation, the technological challenges that would hit them from nowhere, that sinking guilt of violating international nuclear protocol to create a bomb for Madam. Was it such a simple ask? Could a reply be even contemplated to such a direct question?

But reply he did.

'Everyone is trying their best to meet the deadline,' he replied flatly, not giving in to her intimidating stare.

She kept quiet and tapped her work desk with a fountain pen. Then, she reached for a file kept beside her and pushed it towards Rhino.

'Read it,' she instructed him.

The file contained a collection of cables from Intelligence Bureau (IB) officials. They all highlighted that the fiery trade union leader, Alvarez, was planning an indefinite rail strike that would cripple Indian railways, and, in the process, perhaps even shut down the Indian economy. Alvarez was not working for Tapash, he was a leader in his own right. But, he was in the same mould as Tapash, and perhaps even an ally of Tapash in his quest to bring down Priya Kaul.

'So, Rhino, these are cables and intercepts from your own officers. When were you planning to bring up the matter to me or were you not planning to do that at all?'

For once, Rhino was at a loss for words. Priya Kaul unexpectedly got up and walked to a side cabinet. She opened it and posed a question for Rhino.

'Macallan or Glenfiddich?'

'Macallan…always,' he replied quickly.

Priya Kaul selected two cut glasses from the cabinet and poured liberally from a decanter. Offering a glass to Rhino, she drowned her drink in one shot. She poured herself another drink.

'I needed that,' she said as an explanation. They settled down with their drinks on the sofa in the room.

She nursed her drink for a while, lost in thought. Then, she opened, speaking in Kashmiri, 'It's not going well for me, Rhino,' she confided in him. 'And I don't mean all this political bullshit. This, I can deal with. I can fight an external enemy, but what do you do about the enemy within? You know all too well of my differences with Prahlad. But I don't even mean him. It is my mind, Rhino, my mind and my overactive imagination, it is always in a spin. Sometimes it rotates with such intensity that the pain is unbearable. It's like being crushed from within.'

Her voice shook as she consumed her drink.

'They call me the Iron Lady of India. But, Rhino, even iron can rust. It needs tempering. It needs care. Of late, this question has been dogging me: for whom do I fight? Why should I even fight? To the victor go the spoils, they say. I thought I was doing all this for legacy, for my kith and kin who would be grateful and proud of what I have achieved. But, no, nothing there…'

Her eyes welled up. The dam broke. She wanted to let it all out. Her body shook with sobs. Rhino thought for a moment and the elder man in him guided him to reach out. He went up to Priya and offered her a shoulder. She put her head on his shoulder and cried inconsolably like a little girl, lost and completely afraid.

After a while, she disengaged, a bit more composed. Rhino took the hint and withdrew to his chair. She spoke with clarity and cold logic.

'Rhino, maybe I am paranoid, or delusional, and certainly not completely self-aware, these are modern concepts. I don't think about them. But there are two things I know about myself. First, I am set in my ways, I won't change them for anyone or anything. And second, I don't let a threat to grow under my feet for long. I crush it. That is who I am.

'So, here's the thing, my friend. I am perfectly aware that my socialistic policies are ruining this country. But I cannot reverse them. I cannot turn into an American capitalist overnight. I cannot become, or allow India to become, a vassal for American capitalism. Besides, I hate men like Fielding, but I love all the socialism spouting dictators, tyrants, despots and communists of the world. I feel at home with them.

'What does this mean? It means socialism will not improve the living standards of my people. And I cannot discard it. So, it means I must create the illusion of good governance. The illusion of a powerful woman who can take on the threats and conspiracies of a string of enemies that surround her. Both within and outside the country. Small-minded, vicious men who cannot tolerate a woman controlling the levers of power. I also know I cannot defeat Tapash, or this Alvarez, by hard, economic logic. I cannot browbeat Fielding who is certainly the most powerful man in the world.

'But, what I can certainly do is to shame and humiliate these men by giving my people the illusion of empowerment through a once-in-a-lifetime explosion. And that is why, I need the bomb. As fast as possible. Because this bomb will wipe out all my past failings and give me breathing space for the next few years to govern in peace. The people of India need a *dhamaka* (explosion) and not a higher per capita income. It is wasted on them.'

Priya Kaul laughed cynically and finished her glass.

'Imagine a bomb heralding an era of peace and calm!'

Rhino stood up absorbing the destructive magic of his protégé.

'You will have your bomb, Priya. I promise you. One last thing. You do what you do not for legacy or securing the affection of those closest to you. You do it because you were born to fight. You define your existence by always going in for the good fight. That is who you really are, Priya Kaul.'

★★★

Chapter 26

The completely naked man hung upside-down from the ceiling and his torturers took care to inflict pain on him without breaking any bones or tearing his ligaments that could result in bluish scarring. After all, the man had to be presented in court at some point for a trial hearing. The subtle art of torturing to elicit information without making a hash of it was best known to the elite interrogation officials of Indian police and intelligence corps.

The man, in the shadows at the back of the torture chamber chain-smoking Chesterfields, nodded his head giving the interrogator assent to step up the pressure. The interrogator did what was asked of him. The inhuman screams of the tortured man filled the chamber and bounced off the walls.

The man was a sight, bloodshot eyes, and sputum hanging from his nose and mouth. He had great difficulty in breathing. Rhino looked at his watch. He knew the man was close to breaking point. Soon, he would either start singing like a canary, or his body would stop functioning permanently.

When inflicting torture, the interrogator cannot be trusted with the task of maintaining a fine line between eliciting information and snuffing out a life. He is way too deeply involved in the act of uncorking information. Only the handler, hands-free as it were, judges when the point of no return has arrived.

Rhino looked at the man's face closely and knew he was ready to talk. He nodded again, and the tortured man was brought down and dragged before him.

Rhino summed it up for him.

'I will give you only one chance to get out of this tub of boiling water, only one chance. Speak the truth. You are already booked under MISA (Maintenance of Internal Security Act). We know you are deeply involved in liquor smuggling and *hawala* transactions. We also know you are one of the main fund raisers for Tapash. You bankroll his movement. I want to know all the details of all the transactions to prepare a case. Remember, if you prevaricate, act smart or fudge the truth, I will simply leave the room. Then, it is between you and the interrogator. And God help you after that…'

The man shivering violently shook his head and tried to croak a reply. He was inaudible. Rhino brought his ear closer to hear what the man was trying to say.

'I used to be the supplier, Sir…' the man croaked. 'No longer. They have found a better source, someone who pays them in dollars. Most of the funding is coming from a *firangi* (Foreigner). He directly pays in Swiss bank accounts and the money is re-routed to India.'

Rhino frowned and pressed on.

'This information is not enough. It could be anyone. Who is this person, what is his name and who does he represent? Remember, no second chances.'

The tortured man hesitated for a moment, then he carefully replied, 'The CIA is funding Tapash's agitation. The man has a strange name, I think, he goes by the name of Freckles.'

★★★

Chapter 27

The Bentley emerged from the village road and ran soundlessly on the main arterial road, the river Cam flowing alongside it. Priya Kaul looked out of the car window, soaking in the green acreage that swept past her. For some reason, the fields next to the Cam River were dotted with horses grazing around haystacks bundles spread far and wide. So many horses in these fields, and if there were horses, there was bound to be horseshit. How did people traversing through these fields deal with that inconvenience? The practicality of the problem brought a smile to Priya's face. She looked out of the car window to take a closer look. The Special Branch policeman seated next to her gave her a disapproving glance. She smiled again and leaned back in the upholstery as the car turned a bend, bringing her closer to her destination. For some reason, Priya Kaul felt relaxed and happy. It was as if a cloud circling her head had lifted. She was looking forward to meeting her son Rajan and his girlfriend Christine.

Her trip to the United Kingdom was a private visit. No official protocol was required or extended to her, yet out of diplomatic courtesy, the British government had provided her with an official car, driver and a senior policeman to look after her security. Narang sat in the front seat, next to the driver. The car came to a stop near an old church building that looked a little derelict, its grounds overrun with weeds. In the bright sunshine, she saw Rajan busy laying a checkered cloth on a trestle table and arranging bread, a cheese platter and a couple of bottles of red wine on it. He smiled brightly and waved to her as she got out of the car.

Priya Kaul warmly embraced her son and held on to him to feel the love. She felt hopeful.

'Did you miss me, son?' she asked him. 'Please, say yes, even if you did not. I feel so hopeful today.'

Rajan broke away and smiled generously.

'If missing you means do I think about you, then I do, mother. Rest assured. Maybe I am not very demonstrative in my emotions, but I do care and think about you. And so does Christine, so does she. Happy, now?'

Priya tightly held on to her son and finally broke away reluctantly.

'So, where is this enigmatic Christine? I am so keen to meet her.'

Rajan took her by hand and walked along with her to

the edge of the Cam River. He pointed in the distance. The river curled under a natural canopy of a giant tree. Some enterprising soul had tied a rubber tubing to a drooping hardy branch of the tree. Many youngsters were taking turns to swing on the rubber tubing before diving in the not so deep waters of the Cam River. Christine had also joined in the fun.

Rajan offered an explanation.

'She's usually quite reserved, but she could not resist the fun. She will join us shortly. Come, let me pour some wine for you, and let's talk.'

She could not remember the last time she had shared wine with her son, talking about matters they had always been reluctant to address as a family. But she soon discovered that something had changed in him. He was receptive to, at the very least, listening to matters close to her heart. And, surprisingly, even if he held a different opinion, he was emotionally engaged. These could have been the influence of Christine on him. Her curiosity about the girl had certainly piqued. She was not sure when and how the subject of family values came up, but he spoke with quiet passion on the subject.

'You will have to forgive me, Mother, but I think we deeply believe in legacy as a tool to perpetuate our power. I wish we had a legacy of genuine compassion, altruism and equal opportunity for all, including political opportunity. But we don't have it. And that is the truth. And deep within, we know this. That is why we communicate at a surface level. We mask our feelings and that is the real reason why your relationship with Prahlad has broken down.

'I am not defending him. But have you ever thought of the possibility that he might be emotionally lost, and he covers it all up with his rough and uncouth ways?'

She was struck with him. He had changed quite a lot during his stint abroad, more questioning, more sceptical, but certainly warmer. She did not in the least think he was critical of her. He had that prerogative. She, in fact, welcomed it. It suggested to her that he still cared deeply for her. Yes, Christine certainly must have had a hand in all this. She was suddenly very keen to meet this girl.

Priya did not have to wait for long. Dripping wet in a two-piece bikini suit, Christine came up running to Rajan. He smothered her in a large towel, and she embraced him with tenderness. Priya could clearly see they were very much in love. She tied the big towel around her, came up to Priya Kaul and met her in a manner she would never forget for the rest of her life.

Christine knelt, touched Priya Kaul's feet and spoke in accented Hindi.

'Namaste, mother. So good to finally meet you. I have been such a fan of your accomplishments throughout my life.'

Priya Kaul instinctively embraced her. She instantly knew she must have done something good in her life to deserve this happiness. The girl was not pretending at all. She was so completely taken in by her. Priya closed her eyes momentarily, in relief and complete joy. There was hope still left in the world.

They all held hands, laughed and chatted, and drank wine in the afternoon sun. As dusk came on early, Rajan gave her another good news.

'Mother, Christine and I have discussed our future options. She is quite keen to settle down in India with me. She will complete her semester at the University and after her graduation she will accompany me to India. Meanwhile, I have accepted an offer from the Indian aviation company as a commercial pilot.

'We will be by your side, mother, but only on the condition that you don't force me into politics. It will be a quiet, civilian life for both of us in Delhi, and nothing else.'

In response, Priya Kaul drew both of them close to her bosom and looked up at the sky. It was a perfect English summer day. She could have sworn there was indeed a silver lining in the blue sky.

★★★

Chapter 28

Ah, the sights, and smells, and sounds of India! For Justine, the Cottage Emporium at Janpath was a microcosm of Indian mystique. It lived up to its reputation on a Monday morning when she walked in without her usual entourage of shopping friends. The smell of *agarbatti* (incense) wafted through the dim-lit corridor on the first floor. Soft, mellifluous strains of sitar maestro Ravi Shankar in *jugalbandi* (concert) with tabla wizard Allah Rakha filtrated the narrow confine. The muted shades of Kashmiri carpets adorned the walls. There was elegant brassware and Rajasthani *juttis* (footwear) on display as well.

There was no salesman in sight. Justine shook her head in irritation. What else to expect? The Cottage Emporium was a public sector undertaking, after all. They must have disappeared for a tea break, all at the same time. Her fingertips traced the elegant workmanship of an enormous brass jar with an inverted siphon. A strange sensation, generating from her fingertips, worked its way up in her body. She felt a humming of sorts. Was it her imagination, or had the smell of the incense suddenly become intense?

She felt a little dizzy and stumbled for support. Someone caught her from the back and steadied her. The safe pair of hands guided her to a nearby couch. She sat down heavily and looked up. A young man in his early thirties stood before her holding a stainless-steel glass.

'Drink this,' the man urged her in a voice and accent that was pitch perfect British, a voice with a conviction of someone who knew what he was talking about. 'It will make you feel better.'

Her head was reeling, and she did not have the energy to understand where he had transpired from and what was he offering her for a drink. Maybe he was one of those charlatan fellows she had read about in Indian magazines, the kind who peddles spuriousness to foreigners, especially white women. She did not care, she wanted to get better fast. She was going to take a chance. She drank the salt and sugary liquid, closed her eyes and leaned back on the couch.

She woke after a while, her head cleared, the enigmatic man sitting on a stool facing her. She could no longer smell the incense.

'Feeling better?' he asked her softly.

'Yes, so much better. Thank you. Can't understand what happened, really? It's never happened to me before...'

The man smiled and continued to look at her closely.

'It was a simple thing really, it happens sometimes. The *agarbatti* is not for everyone. Your body reacted against it. I have put them out.'

'And, what did you give me to drink?'

'It's Indian lemonade. We call it *shikanji*. It is a wondrous drink for hot afternoons. Revitalises the body.'

'Well, it has worked wonders. Thanks, again.' She got up carefully, took out her compact from her purse and dabbed her lips with a tissue. She snapped the purse shut and a smile flitted across her face. She looked at him carefully. He was wearing a batik kurti, blue jeans and sandals. The buttons of his kurti were open, exhibiting his muscular frame. He had long and messy hair like a pop star. And, he had the most enticing ivory skin she had ever seen in a human being.

'You always keep a bottle of, what you call, shikanji with you? It sure came out fast, did it not?'

He replied with just a hint of sarcasm, 'Dead right, lady. A glass of shikanji for every American woman I find in distress.'

They laughed in unison. She stood unsure whether to leave or linger on for a conversation.

'So, what's your name, shikanji man?'

'Sunflower,' he replied deadpan.

She looked at him quizzically, and then she laughed full-throated.

'Really! Sunflower, you said. And that would make me

Mary Poppins, right! And, what are you? I mean, what do you do, Mr Sunflower? Are you a manager in this place?'

His eyes bored into her. A sardonic smile played on his face.

'I am at the bottom of the food-chain, lady. A humble salesman, the kind nobody remembers. At least, Arthur Miller's salesman gained international recognition. No such luck here. You want a nice Rajasthani jutti, I am your man.'

She watched him carefully, unable to take a decision. A bit of mischief lurking in her eyes.

'An Arthur Miller-name dropping, Brit-speaking, humble salesman. You intrigue me. Okay, let's try that *jutti.*'

He escorted her to another section on the shop floor and guided her to a comfortable chair. He sat down on the floor, slowly removed her heels, and gently eased her feet in a pair of juttis. She made appreciative noises, tried on different pairs, walked around a little, and admired a potential buy in a full-length mirror.

She never knew when, in the artistic garb of his salesmanship, he had started to play with her feet. Suddenly, she jerked back to reality as he pressed a point somewhere below her big toe. A tingling sensation traversed through her, easing up a stress point at her nape. Getting up immediately, she walked towards the full-length mirror, rubbing her neck.

'What did you do? I have had a pain at the back of my neck for months now. It…it just disappeared…as if by magic…what did you do…'

He slowly got up from the floor and bowed before her. 'Madam, as you walked in, I knew from your posture that this pain was bedevilling you. I just pressed the right point to ease it. The foot is the nodal area for nerve activity, one needs to press the right points for pain alleviation.'

She kept quiet and eyed him with a mix of discomfort and curiosity. She paid for a pair of juttis, collected her bag and walked towards the wooden staircase meandering down to the ground floor. She stopped near the stairs and looked back.

'Care to join me for a cup of tea at the Bankura, Mr Salesman?'

'Thought you would never ask, American lady.'

★★★

Chapter 29

Over sips of Darjeeling tea, she realised that, besides his other talents, he was a master storyteller. It did not matter whether his stories were blatantly false or perhaps had some kernel of truth in them. She had been warned time and again that India was ridden with deceiving characters, termed '*chalu maal*' in the local lingo. These were charlatans who came out of the woodwork, offering God, instant nirvana, karmic salvation, marijuana-ganja bliss and many other varieties of Indian pleasures as soon as they laid eyes on white, gullible, western women.

Well, she was not one of them. She was sure of that. For starters, she was not the garden-variety bimbo. She had seen the world. She loved the contours of Indian culture and experiences, but always within the confines and rigours of western scepticism. Moreover, she was not a spring chicken; she was fifty years old. And this person sitting in front of her could not have been a day older than thirty-two years. What could he offer her that would deceive her?

She focused on his story. He was the accidental offspring of a one-night union between a robust, adventure-seeking Sikh man and an Italian woman, a hippie. He was abandoned in the crib of an Irish missionary ran orphanage in Bombay. That accounted for his pucca British accent. He claimed that when he grew up, he landed in Europe where he took up odd jobs to make a living. In his spare time, he hung out with the art crowd around river waterfronts. He would visit art galleries, and museums to–educate himself about western art, literature and philosophy.

When he returned to India, he realised there were no takers for his self-taught education and his appreciation of western thought and manners. He roamed on the streets of Bombay, especially the Colaba area, and adapted to survive taking up petty jobs. And then, indulgence in petty crime followed to make ends meet. A ragged existence followed, as he survived on personal charm, used or misused, in a manner of speaking.

It was an interesting story, and Justine was not sure how much she believed in what he told her. Her scepticism showed on her face.

If nothing else, he could put a finger on the pulse and know the feeling.

'You don't believe me, do you?' he asked her in his trademark soft tone.

'Does it matter, Sunflower?' she said. 'I don't think I will ever see you again after today.'

He smiled and continued unruffled.

'Of course, that is your prerogative. But before we part, do you want to see the real India?'

'What do you mean?' she countered. 'Whatever I see around me is an illusion or *maya*, as your people would say?'

'No, I am not disrespecting your insights on what you have seen or encountered in India. I am talking of real India which is hot, dusty, and unpredictable, often violent yet compelling. This air-conditioned bubble called Cottage Emporium is not real India.'

She kept quiet, contemplating his offer. She felt he was speaking the truth for a change. Her curiosity was aroused. What did he mean by real India?

She paid the bill at the Bankura, and they both stepped out in the mid-day sun.

'Another day with you won't kill me. Okay, let's see your version of real India.'

They met again the next evening. He would be taking her to a place that, he said, came alive only in the evenings. Sunflower picked up Justine from the Oberoi hotel where she had spent the afternoon getting her hair done and nails manicured. His preferred mode of transport was the Lambretta scooter. Though Justine was surprised at the unorthodox means of transport, she did not show it. She wanted to play along. Where would it lead to?

Sunflower picked up his ride and threaded his way through the neat, landscaped drive of the Oberoi hotel, all the way to Nizamuddin in central Delhi. A psychedelic gauze of colours had infected the late evening sky. It was still quite hot for a spring day. Sunflower brought the scooter to a halt near a narrow lane. Suddenly, from nowhere, streams of people from all directions converged at the narrow lane. There was a tense excitement impregnating the air. The narrow lane was dimly lit and there were rows of people sitting at either side of the lane begging for alms. The light in the evening sky was almost gone and Sunflower whispered in Justine's ear, 'Whatever happens, hold my hand tight and don't let go.'

'Where are we and what is this place?'

'This place, Justine, is the shrine of the Sufi saint Nizamuddin Auliya. I am taking you for an out-of-body experience. Do you trust me with it, or shall we retreat to the safe, antiseptic confines of the Oberoi hotel?'

Justine could hardly see Sunflower in the ebbing light of the day, but his coal black eyes shone with a strange kind of animism. She found herself agreeing to his proposal.

He guided her through the lane, a short walk through dirt and hell. Practically all the beggars that choked the lane were lepers. They were not merely begging for alms. They fiercely grasped at the ankles and soles of the devout, demanding compensation for being sentenced to a life of misery, disease and filth. Justine screamed, and grasped

Sunflower's hand as if it were a lifeline. He dragged her through the wretched sea of humanity.

In an instant, her coiffure was disentangled and one of her manicured nails broke. Rivulets of sweat broke over her forehead and trickled down her face, seeping through her dress. Her make-up smeared and mottled on her face. Her heart was thumping with fear of the unknown. Vistas of animal attacks on human beings swam before her eyes.

They came out of the lane and stood facing the *Baoli* (stepwell) of the *dargah*. It was a surreal sight. Hurricane lamps lit up a cavern-shaped, 100-foot deep Baoli filled to the brim with greenish water. Even at this time of the night, intrepid boys were jumping in the Baoli for a shout and a swim.

And then, in that instant, the mood, the texture and setting of the entire place completely changed. Lights came on in the main dargah. The Sufi Qawwali singers had settled in for the evening. Soon, the tenor and the lyrics of the Sufi singers filled the place like a rain-bearing cloud that settles atop a hill. The lyrics in praise of the Almighty, sung with great vigour, pitch perfect with soaring cadences, deeply affected the faithful. The audience was already swooning with the very first rendition. Skull-capped faithful rocked their heads in a beat and unison as if egged on by an invisible force.

Masses of people occupied every inch of the space. Justine and Sunflower were crammed by people from all sides. But there was no misbehaviour. A state of ecstasy was building up in the audience.

At some point during the rendition, Justine forgot the discomfort, the squeeze in, the hotness, the conspicuous dirt and filth bogging the place and all other external distractions. She did not understand a word of what the Qawwals were singing. She did not need to. Their rendition was so powerful and energetic that she felt lifted, the music streaming in and about her.

She never knew when Sunflower whispered something in her ear to consume the substance that would enhance the audio-visual sensory experience. She went along with whatever he said or did. He rolled a ball of opium, and she consumed it from an opium pipe.

The world around her exploded in sensory fireworks of colours and sounds she had never heard, seen or experienced before. She felt elevated as if she had climbed a mountain and could afford to look down. The girl from Maine was far away from home, caught in a stream of sub-consciousness that did not bear the stamp of the world she had been inhabiting so far.

★★★

Chapter 30

Her discovery of real India did not end that night at Nizamuddin Auliya. It continued next afternoon at the Purana Qila fort. She and Sunflower took a trek around the ramparts of the crumbling fort, walking past the nettle and thick undergrowth circling the fort. It was unusually hot in the afternoon. But Justine was in a mood to explore, discover and experience new things. In less than twenty-four hours, she had left her usual sceptical self behind. She followed Sunflower around like a giddy schoolgirl who has just been released from a cloistered convent to go on a school picnic to a shady place that promises unknown adventures.

They spent the large part of the afternoon walking around the place and Sunflower was unusually reticent, not his usual voluble self. During their afternoon sojourn, Justine wondered the point of coming to this place. Sunflower did not even fulfil the role of a tourist guide rattling off the history of the fort. It was unusually quiet in the environs and the heat was oppressive. Her sweat-filled cotton shirt clung to her skin, showing her bra prominently. Her make-up had again become mottled in the heat. There were no uplifting strains of Sufi music to take her mind away; she was increasingly beginning to feel scratchy, irritated and intolerably thirsty.

The ramparts of the fort were broken in several places. Constructions wedged between these gaps appeared to have been added much later in the fort's architectural history. A short flight of stairs led to a canopy. Sunflower quickly climbed up the stairs and looked down at Justine. She met his gaze as he signalled her to come up. She was beginning to be just a little mad at him. Maybe all this had been a big mistake, maybe he was just a pretentious, untalented, little ferret out to make a quick buck, a glib talking conman leading her up the garden path, or a weed path in this case.

Nevertheless, she climbed the flight of stairs and walked up to him.

'What is it you want to show me in this God forsaken place?' she asked brusquely.

He pointed to the wall adjacent to him. She squinted in the afternoon gloom and tried to make sense of a scribbling on the stone wall. Someone had put a penknife to etch names on the wall, probably in Urdu.

'Well, what is it? What does these etchings on the wall mean?'

He was again looking at her with his trademark intensity. He softly whispered, 'Rumour has it, these etchings are hundreds of years old. Two lovers, Fiza and Jabbar, would climb up to this ledge on hot summer days, like this one, and make love. There are many other similar etchings spread across the wall. Rumour has it that over time this spot became a favourite bedding place for lovers maddened by lust.'

He stood before her, suddenly transformed into a dark, ivory-skinned entity, radiating immense power, even magnetism. Justine's anger spiked uncontrollably. She briskly walked up to him and slapped him hard on his face.

'You bastard! This was what it was all leading to, wasn't it? Your cock-and-bull stories about real India! Your concocted story of ancient lovers making out under a canopy? You take me for a fool? Passing on unemployed youth desecrating ancient monuments for ancient folklore? The nerve of you to take me for a ride! All you had to do, you bastard, was just to ask! I would have given it to you the first time I laid my eyes on you!'

Justine then took charge. With complete authority, she roughly opened his belt, unzipped his bell bottoms and pulled down his trousers. Swiftly, she unbuttoned her shirt and pulled up her bra. And, she challenged him.

'Enough of talk. Show me what you are really made of, you low-life! Fuck the brains out of this old hag! Do it now!' Sunflower, once unbound, came into his own.

Like a proverbial beast unleashed, he ravaged her in every possible way—in every position known to man and woman, in durations of love-making that were unheard of, exploring body spaces and points that would intellectually appear ridiculous and off-limits.

The sounds of their love-making were ultra-low, the barely heard, tiniest sound of the release and drawing of air in the chest, like insects chirping at the sunset. It got dark, but there was no cessation of desire. It went on and on, interminably till Justine broke away, around midnight, convinced that by now her husband would have alerted the police at her disappearance.

They came down the citadel in complete silence and walked up to her Plymouth Gran Fury parked outside the Fort. She fished in her purse for her car keys. He asked her with a degree of concern, 'They would be looking for you. Do you know what to tell them?'

She took out a cigarette from a silver case, lit it and inhaled deeply.

'My husband and I have an understanding. I will handle my end. You get yourself primed for me tomorrow afternoon. And, the next afternoon. I am not letting go of you so easily. I want more of you. I am walking in a tunnel of sexual rekindling. I need to cross it. Do you understand?'

It was pitch dark by now; she could not see his face when he replied, 'I am there…for you…'

She went for the car door and opened the glove

compartment. She pulled out a bundle of dollar notes.

'Here, take it,' she said, again taking charge. 'Rent a convenient pad away from prying eyes. I would suggest the Ridge area. You could rent a nice one-room top-floor apartment terraced in Civil lines.'

She took a deep drag and closed the deal.

'We understand each other perfectly. I am…what is that word I am looking for…yes, I am "keeping you". Any objections?'

He smiled wolfishly in the dark, 'At your service, Ma'am. I am here to please.'

If a film camera attached at fan length could record the afternoon trysts of the desirous and her 'keep', then it would show that exploring human body for satisfaction is a journey of unbelievable metamorphosis. The camera film would record the limits of human imagination and ingenuity. The 'keep' had begun to draw out the deepest desires and fantasies of his benefactor. Justine would scream, cry, laugh, slap him, scratch him red, and beg pitifully as he unfailingly bored into her like a machine that does not know how to stop.

The passion of their love plays turned into kinkiness. Justine gifted Sunflower with the latest Kodak camera.

'A camera? What for?' he queried.

'To take my photos. Put me on film. My nudes, our bouts of love making. The entire act.'

'To what end?' he questioned her. 'You want reels that

you can put in your safe and view them at leisure?'

'No, you idiot! I don't do closet. I am giving you a gift, baby! Take these prints and sell them to pornographic magazines. Sell them in the bazaar, for all I care!'

'You are mad, you know that, don't you?'

'And, you are stuck with me. I hope you know that.'

But even a tryst outside of human imagination has to end. In the case of Sunflower and Justine, their afternoon trysts came to an unexpected and scruffiest end.

One late night, as Sunflower got off a cab and walked the quiet street to his pad, a car with tinted windows drew alongside him. Two men, with mufflers masking their faces, emerged. Sunflower tried to run, but he could not outpace them. They caught up with him, pinned him, and bundled him in the car with professional swiftness. His hands were tied behind his back and a black sack cloth was pulled down his face to cut his vision. The only sounds he heard was the purring of the car as it sped out of the Ridge to a pre-arranged destination.

★★★

Chapter 31

A splash of cold water on Sunflower's face alerted him to his new bearings. He was in a non-descript room, tied to a chair, looking up to a brawny man, a foreign national. Another foreign national, at the back of the room, paced around with slow, deliberate steps.

He attempted a bit of bravado to reverse the situation he found himself in.

'You are a foreign national who has kidnapped an Indian citizen. This is what it is. There will be hell to pay for this. Release me immediately.'

The man at the back stopped pacing the room and looked at him curiously.

'Despite being a low-life, you have a fine British accent and a surprising attitude. That is a bit of a surprise. I will do the talking here irrespective of that. Who are you and what is your interest in the wife of the United States Ambassador to India? To put it more bluntly, you really imagined that you could have an affair with the Ambassador's wife and get away with it? We have been keeping track of your activities for quite some time now.'

Sunflower spat on the floor.

'Who's the "we" here? Care to specify? Oh, wait! You jerks are the morality keepers of the American Embassy. Well, if you watched us so closely, tell me, did you enjoy your peep show?'

The burly man who stood glowering slapped him hard. The man at the back held up his hand.

'We don't do that, Steven. We don't need to. He's wanted for murder in Bombay. I checked on him. Now, before we hand you over to the police, mister, I will ask you one more time. What is your interest in the Ambassador's wife? Why did you befriend her?'

Despite his situation, Sunflower smiled.

'You mean why was I screwing her day and night? Last I checked with her, she was a full-grown adult, someone who has a mind of her own and takes her own decisions. In any case, why don't you ask her the same question? Why she was so keen to jump into bed with me? Well, to cut a long story short, friend, she was paying me to do that. She "keeps" me, if you can wrap your head around that. Satisfied?...now let me go.'

The man in the shadows thought for a moment and persisted.

'You haven't answered my question. Who are you? I

have a feeling you are more than a confidence trickster. I grant you that you have an…allure, a certain kind of an appeal. You have the looks for that. But, why the Ambassador's wife?'

'Release me, and I will tell you the truth,' replied Sunflower impassively.

The man in the shadows deliberated and then nodded to the burly man. Sunflower was released, and he rubbed his wrists for circulation. He looked at Freckles in the shadows and smiled slyly.

'It's simple really. I was using her so she would sponsor me for a green card to America. You see, mister, I love America. I always wanted to settle down in America. Look at it from my point of view. There is no opportunity for me in this country. I know I have a personality and looks which appeal to…well…a certain kind of white women. I am just a hard-working person end of the day, using my talents to secure a passage to America.'

Freckles emerged from the shadows. He could not help but smile.

'There's one thing I like about you though. You are a low-life, but you are upfront about it. Let me educate you then, mister. The US does not care for your talents. We have more than enough of your garden variety in the US. You seriously think the Ambassador's wife would have helped you? You used her or she was using you. It does not matter. It all ends here.

'I am releasing you. My advice to you is that you take the first train out of the city. If I find you stalking the Ambassador's wife again, I will notify the police. Knowing the reputation of your police force they will, what you call it, do a "police encounter" with you. Okay, scram away. Enough of you.'

Freckles and the man called Steven briskly walked to the door. Sunflower called after them. He spoke softly, pleading with them.

'Mister, we got off to a bad start but just hear me out. Please. Yes, I am a degenerate and a desperate man because I want to get out of this country. Yes, the police have a case against me. Yes, if they find out my whereabouts, they will get rid of me. I am quite willing to do anything for you to get out of here. I love America, hand on my heart.'

Freckles was almost out of the room when he turned, barely able to stop laughing.

'You will trade for a green card with what? Your body? I don't need it.'

Sunflower's voice was a mere whisper now, but it was still audible to Freckles.

'Sir, I am gifted with other skills. Extraordinary skills. You see, I have done stints with some of the biggest crime lords in Bombay. I have worked at the docks in Bombay, and covered the by-lanes of Colaba where some of the sleaziest, dangerous transactions of the world happen. I possess a talent for surveillance, interdiction and even elimination, if the need arises. You can use me any which way you want to, and against anyone. I owe no allegiance to anyone, not to this country certainly, and to no one. Except to my goal to reach America. Please, Sir, will you give me a chance?'

★★★

Chapter 32

Dr Iyer looked closely at a Japanese toy placed on his worktable. A visiting Japanese delegation must have gifted it. He had placed it carelessly next to a picture frame that showcased baby Tara in the arms of her mother Jayasudha, with the proud father, next to them, beaming for the camera. The innovative Japanese toy was a small globe that kept bobbing up and down and spinning simultaneously, with the message appearing 'Happy family, happy workplace.'

Dr Iyer wondered at the incongruity of it all. He could not recall the last time he had been happy. And it was probably worse for his colleagues working on the project. They were all stretched thin. Days and nights merging into one, there were endless cups of coffee, frequent cigarette breaks in the cafeteria and the toilet, constant complaints of gastritis and acidity among the staff, and even a burst ulcer for a colleague last week. These were the external problems. The pressure of completing the project on time was playing out in the minds of his team. Many had started hallucinating, forgetting what was real or unreal, possible or impossible. They all wondered whether they would survive the sheer pressure of their situation.

Dr Iyer looked out from his glass panelled office. His line of sight afforded him a view of the metalled gangway that encircled top of the CIRUS reactor. A senior project manager was walking along with a Canadian team, explaining the workings of the reactor. And that was the external challenge, much worse than the internal, the technological glitches that kept cropping up. Yet, they could somehow manage the technological inadequacies springing up in their quest to assemble the bomb. They had the brains and the innovations to do that.

But, how to manage the moral guilt, the uneasiness and the repulsion of lying with a straight face to the outside world that they were using atomic energy for peaceful purposes when they were clandestinely siphoning off fissile material to assemble the bomb? All this in a secret facility inside the dome located not even a few feet away from the visiting Canadian delegation. That was the problem wearing them down. Due to international pacts and agreements, they could not shut out the outside world. It would often intrude their mind space in the forms of these visits, or inspections really—a polite but determined check to monitor what exactly were the Indians doing with the imported uranium supply.

Dr Iyer looked at the Japanese spinning ball. He felt like picking up the piece and throwing it against the glass enclosure directed against the Canadians. He felt like a thief in his own house. Rage engulfed him because of his situation. The phone on his desk rang shrilly. His secretary was on the line. There was an urgent message from home. *Jayasudha had rushed Tara to the hospital. Tara was in a bad condition.*

★★★

Chapter 33

Even if Dr Iyer knew about it, he couldn't care less about it sitting by Tara's bedside in the hospital holding her hand. He always knew that he had been blessed with an innate sense of mental acuteness and extraordinary calm even in the face of the most difficult situations. That elan deserted him when he saw his daughter struggling on a hospital bed. He was panicking and sweating profusely as the visiting senior doctor checked Tara's vitals. Not surprisingly, Jayasudha was unflappable in the face of the new situation. She kept rubbing Dr Iyer's back and whispering in his ear, 'This too shall pass. Don't fret so much. It's alright.'

The doctor completed his check-up and deferentially gave his prognosis to the senior scientist.

'Sir, Tara had an episode which I can best describe as a mild seizure. We have completed all our tests. There appears to be no organ damage. We will, of course, continue to monitor her and conduct some more tests later in the day.

But, I can say with conviction, she is out of the woods.'

Even if Dr Iyer felt a wave of relief wash over him, he did not show it. He questioned the doctor, 'But...but what brought on this attack? We are by her side almost 24*7. It's inconceivable, something like this could have happened.'

The visiting doctor knowing the status of the senior scientist, chose his words carefully,

'Sir, she has a severe autistic condition. Such a reaction, therefore, cannot be entirely ruled out. Having said that, it would be impossible to lay a finger on what brought on this attack. Maybe...and this is just an opinion, maybe something in her immediate environment or in her ecosystem stressed her out. We will, of course, be conducting more tests...'

Dr Iyer's face registered complete exhaustion. The visiting doctor smiled nervously, nodded and took his leave. Jayasudha whispered in his ear again, 'She's resting. The nurse is taking good care of her. A word with you, please, outside this room.'

Jayasudha guided her husband in the dim-lit corridor to a corner near the water cooler. A look of distress clouded her usually serene face.

'Venkat, just because I don't protest it does not mean that I have an endless capacity to put up with your moods. It's all very well for you to become emotionally distraught, but can you even understand the pressure you are putting me under? You are, in a way, pointing a finger at me! That all this is my fault…'

'No, I make no such assumption…'

'Learn to listen to me for a change, without interrupting me, will you!' she retorted with unusual fierceness.

'You know, Tara is not the issue here. It is you. How do you expect me to constantly be attempting to live up to your expectations and looking after Tara at the same time! You don't think your late nights in office, your continued absence from home, your workaholism, all this is not wearing me down? And what about Tara? Can you even begin to understand why she had this episode? She misses her father! With almost clockwork precision, she expects you back from office at a particular time and spend time with her as she has got used to doing. People like you and me cannot grasp the importance of routine and time. But an autistic person does. It is their lifeblood. Hand on your heart, tell me when in the recent past you have spent time with her?'

He replied weakly, 'Lay the blame on me. You have no idea the pressure I am under at office.'

'So what?' she exploded. 'There are things we must do for our children. Do I need to educate you about it? Expect no sympathy from me on this issue, Venkat. If something happens to her, I will never forgive you. You, and you alone, can balance your work with our need to look after our only child. Only you can find a way. I can support you, but there are responsibilities I cannot take. We all have our limits.'

Dr Iyer took off his spectacles. Pressing the tap of the water cooler, he cupped water in his palm and splashed on his face. He wiped his face with a hanky and put on his spectacles. He looked more composed, almost thoughtful.

'You are right, Jayasudha. I have been selfish, self-contained. I was sinking into something which terrifies me when I think about it. You have dragged me out of it. I will find a way between these two worlds. That's a promise. A smile on Tara's face matters more to me than any credit or responsibility which I must shoulder. Stay by my side, my love. We will get through this.'

★★★

Chapter 34

The news photographer D'Souza searched at the empty railway tracks of New Delhi railway station looking for a frame. A frame, a photo that could somehow encapsulate the near-total success of all India railway strike call given by the trade union leader Alvarez. Government propaganda over radio and black-and-white television sets blared incessantly that the strike called by Alvarez had been ignored by the trade unions. They also mentioned that passenger and cargo rail traffic had not at all been affected by the strike. However, the reality of the situation was completely different. Railway stations across the country were deserted, all traffic had ceased on the tracks and trains were idling in their yards. This meant that movement of ordinary people in the country had been completely disrupted. The spin-off effect of the strike deeply impacted the ferrying of cargo, vital goods, fresh fruits and vegetables and essential commodities.

Retail prices of food grains and fruits and vegetables had shot through the roof.

The unionised railway workers had grown increasing belligerent as the days passed without a breakthrough in sight. The government adopted a hardline stance, refusing any parleys with the striking workers or the possibility of back-channel talks. Priya Kaul, true to her wont, refused to budge. The corridors of power in Delhi were full of rumours that Priya Kaul was planning a severe crackdown on the striking workers. There was even talk of curtailing civil liberties and prison terms for the ringleaders of the agitation. Both Tapash and Alvarez had not recently been seen in public. There were grounds to fear that they had been taken into custody.

Delhi was shot with tension. Photographer D'Souza was determined to find an inspiring frame that told the complete story at one go. So, after a lot of work, D'Souza settled for a frame that showed a black crow perched on a platform bench pensively looking out at deserted rail tracks. The photo appeared the next day in a leading national daily, but the headline and body of the report was blacked out to protest a crackdown on civil liberties.

D'Souza's solitary photo on a blacked out-front page became an instant hit, photographically symbolising the state of despair and anger that had engulfed the country.

The crackdown on civil liberties took on a different hue when Prahlad's youth storm troopers fanned out to silence protest and restore their kind of normalcy. A small group of senior journalists had collected near the Jantar Mantar, a stone's throw away from the Parliament building. They were holding placards and loudly protesting the imposition of strictures on press freedom. Prahlad's storm troopers took it upon themselves to teach the journalists lessons in journalistic propriety and responsibility.

They broke up the gathering with force and violence. Veteran journalists were slapped, kicked and punched repeatedly, and their placards torn, leaving them writhing in the dust smeared in their own blood crying, whimpering for help.

To be brutalised by the police was one thing. But to be brutalised by a political outfit which functioned more like a rogue paramilitary outfit was another.

The news of the brutalisation of senior journalists quickly spread by word of mouth. There was dismay, outrage and anger in the public at the treatment meted out to the journalists.

Word of the horrific events of that day quickly reached Priya Kaul. She slumped in her chair when she heard of the full report. Later, a close confidant of the Prime Minister swore she muttered under her breath, 'Prahlad, what should I do with you?'

On the evening of the same fateful day, Priya insisted on a meeting with her recalcitrant son in her office. Prahlad arrived for the meeting in a very aggressive and dark mood.

★★★

Chapter 35

Prahlad paced his mother's office like a gladiator in the ring, determined to tame the lions. He was clearly in a state. Priya Kaul sat shrunken in her chair, wondering how things had deteriorated between them so quickly. Her son was lecturing and blasting her like she was an errant child daring to cross red lines set by the parent. And yet, despite his aggression, Priya was determined to get in a word of caution.

'You know, Prahlad, one of these days you will be the death of me. I will not mince my words today. They all call you a dictator in the making. I gave you charge of the youth brigade to supplement our hold over political narration, and not to create a parallel power centre, a political entity of revulsion. Why don't you get this in your head? I am on your side. I want to eventually pave the way for you to take over. But you always behave as if I am antagonistic to your aspirations. But know this, son, and I speak from years of political experience, the road to ultimate power in this country travels a minefield of discretion, negotiation and even compromise. Everyone in our history who have seized power through brute force have eventually been consigned to the dust. You are headed that path, and, as your mother and your political benefactor, it is my duty to caution you. What was the need to beat up those journalists? They are non-entities and would have dispersed after venting spleen. No one would have even noticed them. But your actions have made them champions of press freedom and installed the halo of martyrs around their heads!'

'Oh, shut up, mother!' retorted Prahlad.

'You drone on and on! Don't give me advice of a "has been"! You are the past. Your experience is of no use in today's India. Look around you. This country is in a mess. We breed like rabbits and the country's resources can't keep pace with our exploding population. Only my outfit, which you so contemptuously call the youth brigade, is bringing sense to our middle-aged breeders who do not know when to stop. The bloody ugliness of the load they discharge on this country! It is I, mother, I, who has taken on this initiative to stop this continuous nonsense. You think sweet persuasion will help them change their minds? You have a hope in hell. Only *danda* works with such people, and I will not hesitate to use it!'

'Then you have already written your political

obituary, son,' warned Priya.

'The hell I have! And speaks the woman who has curtailed civil liberties and is throwing Opposition leaders in jail. And even though you may hate to be reminded about it, but we are peas of a pod, mother. Guess you had shut your mind to that fact of life! We are both tyrants, dear mother, masquerading to the world with our charm and lineage. So, don't have the temerity to lecture me about my affairs! You manage yours and let me handle mine!'

'There is a difference, Prahlad, between what I do and what you are always attempting to do. I have taken temporary firm measures to steady a situation in the country spiralling out of control. In your case, rudeness and violence is becoming a way of life. Sometimes I wonder, from whom you got your sadism streak? It worries me no end!'

Prahlad stopped pacing the room. He was shaking with a fury. He almost spat out what he said next.

'And I also wonder about the succession of undesirables that frequent your private quarters! That Rasputin like hirsute Yoga guru, that podgy *bandhgala* suited ex-diplomat! Let's talk about them, mother, instead of you psychoanalysing me! The shame and sense of betrayal I feel at your behaviour…'

Priya Kaul suddenly felt completely devastated. It reached a level she never could have imagined. She felt completely out of control.

And then, out of character, she wrung her hands and slapped her own face hard. Prahlad took a step back in complete shock. Her eyes were blazing when she looked up.

'I am cursed that you were born to me... in what moment, what folly, the price I must pay for my thoughtlessness...'

And just for a moment, the fight went out of Prahlad Kaul. He looked caved in like a little boy lost in a crowd desperately looking for his parents. Tears stung his eyes. Words escaped him.

And as he recovered, anger filled him. He raised his hand and swiftly came up to Priya Kaul ready to strike her across her face. He would have done that if he had not recoiled back from the horror-stricken face of his mother. He slapped his hand hard against the table and stormed out of the room, banging the door shut after him.

There was complete silence in the room. The image of Prahlad raising his hand against her. It deeply settled in her. She knew it would haunt her for the rest of her life. A voice, almost as another entity, was speaking to her. Had she reached the bottom of her misery, her hopelessness and helplessness? Or was there still some distance to be covered? The voice in her told her she was a fighter, and not a loser. Come what may, a sea of blood was before her. She would have to cross it. There was no escaping it, no turning back. She understood it was a point in time when even a parent separates from a child and the filial narrative changes. Call it a second cutting of the umbilical cord. That time had arrived now. She was a surviving dark force of nature and in a sense her own son had made her aware of it. So, be it.

She gathered her courage and walked out of the room knowing that her staff in the adjoining room was listening to every word that had transpired in her office. So, be it.

★★★

Chapter 36

Priya shut herself in her room back home. She desperately tried to make sense of what had happened in her office some time back. She could not. The shock of Prahlad raising his hand against her hit her now. She felt her resilience crumbling from within. Her eyes stung with tears. She felt alone, humiliated and abandoned. Her mind was numbed with shock. The image of Prahlad towering over her like a vengeful, wild beast haunted her. Her mind was like a dervish spinning out of control. Her rational self told her she was going through a low; a high would come later or maybe another low. She was caught in a spiral. There were voices in her head that were beginning to speak to her. Should she abandon all and flee to some desolate place and bury her head in the sand? Maybe she could slap Prahlad tight on his face and assert parental authority. Or would he see reason if she prostrated herself before him and begged him not to break the bond between a parent and a child?

She never knew when she started to speak to herself in the dark. She spoke staccato, unhinged; the gist of her talk to her own self being that Kamini had conspired to destroy her relationship with her son. She then switched tack. No, maybe it was the United States that had brought on this situation. So many journals and magazines were full of articles that the US was conducting research in mind, altering experiments to use research against heads of government they despised. Surely, she would be at top of that list.

And then, she sank on the bed and started to speak gibberish, incoherent stuff. After a while, listening to her own self, she suddenly fell quiet. Her mind was out of control. She understood that. It was racing at incredible speed. She would have to slow down if she wanted to survive the night. Anything could happen. After all, there was only so much pain, emotion and pressure that even her mind could take.

She lay still on her bed, quietened down. After a while, when she was somewhat calm, she wearily got up and staggered to the en suite bathroom. She did not switch on the light. She splashed cold water on her face and rubbed her face with the folds of her night dress.

She breathed a little better and purposefully returned to her bed, picking up the RAX handset. She knew there would be an operator at the other end, a senior member of the intelligence staff. They were on a twenty-four-hour shift. She connected to the operator.

A terse command.

'Connect me to Swamiji.'

There were clicks and transmission sounds in her handset and Swami Dharmachari took the call.

'What is it, Priya? It's late in the night. Hope all is well?'

'No, it is not. Take out your plane from the hangar, and come to my place immediately. I need you here.'

'Child, can this wait till the morning? You sound deeply unsettled and upset. Perhaps, morning will bring more clarity?'

'Listen, you pompous, Yogic world healer! I have just taken a lot of shit from my son because of you! When I say get your ass out of bed, then do it immediately! Now means now! Get moving!'

She shut the handset and switched on the bedside lamp. Her frenzied mind was slowing down which was good. Maybe, there was hope yet.

Closer to the first flush of dawn, the motorcade of the Swami arrived at the gates of 7, Race Course Road. He was given immediate access to come in. The security set-up at the residence had already been notified. After a while, the Swami entered the house and gently knocked at Priya's bedroom door.

'Come in,' commanded Priya. 'And close the door behind you.'

The Swami walked in and though he was shocked to

see her in a state, he did not show it. Her eyes were blazing, hair unkempt. He stood near the door with a neutral expression on his face. He was wearing his morning Yogic attire, displaying his hirsute self.

She picked up a book lying at the bedside and violently threw it at the Swami's face. It hit him right in the middle of his face, and though he was stunned by her reaction, he did not show it. He stood impassively near the door, waiting for more. She screamed at him and then collapsed in a paroxysm of choked tears.

He carefully walked up to her and sat by her side without her approval. He gently stroked her head. 'What is it, child, what ails you? It saddens me to see you in this state. Tell me about it.'

She clenched her fists and spoke with gritted teeth, her body shaking uncontrollably.

'He almost hit me. My own son. The depravity, the horror of it! I, the most powerful woman in the world, helplessly writhing in front of him. How have things come to such a pass? Has he no shame? Why does he hate me so much? Why? Why? Why?'

The Swami did not respond immediately. He continued to stroke her head till she calmed down. He softly whispered, 'It happens, Priya. Nothing in this world is inconceivable. We live in Kalyug. The son turns on his mother. The jackal mates with the dog. The parrot pierces the eye of the benefactor that extends his hand to feed it.

Nothing is what it seems, child. This too shall pass…'

Priya Kaul suddenly got up and started to laugh maniacally.

'I now know, Swami, why I tolerate you. It's not for your Yogic prowess. It's for your bullshit that's so entertaining! It really has lifted me from my mood of despair.'

'Happy to oblige, Prime Minister,' muttered Swami Dharmachari weakly.

Priya Kaul set her steely gaze on the Swami. She tersely told him, 'You and I will not be seen in public from now onwards. Discretion is the key here. I don't like tongues wagging. There is a crisis I need to handle. I cannot be distracted by rubbish gossip. But, since you are here, I would expect you to comfort me. After that, you should disappear back in the wilderness from where you come.'

★★★

Chapter 37

Rhino lit a cigarette and inhaled deeply. His mind was working in top gear. He sat in his favourite chair in the attic of his small, two-roomed flat in Sujan Singh Park. The attic was his place of escape, his sanctuary where he collected his thoughts and made sense of the way forward. It was a dimly lit, musty place, full of mementoes. The walls displayed photographs, framed cuttings of creative writing, science-project conclusions and even a report card with a big circle in red pointing to the subject he had failed that year and the marks he had scored. The report card kept him grounded, reminding him that he was not infallible. Even the best of the best trip at times, make mistakes, and even fail.

There were also some papier mâché miniatures and models of World War II fighter aircraft, like Spitfires, Hurricanes and Mustangs, hanging from the ceiling from wires.

Rhino was a boy, man, and an old man, all at the same time in this attic. His place of refuge. A place that gave him time to think and connect the dots. He smoked languidly and sipped his whisky. He needed that drink. He had come home a while ago after a stormy meeting with Priya Kaul. She had largely been raving in that meeting as a woman on the edge, clearly someone who, like the Shakespearean general Macbeth, was convinced that her enemies were closing in on her.

For the first time during that meeting, he was convinced that maybe there was a method in her madness. The stifling of civil liberties in the country and the crackdown on Opposition luminaries, like Tapash, and union leaders, like Alvarez, had boomeranged. There was an outpouring of support for them in the country. The increasing unpopularity and chronic dislike for Prahlad Kaul was a huge contributing factor.

But, Rhino was a loyalist and even though he personally disapproved of how Prahlad Kaul functioned, he never raised objections to his behaviour and trajectory with Priya Kaul. He accepted fait accompli. Not because he was afraid of Priya Kaul, but because he loved her too deeply, and firmly believed in the dynastic principle of succession and its grip on power.

And so, keeping these complexities in mind, intensifying the overall crackdown was not the answer. Hence, Priya's assumption that a nuclear test would shake things up, directing protest and opposition and discontent in a completely new non-threatening direction, made complete sense. The test would have to be actualised sooner than later.

But a spanner in the works had appeared.

A report in his briefcase indicated trouble was brewing from an entirely unexpected quarter.

Rhino crushed his cigarette, his mind made up, and went to his desk for another look at the single-page report given to him by the IB.

Three of their double agents in the northern sector, all housed and operating near major Indian army bases, had been eliminated in the most brutal manner. This meant only one thing. An asset, an entirely new entity, a sinister, ruthless and very capable agent of the ISI had infiltrated the country and was working overtime in the North.

The timing of this agent's ingress and operating methodology made Rhino deeply suspicious. The reason behind these targeted killings was a cause for worry. Had their plans been leaked? Was there a mole in the establishment that had leaked Priya Kaul's nuclear doctrine to the Pakistanis? Or, were the killings a reaction to something else, a new danger not visible on the horizon, but brewing rapidly?

So many questions, so few answers.

Counter measures were required to cocoon Priya Kaul's initiative from a hostile foreign attack, and to track down and eliminate the killer of the double agents.

Rhino picked up his RAW handset and dialled a number. His man for all seasons picked up at the other end.

★★★

Chapter 38

The man, with a half-opened skull and brain matter seeping down his forehead, crawled the soot-ridden floor on all fours, inch by inch. He was trying to get somewhere, anywhere to escape the wrath of the assassin and his accomplice. Both men dressed in black, took slow, deliberate steps, trailing the dying man. Both men appeared to be in no hurry.

The man with the shattered skull had a great will to live. His tedious crawl led him out of the room, into the hallway, in a scene straight out of hell. Small, little fires burnt everywhere, consuming, licking and sputtering, sucking oxygen from the air, and making unearthly sounds. Somewhat like a beast feasting on a kill.

Through his blurry vision, he made out two bodies lining the doorway. Smoke rose from the upturned body of his son, blackened and charred from the fire. His wife lay next to her son, looking upwards at the ceiling, breathing slowly, her last breaths rising and falling unevenly. Peeling flesh hung from her cheekbones. The remains of her burnt, smouldering burkha were plastered on her forehead.

His will to live escaped him.

He saw them clearly now, and a deep, wracking cry of pain grew in him. But there was no release because his facial muscles were atrophied in extreme pain. Nevertheless, he somehow managed to turn over and look at the face of the pitiless marauder who had done this to him.

'You bastard!' he whispered and cranked up his burst head to spit in the face of his tormentor. It was of no use really. More streams of blood streamed down his face.

Viper observed the dying man with no emotion. He looked at his wristwatch. It was time. He nodded to the recruit standing next to him.

'You do it,' he said quietly. 'Don't mess it up. I want to send a message to all.'

The recruit also showed no emotion, much like the mentor. He took out a knife and methodically sliced off the dying man's neck, slowly with controlled savagery.

The decapitation involved tremendous force, but the recruit carried out the task effortlessly, without hesitation and with complete, utter calm. The neck lolled off the severed torso and a fresh geyser of blood erupted. The protégé got up and kicked the decapitated head in the direction of the dying wife. It rolled next to her. Her pupils dilated with the horror of the situation; she was unable to breathe.

Later, the two killers exited the flat silently, unseen, without leaving a trace. By evening, Viper and his protégé settled in their hideout, a safe house for infiltrators coming over from the other side. The safe house had a window which gave a good view of the Badami Bagh cantonment in Srinagar.

Viper prepared an evening meal for both which could be best described as part Wazwan cuisine and the other part Lahori. So, a feast really. A table was laid with Kashmiri-style meatballs dipped in sauce, accompanied by saffron rice and tandoori chicken. They ate heartily and drank kahva along with their meal. After the dinner, Viper offered his protégé his special brand of Turkish cigarettes. The younger man politely refused, and Viper smoked his cigarette without a word. Both men sat in chairs facing each other.

Viper smoked his cigarette and crushed it under his foot. He spoke matter of fact to his protégé.

'A job well done today. I am impressed. You held your nerve. You might go far. But I am still tasked to ask you a few questions, complete a formal interview as it were. I have been asked to send your assessment to the higher-ups.'

'Of course, Viper. It is your prerogative.'

Viper scanned the man facing him. He questioned him.

'For the record, Mushtaq, what was your original name?'

'Tikka Ram,' replied the protégé unhesitatingly.

'Why did you convert to Islam? Was it under some kind of duress?'

'I converted out of no compulsion. It was a decision of free will. I was a Kashmiri brahmin by birth. I have been exposed to Islam from an early age. Most of my friends in school were Muslim. Over the years, I grew more and more disenchanted with my religion. Meanwhile, I got increasingly absorbed in understanding the tenets of Islam. They appealed to me, made sense to me. And so, I decided to convert. It's as simple as that.'

Viper kept quiet for a moment and then continued.

'Let me say, Mushtaq, that I am still not fully convinced by your assertion that you converted to Islam out of free will. I find it hard to believe. I have never known a case where a Kashmiri brahmin converted to Islam out of choice.'

Without a moment's hesitation, Mushtaq answered, 'Then that is your problem and not mine. I know about the faith I have chosen. I don't have to prove to you, or for that matter to anyone, the reasons for my decision.'

Viper leaned forward.

'The passion of the newly converted. Question is, how real is it?'

Mushtaq shrugged his shoulders. Viper got up and took out another one of his Turkish cigarettes. He smelled it and licked it with his tongue without lighting it. He paced the area around Mushtaq.

'Let's assume, you converted out of conviction. But not every convert would also switch loyalties to an enemy country, I mean, to my country that is Pakistan. I find it a little unnerving that you are as passionate about Pakistan as you are about Islam.'

'Well, I proved to you, did I not, this afternoon, what I believe in,' answered the protégé rhetorically.

Viper carefully studied the protégé's face.

'An experienced, Indian intelligence agent would do the same what you did in the blink of an eye. To ingratiate himself with the other side. So, Mushtaq aka Tikka Ram, are you an Indian intelligence agent masquerading as a soldier of Islam?'

Mushtaq moved uneasily, and Viper, with lightning reflexes, pinned Mushtaq to the chair, locking his arms behind with handcuffs. If the younger man was caught by surprise, he did not show it. Viper proceeded to squeeze the man's throat, snuffing the air out of him.

'Die, Indian agent…'

Mushtaq somewhat struggled, but gave up after a while, strangely looking composed accepting death. The veins stood out in his neck and his eyes were popping, but he showed no panic. Viper kept on pressing till a point came when both the killer and the would-be-executed know the end was not far.

At that point of termination, Viper let go. He had never encountered a man completely unflappable in the face of death. He knew such acceptance came only from a man of faith, the faith of the newly-converted.

He slapped the man hard, unlocked his handcuffs and

helped him on his feet. Mushtaq gagged and coughed violently and rubbed his sore neck, but he was alright.

Viper lit his cigarette and led Mushtaq to the window that gave a view of the distant twinkling lights of Badami Bagh cantonment.

'Mushtaq *mian*, I am going to believe in you. You will be my second in command in India. My mission is to place my agents, my kind of men, answerable only to me, fiercely loyal to me, around India's premier offensive armed strike units. This also means that many of our agents in the past that have been compromised by Indian intelligence over the years have to be eliminated. Call it the weeding of the old and the creation of a new cadre. You will help me do that. Is that clear?'

'Absolutely,' replied Mushtaq quickly. 'You will have my full support. Can I ask a question though?'

'Sure. You have earned that right.'

'I am no stranger to killing, *Bhai*. But what is the need to kill these traitors in such a gruesome manner? Aren't we inviting attention from Indian intelligence to our plans?'

Viper flicked an imaginary hair from Mushtaq's bulky phiran.

'These killings are my signature card, Mushtaq. This is the first and last time you will ask me this question. There is a method in my madness. Know that. India is a soft, lumbering state. Our brutal methods strike terror in the hearts of the Indians. It confuses them and leads them to make more mistakes. That is what I want from them. Because what is coming in the not-too-distant future will be nothing less than the clash of two civilisations, the ultimate test of nerves, deceit and betrayal. That is what is at stake here.'

★★★

Chapter 39

Viper took a seat in front of his boss, the ISI chief in the Islamabad office.

The older man took out a cigar, cut it and lit it, blowing blue smoke to the ceiling.

'What shall I do with you, Viper? If you had not been my best agent, I would have put you to pasture a long time back. What shall I do with you?'

'Let me work without interference, Sir, that's all,' answered Viper confidently. 'If I can ask, what has offended you so much this time?'

The ISI chief blew a smoke ring towards Viper.

'Nasir Rahmatullah Sahab, aka Viper, let me rephrase the question. Will a time ever come when you will be an asset and not a thorn in my foot? Will the day ever come when by your actions you do not end placing me on the horns of a dilemma?'

Viper did not bother to reply. The conversation he

knew would follow a familiar pattern. It always did. The boss would fret and fume, but, ultimately, he would give in. Not because he believed in the operational methodology Viper practised, but because he feared him. Viper was not an ordinary operative of the ISI. He was, in a sense, the pack leader of an entirely new cadre of younger, fitter, ruthless ISI agents, driven both by religious and ideological fervour. Many of these agents were desirous of exacting revenge against India for the humiliation their country had suffered in various conflicts. They could go to any extent to achieve that. Their role, and even hold, within the organisation could not be challenged. The ISI in that sense was a peculiar intelligence agency. Its ruthlessness and even deviousness for conducting operations was proven. But it was still an organisation riven with various factions supported by different power centres. No one so far, and certainly not the present ISI chief, had been able to clean the Augean stables and streamline the command-and-control staffing of the agency. The job requirement of the top man of the agency was to keep the various factions under check and relatively happy. That was the only way to survive the job.

The ISI chief continued.

'Okay, Viper, let me come to the nub of the matter. I know all about the manner you have been eliminating those so-called double agents in India. I don't care about the methodology. But I am deeply concerned about the brazenness with which you are going about the job. The entire affair smacks of some kind of personal vendetta. You would have already alerted Indian intelligence by your actions. Besides these agents, we also have dozens of other sleeper cells operating in India. Cells and operatives you are not aware of. All of them will come under the scanner because of your intemperate actions. Your kill list will boomerang against us.

'You might be thinking tactically, but I must have a strategic overview of things. There is a time for action, but there is also a time for plotting and planning. You just don't seem to understand the difference.' Viper answered respectfully but firmly, 'I hear you, Sir. In my defence, I must say, I have not done anything against the interests of Pakistan. India is our number one enemy and my actions in that country are small, but necessary, initiatives to eventually deliver a crushing defeat to India. Now, is there anything else for me, Sir?'

The ISI chief got up and made a show of crushing his cigar in the palm of his hand. He walked slowly and deliberately, circling behind Viper. He knelt and whispered in his ear,

'Listen, you overrated thug. I have news for you. I know all about your support base. But don't push it with me. I am denuding your support base even as we speak. And they are listening to me and agreeing to what I am promising them. Know why? Because they are human beings at the end of the day and not mindless freaks like you. They all want what other human beings want.

'But know this, Viper. The priority is no longer India. It is the Afghanistan-Soviet frontier. Everyone agrees to that, even that son of a bitch head of state that we have. Now, ask me why is that the case? Because a once-in-a-lifetime opportunity has presented itself in front of us. The Americans are desperate that we fund and arm and train the Mujahideen to wobble the mighty Soviet army. This means they are willing to flood our coffers with hundreds of millions of dollars. This also means we get to buy all the fancy tanks and aircraft and guns from the Americans at basement sale prices and replenish our army and boost our economy.'

The ISI chief's voice dropped even further.

'It also means, you fucking dolt, that everyone in this food chain, especially those who matter, get a piece of the pie. Even the top man who rules our country. Translated, it means many of us get to own farmhouses around Karachi, the latest Bentleys and holidays on the Riviera with our families and kids. All on the house. The American house foots the bill. And it does not stop there. It also means out of turn scholarships and entry-level admissions for our kids in top Ivy League colleges in the US. And not to forget, the prestige of attending those coveted courses at the West Point academy in the US where we rub shoulders with the best of the best of their armed forces. We get all that, you fucker, and I, and everyone else in the food chain, will not be denied those essential pleasures of life. Because of the actions of a screwball like you. I hope what I have said is not lost in translation to you.'

Viper knew it was time to leave. He got up with the painful gait of a man which had just been rammed in the solar plexus by a car.

His boss was, however, not done yet.

'You leave when I tell you to leave, you fucker! Sit down.'

The chief circled him again, eyeing him like a bird of prey. He held up three fingers and waved them before Viper.

'Three months. That's all you get to complete your project in India. If something comes out of it, we will do something about it. If not, we end that project. The agents will function as they have always done. No more cutting and pruning by the likes of you. No more looking into darkened corners, fishing for conspiracy projects. We relocate physically and mentally to project Afghanistan. All resources and all assets will be utilised there. And that includes you.

'I am giving you a last chance, not because I am afraid of you but because I still have some honour left in me. Now, you can get up and get the fuck out of my office.'

Viper got up silently and made his way to the door. His boss stopped him there.

'One last thing, Viper. I know you are an obdurate fellow. For whichever reason you are obsessed with India, you must back off. It might be too late, later. Not a day passes by when unknown gunmen riding scooters and motorcycles don't shoot dead their targets on the street in broad daylight. Just saying, you know.'

★★★

Chapter 40

Back home, Viper insisted on feeding his seven-year-old daughter with his own hands. It was a simple meal of chicken curry and rice, Viper's favourite. His wife Salma looked at both with indulgence and happiness, as Viper showered his daughter with affection and care. They had some *phirni* after the meal; Viper sipped a cup of kahva while chatting with his daughter about her school activities. Not too long after that, her eyelids became heavy with sleep. Viper gently lifted his daughter, carried her to her room and tucked her in bed. He quietly closed the door of her room and returned in the dining area to join his wife. She stroked his head, and he continued sipping his kahva.

She spoke soothing words to him, 'You look exhausted, Nasir. I never ask you about your work. But, is there something weighing on your mind? I am worried about you. And, laughable as it might seem to you, but even Dua worries about you. She keeps asking about you during your long periods of absence from home.'

Viper could not help but smile. He pressed Salma's hand to comfort her. He had grown up in a stoic, never-share-your-feelings environment and was not about to change demeanour anytime soon. Salma was his wife, the repository of his secrets, or at least some of them. But today, out of nowhere, he felt like venting.

'You know, Salma, I have always disciplined myself to keep my passion ringed deep, deep inside me, for your sake, for Apa's sake, and now for my dearest Dua's sake, the three women in my life. Because my passion is scalding. It burns and scalds and leaves marks. I have always sought to protect Dua. I want her to be innocent and carefree when she grows up.

'So, what I say to you today stays in this room, not to be told to anyone. Ever. Dear Salma, I will always fight to be with you and Dua, but at some point in time that might not be the case. There are men out to get me. My own people, men from within the organisation.

'These people are venal and corrupt to the core. They are the biggest hindrance to my dream of a *Naya* (new) Pakistan. And, they will stop at nothing to remove me from their way.

'So, tomorrow, if I don't return home you have to brace yourself. You will have to raise Dua with both your and my absentee love. I am preparing you, Salma, because at some point in time the unthinkable can happen. Hopefully not today…'

Salma collapsed in a paroxysm of tears. He comforted and soothed her without misleading her. In his mind, she was a soldier's wife. She had to be prepared for the worst.

They went to bed late in the night. Before putting out the lights, he asked her.

'How is Apa holding up? She was asleep when I came in. Everything alright with her?'

'She has her good days and bad days. She has been quiet of late, sleeping a lot. Sometimes, I feed her in the room. Don't you worry about her. Get some rest.'

At 2 am, both of them woke up with alacrity. They heard low-pitched wailing and moaning outside their bedroom door. It could have been the sounds of an animal in distress. Viper rushed to the door and opened it. Apa stood at the doorway, stark naked, convulsing violently, her eyes unnaturally widened, hair streaking in all directions. Salma shrieked in horror, but collected her senses to snatch a cover from the bed and throw it around Apa to cover her nakedness.

But it was of no use.

Apa began to thrash around even more violently and her low-pitched moaning and wailing increased in intensity. Salma was finding it difficult to control her. She needed help. Where had Nasir disappeared?

She tried to drag Apa to her room, and screamed for Nasir to come and help her. Nasir had locked himself in Apa's room and was scratching the walls of the room with his nails. Salma felt she would soon lose control, but she managed to drag Apa to her room. She pounded on the door and begged Nasir to open it. But Nasir, in Apa's room, was lost to Salma and the world.

He felt murderous and an urge to inflict incalculable violence had gripped him. The walls of Apa's room were melting and columns of fire were spreading all around, enveloping the furniture, linen, plastic and even the footwear. Everything was melting, reducing and turning into gnarled, grotesque, charred, lumps of inanimate matter.

And then, with a whoosh, the fire and the destruction disappeared. Nasir was looking at clear, blue skies and an unending field of corn stretching for miles. It was a time in his life thirty years ago. He was a six-year-old boy holding on to his Apa's hand, Apa, his elder sister, who loved him the most in the world.

Brother and sister entered the frame of a world that had gone by. But, something was wrong. There was death and destruction brewing under idyllic skies. They were both running for their lives in a cornfield, running away from their own village, fearing the villagers who were not from their religion, and who chased them like a pack of wolves.

It had all changed in a day. Some wise men had drawn a line across a map. And in a single day, man had turned against man, in village after village after village, in an undivided country.

They were running through the field. They only heard the sounds of their rasping breath, and the crisp sounds of the bending and breaking of corn stalks as they plunged deeper into the field to escape somewhere.

And then suddenly, the field gave way to a clearing. A fire was burning in a circle in the clearing, with men standing at the edge of the circle of fire. They wore *kurtas* and *lungis*, and so many of them had twirling moustaches.

Many of them were the uncles he knew in the village. He was sure they liked him—sometimes they would indulge him with *Jamun* or *shahtoot* fallen off the tree.

They looked at the brother and sister, smiling knowingly. They carefully upended their lungis till their flaccid members could be seen clearly. All the uncles, who had indulged him in the village, had no time for him now.

They had eyes only for Apa. They carried her in the ring of fire and tore off her clothes. For some strange reason, they left only her *dupatta* draped around her neck. He would understand the reason later.

They stroked their members, bringing them to life, and then one by one, all of them descended on Apa to have their fill. He could not remember the exact number of them, but there were many.

Apa incessantly wailed and moaned with pain in low-pitched tones through all that. She kept looking at Nasir standing outside the circle of fire, as men descended on her. He was sure she was struggling to say, 'Run away,

Nasir. You will be next. They will not leave you.'

The last man on the job finished what he had to do and proceeded to choke Apa with her dupatta. Her eyes became bloodshot and popped out.

It was all so quiet. She was almost out of breath, but then suddenly, a large red hole erupted on the forehead of the man on top of Apa. He fell and a volley of shots rang out. In the distance, a British army officer in a jeep was firing from a Colt pistol. Both the brother and sister were saved.

Salma broke through the door. As Nasir, scratching the walls with fury, turned, Salma rushed to him and took him in her arms. He collapsed in her arms. The frenzied agony of the brother and sister perceptibly subsided after that. A little later, after recovering, Nasir administered a sedative to his elder sister. She went to sleep, and he sat by her bedside for long, a cold light shining in his eyes. His face was a mask again as he looked up at Salma.

'They want me to move on and forget all this. As if all this never happened. This is not in the past, Salma. It is a living, present-day ember that burns fiercely in me. I will avenge my sister, Salma, come what may. The Indians will pay for this. Oh yes, they will pay for this. And nothing, and no one, will be able to stop me from doing what I must do.'

***

Chapter 41

Sunflower was living his dream having secured his passage to America. It had been three months since he had landed in America as part of a secret international training programme called 'Special agents'. The men and women selected in this programme were not citizens of America. They came from what then used to be called the 'third world' countries, countries the US was interested in to wean away from the Soviet Union's global influence, bringing them in the orbit of American interests. These special agents in the making were men and women of extraordinary potential. At the very least, they possessed gifts of carrying out surveillance, interdiction and elimination, unlike anyone else. The basic requirement of the job was an unwavering commitment to American interests, even if they were asked to turn on the country of their birth and origin.

So, how did a man like Sunflower, wanted for murder

in Bombay, manage to become a part of the elite group and travel to America?

Freckles spotted the man's hidden talent. When Sunflower had begged Freckles to give him a chance, Freckles, in a moment of indulgence and out of boredom, did precisely that. He assigned Sunflower the task to find out the exact name and number of Indian Intelligence Bureau agents tracking senior staff and their movements in the American Embassy in Delhi.

A week later, Sunflower submitted his report. He gave the exact number and names of IB agents on the job, carrying out the surveillance. The names matched the list of IB agents that Freckles had already prepared, courtesy other sources and means available.

The tallying of Sunflower's list with his own deeply impressed Freckles since a conman, a petty criminal and a rank amateur had come up with top-grade spying stuff. But, what really stunned Freckles was the finding by Sunflower that Indian intelligence had zeroed in on Freckles himself. They also know Freckles' modus operandi of funding Opposition politicians in India to bring down the present government and the Prime Minister. Despite knowing all this, they were still being discreet to beat the Americans at their own game when the time came.

Freckles made up his mind to send Sunflower to America to enhance and sharpen his talent and use him for covert missions in India.

And so, Sunflower, the man so fond of saying 'I love America', landed in snow-bound Virginia in America for a CIA training programme. Sunflower cradled a Glock automatic at a shooting range in the icy hills, awaiting next instructions from a small arms instructor.

The cardboard cut-outs of a mean-looking enemy popped up from the ground and the small arms instructor barked, 'Fire!'

With great deliberation, Sunflower fired, unloading his full clip. So did ten other recruits in the programme. Only Sunflower maxed the perfect score, bullseye bullet holes in the forehead of the enemy target.

The next day, Sunflower was taken out of the training programme to sit down for a debriefing with a senior instructor in a closed padded room.

The man came straight to the point of the 'interview.'

'We are pulling you out of this training programme because there is nothing more that we can teach you. Your skill sets, aptitude, attention to detail, planning and execution is extraordinary. Frankly, your peers in your batch appear to be fumbling novices when compared to you.

'And so, in the light of your immense talent, I am constrained to ask the question, Sunflower, how the fuck did an agent of Indian intelligence infiltrate this top-secret programme? Just tell us how, and all is forgiven!'

And in a blink of an eye, Sunflower's American dream was over. His American nightmare began. Two tough-looking men rushed in the padded room, and started working on Sunflower, slowly, ruthlessly and efficiently. They stripped him off all clothes and tied him naked to the chair. His eyelids were stapled wide with tape so he could not close his eyes. All the men in the room exited and the lights dimmed. A screen came down opposite Sunflower's line of sight. And then began a non-ending assault on his auditory and visual senses. Harsh, loud, punk and rock music boomed in the small room. Grotesque images of death, destruction, barbarity, sadism and necrophilia lit up the screen. The sound-and-light show went on and on, without a respite till Sunflower screamed like a man whose head had been cleaved in half. And then abruptly, it stopped. Pin drop silence. The lights went out completely. It was pitch-dark. And suddenly, the floor beneath his chair opened. Still tied to the chair, he plunged several feet in the ground in an underground shaft. He landed maybe 40-50 feet deep in the ground, with the opening above closed. Pitch-dark. Nothing could be heard. A dark silence enveloped him.

After a while, he thought he could hear his heart beating loudly. At the very least, he heard his own voice. Loud and strong.

'You think you can frighten me, you bastards, by these cheap, parlour tricks! By these gizmos and theme park lift stunts! I am made of sterner stuff. You bastards, I still love America despite you! Do your worst!'

But this time, there was no response. There was only the sound of silence in the dark. They would try new tricks soon, he thought it over in his head. Best to get some rest. He tried a shut eye, but it was of no use. He could not sleep. The dark was crawling on him like a living entity. After a while, he suddenly realised with a shock, he had lost sense of time and space. A sinking feeling grew in him.

Was he beginning to panic? After all, it was not every day that a man of strong mental disposition is thrown and abandoned in a 50 feet deep hole in the ground.

No, he was not panicking. He was made of sterner stuff. But what if no one pulled him above? What if the switch controlling the lift had malfunctioned? What if rats deep in the ground started to crawl over him?

He was at the edge of panic. He could not even close his eyes that were stapled wide. He was looking at the horror of his own existence.

Time must have elapsed because hunger was gnawing at him, his mouth was dry, and he had, perhaps, urinated on the chair. If oppression had a sound, then he was hearing it. But not much else.

After a while, he knew no one was coming for him. He had been left alone in that hole. End of story. The only thing working for him at that point in time was his mind. And soon, his mind began to play tricks with him. He was transported to his childhood. He could not weep, laugh or emote when he saw his childhood images in his mind. At times, his mind became a blizzard of images, some real and many more imagined. At other times, the images in his mind slowed, moving glacially at, perhaps, a hundredth of a second.

First time in his life, he realised the mind was a wonderful vessel. It could be filled with anything and transported anywhere after it had set sail.

And then, when a lot of time had passed and he shat on his chair, covered in faeces, urine and sweat and ravaged by hunger and thirst, he suddenly grew tired of his mind. He just wanted to get rid of it, discard his only live companion in the dark.

And then he saw it clearly, he had to make a choice.

He could either die in despair or go down fighting in the hole. A fight to the finish, a fight set by him on his own terms and not someone else's. He chose to make a song, but not a dance of it, and not die in despair.

He began to sing aloud with passion.

'I love America but not you, you bastards! Hip hip hurray, America! Fuck your mothers', you bastards! Hurray hurray! I love America, hip hip hurray!'

He sang till his vocal cords became strained and his voice dropped to painful pips and squeaks, a mere twittering of a bird.

And yet he sang on, fiercely and passionately till he heard his own whispers in the dark. And then, the sound of silence.

He woke up, not in a dream but handcuffed on a hospital bed. A Caucasian nurse fussed over him holding an injection in her hand, the needle bristling with an overflowing chemical.

She chimed in melodiously.

'Sodium thiopental, the truth serum, dearie! Now you go to sleep again, and tell us all your little secrets, dearie!'

He was transported to another world but even in that world he was sure, rather he was convinced, he was singing the anthem of his life, 'I love America!'

Forty-eight hours after his test began, he found himself in a large airy room, not tied to a chair, sipping a can of Coke, agreeing to a lie-detector test. The needle swung manically on paper, revealing his true state of mind. He continued sipping the can of Coke.

That same afternoon, a grizzled man with a stoop visited him in the garden where he sat in an easy chair reading, or rather looking at, the *Playboy* magazine.

The man without an introduction sat opposite him, looking at him quizzically as a species.

'You can't be real, can you be?'

'Well, I am, old man. So beat it, will you? I think I am done with America.'

The man with a stoop smiled and took his hand.

'You are the real deal, son. You sang in your audition. I don't know anyone who has ever had the guts and the gumption to do that in the "audition". A splendid rites of passage, I say.'

'I don't think I need your approval, old man. Leave me alone to savour the beauty of these provocative playmates…'

'Will do…will do…son….you passed the test. Now, just tell me where you picked up your skill set? Satisfy an old man's curiosity, will you?'

Sunflower folded the *Playboy* magazine and tossed it in the bin nearby.

'After what you did to me, that's an ask. But since you are feeding me and keeping me alive, I will oblige, old man. And I will say it once. The docks in Bombay and the tutelage provided by the smuggler kings of the docks are unlike any other training any intelligence outfit can provide. You learn to survive in that training. Your trainings, even your interrogations, are cliché, propped up by gizmos. That is not real life. Real life moves to a uniquely different beat. We, in the East, understand that. You, in the West, still have some catching up to do.'

The man with the stoop gazed at Sunflower in silence; then he smiled and patted Sunflower's knee and took his leave.

One week after that visit, Sunflower found himself sitting in Freckles' office in the embassy in New Delhi. He watched the man carefully as he slowly paced the room.

After a while, Freckles broke his stride and thoughtfully looked at Sunflower.

'It had to be done that way. To find out the real you.

I am truly sorry about it. I was convinced of your skill sets even when you had seduced the Ambassador's wife. But I had to make sure of your intent. The good news is, we are convinced you really love America. Now, are you ready to work for us?'

★★★

Chapter 42

The world changed in the blink of an eye. US president Fielding realised it was time to go. He could no longer hold on to the reins of power. The wiretapping scandal had sapped his equity, destroyed his credibility with the public, the media, and with politicians both sides of the aisle on Capitol Hill. He resigned not unexpectedly one afternoon, and his Vice President took charge of the presidency.

It did not matter that Vice President Douglas Smithson was from the same party as Fielding. With Fielding's removal, the entire tone and tenor of the new administration changed. So did its priorities. New power centres and power brokers emerged. Old ones got replaced.

Around the same time, the Mujahideen launched a fierce attack on a Soviet convoy of military vehicles in the Panjshir valley. Though the Mujahideen launched an attack with outdated weapons, and despite suffering several casualties, they destroyed dozens of Soviet armoured personnel carriers and killed scores of Soviet troops.

One of the most remarkable aspects of the attack was how the untrained Mujahideen banded themselves, brilliantly using sticky bombs, Molotov cocktails and primitive weaponry to give a knocking to Soviet might and pride.

The two developments rang alarm bells in major world capitals. Tele printers relaying secret communication, messages and code began chattering incessantly. Intelligence heads ordered reviews and called strategy meetings. Section heads of intelligence gathering units were summoned from all over the world to Washington.

Freckles was no exception to the frenetic activity. He was asked to board the first flight from New Delhi to Washington.

At Langley, Freckles met his old boss collecting his hat from the concierge in the foyer of the main hall. He looked pale, not his usual robust self.

Freckles could not help but ask his boss.

'You don't look well, Sir. Hope everything is in place?'

Joe Stanstedt wore his hat with a tilt and weakly smiled.

'I have seen better days, Freckles. Well, everything's changing around me, rather has changed. The world's turned upside down for so many people. I can't be an exception. You no longer report to me, Freckles, you have a new boss now.'

'So, I am given to understand, Sir…'

The old, dying spymaster placed his hand on Freckles shoulder affectionately.

'Watch your step with them, Freckles. They are reshuffling the cards there. In a card game, different cards have different values. Sometimes a seemingly lower value card holds the key to the game. You would do well to remember that.'

A little later, Freckles was ushered in to meet his new boss, a career officer who had been sidelined in the earlier dispensation, a man with a point to prove.

Roger Fairbanks was blunt and to the point in the short meeting.

'We are spicing things here, Freckles. I don't need to tell you that. We are clear on our priorities, some of which are new ones. You are the section head for India. But, you also look after Pakistan and Afghanistan, well, at least temporarily. I will assign new heads to those countries eventually, but that could take some time. And time is what we don't have. What are your thoughts about the Mujahideen attack on the Soviet convoy?'

'Brilliantly executed, Sir,' replied Freckles without hesitation. 'They accomplished their task with raw courage, ingenuity and not much else.'

'Well put, Freckles. And that's the point of this meeting. If a bunch of sheep farmers called Mujahideen have given the Soviets a kick in the pants, imagine what they could do if we train them, and equip them with Stinger missiles, bazookas and M18s. They could cripple the Soviet army. But that's not happening. Know why, Freckles?'

The new man on the job leaned forward, wagging a finger accusingly at Freckles.

'Because the Pakis won't play. All roads to the Afghans cross through Pakistan. But the Pakis can't get their minds off India. They are still not doing enough for the Afghan cause even though they agree with us in principle. I wonder why, Freckles?'

Freckles knew it was not so much the Pakistanis that were under the scanner but him. He would have to navigate between treacherous waters if he were to keep his job.

'Here's the thing, Sir,' began the section chief. 'To co-operate with us fully, the Pakistanis will have to divert and reallocate major assets and resources from the India front to the Afghan front. If they do that, they would naturally feel vulnerable. They are still hedging their bets about this move. I am trying to persuade them…'

The new boss cut him short.

'You still don't get it, do you? The priorities in Washington have changed. Fielding and Priya Kaul could have been India-Pakistan. They had mutual hatred for each other. Fielding's gone and the new President elect gives a hang about India. That country is a basket case. No one cares about Priya Kaul in Washington. Her government will probably collapse under its own weight soon. We have eyes only for Afghanistan. Because the sheep and opium farmers in that country are our best bet to kneecapping the mighty Soviet army which in turn will splinter and break up the Soviet Union. Is that not clear to you?'

Freckles ignored the reprimand and moved in determined to put in a word.

'India cannot be underestimated. It is a major military power and has a fledging atomic power programme…'

Roger Fairbanks burst out laughing.

'Their nuclear programme! Are you nuts! They don't have the balls to make the bomb. They know perfectly well we will wipe them off the world map if they even have the temerity to think so! In any case, the Canadians supply them with uranium, and we get regular briefings from them that the Indians are model and textbook practitioners of peaceful uses of atomic energy, or whatever shit that means. Look, Freckles, you need to stop looking in the wrong places and develop a spine! Let me lay it out to you in clear terms.

'I couldn't get careless about these three categories of brownies we deal with. The Indians smell of curry and coconut oil, the Pakistanis of chicken kebab and the Afghanis of skewered lamb! That best describes these three sets of actors in that part of the world. What do we care if the Pakis and the Indians keep lobbing shells at each other or if we use the opium-drug money of the Afghans to fund and fuel insurrection against the Soviets?

'The endgame is to kill as many as Soviets as possible

without blowback to America and without our boots on the ground. In the process, if all three categories of brownies kill and maim each other, well, be my guest!'

There was nothing more to be said after that. Freckles looked closely at the new species in charge of intelligence gathering in Langley. He felt the bile come up in him. But he also knew his career was on the line. He would have to comply, there was no escaping that.

He gave a guarantee to the new boss. 'I will get the job done fast, Sir. Come what may. Rest assured, Sir, it will be done.'

★★★

Chapter 43

There was something about winters in Delhi in the mid-seventies. It was the best time of the year in the city. There was a crispness in the air and affability in the warmth of the winter sun. There were the red star of Bethlehem and string lights-dotted landmark restaurants and retail outlets in Connaught place. Delhiites, clad in woollies, mufflers and the in fashion and anti-establishment corduroy trousers and coats, thronged restaurants like Ramble in the middle of Connaught circle, Volga and United Coffee House in the outer circle. The movie theatres in this zone were also playing the latest potboilers from Bombay and Hollywood to attract cinema lovers. Regal cinema was screening a Raj Kapoor film, Plaza cinema was handling huge rush from the mega release of *Sholay* and two blocks away, Odeon cinema screened *Deewar* in the morning and matinee shows. Only Rivoli cinema, situated not very far from Regal cinema, was playing a Hollywood masterpiece, the Marlon Brando-Al Pacino starrer, critically-acclaimed *The Godfather*. The film had arrived rather late for a limited release in India.

It was not only restaurants and cinema that reflected the winter and Christmas spirit. A lot of discounted book pop-ups spread over pavements appeared this time of the year. One could as easily lay hands on an old, florid issue of a *Debonair* magazine or a *Penthouse*, as one could bargain a *Ulysses* by James Joyce lying cheek by jowl with *The Outsider* by Jean-Paul Sartre. Connaught place had something for everyone in the winters.

The Embassy official car dropped Sunflower and Freckles at Janpath, and the two men walked the distance to an outlet euphemistically called Depaul's coffee.

Freckles treated Sunflower at the well-known coffee bar. The two men munched veggie (potato) patties and drank Depaul's cold coffee in the frigid weather.

There was an awkward silence between the two. Freckles frowned and tossed the emptied Styrofoam cup in the bin and came to the point.

'Good coffee. Could give a run for money to a Starbucks coffee vent in downtown Washington. So, Sunflower, my man, I have an assignment for you. I wanted to discuss it with you. I want you to infiltrate into Pakistan, specifically Islamabad. You will tap a source in the ISI to do a job for us.'

If Sunflower was surprised, he did not show it. His

face was expressionless as he continued sipping his coffee. He took his time to reply.

'Of course, Boss. If that's the job, it must be done, it will be done. Rest assured. Can I ask how do I make passage into Pakistan? The Pakistanis would not be too hot in giving a visa to an Indian national seeking to spy on their premier intelligence agency.'

Freckles could not help but smile.

'You are a smart guy, Sunflower. I have no doubt you will find a way. The only help I can give you is, an intelligence operative of the US embassy in Islamabad will give you the keys to a safe house in the city. Other than that, you would be on your own in that part of the world.'

Sunflower shrugged his shoulders.

'And the job?'

Freckles carefully looked at Sunflower. 'You will find a source in the ISI and persuade it, by whatever means you wish to, to tell you the real reason why the Pakistanis are dragging their feet on Afghanistan. Understand this, Sunflower. Priorities in Washington are different now. We are in an existential war with the Soviet Union. We will not rest till we have broken them up. The Afghans and the Pakistanis are essential to this puzzle. India is not. It is an outlier in the scheme of things.

'One more thing. There are far more experienced operatives than you to do this job, both in New Delhi and Islamabad. But you hold an advantage over all of them. You are an unknown entity in the scheme of things. And, pardon me, you are also a brown man. Indians and Pakistanis in that sense are indistinguishable. A white or a black American operative from the embassy in Islamabad will stand out for trying to tap into the ISI. On the surface, we share a great rapport with the Pakistanis. But we know, deep down they hate us. They do many things behind our back. Plus, the ISI has a file on almost all our personnel, both in New Delhi and Islamabad. But not on you. I am sure of that. That is why you are the perfect man for the job.'

Sunflower replied with all seriousness, 'I am listening, Boss.'

'Good. Let us enjoy the winter sun. Walk with me.'

They circled behind the Janpath building housing the Depaul's coffee outlet. It was a relatively quiet area where the crowds thinned out. Freckles led the way to the back of the building. It was deserted. The two men faced each other under the overhang of a metalled staircase that went up to an office block.

'There's this other thing, Sunflower,' spoke Freckles. 'This is a very critical assignment. And it has a timeline. We need results as of yesterday. Time is of the essence here. Washington is extremely anxious. Your first major assignment under my watch will not be an easy one. Not because you can't do it. I am completely confident you have the skill set to complete the assignment. But at some point in the assignment you will get conflicted.'

Sunflower looked his boss in the eye. 'Can you be more specific?'

Freckles briskly replied, 'You are an Indian at the end of the day. And some of the work you will do for me, will make you feel a traitor to your country. That is the dilemma.'

Sunflower looked down at his scruffy shoes. He made a mental note to polish them for next time. He looked up smiling.

'Did I not tell you I am a citizen of the world? And a citizen of the world has no allegiance to anyone but to his or her own self-interest. So, quit worrying, Boss, on that quarter.'

Freckles response was a whiplash, 'Stop horsing around, Sunflower. Don't give me Miss World responses. This is a serious question. You will face an ethical dilemma at some point. What will you do about it?'

Sunflower looked his boss squarely in the eye. 'My turn to ask you a question, Boss. Why do you think I am working for you? Have you not figured it out or are you pretending?'

'What the hell are you talking about, Sunflower?'

He replied deadpan, 'I am doing this job for love, Boss. Yes, I need the money and the 'I love America' bit is all too real. But there are considerations higher than that. I am doing this for love.'

Freckles face took on a harassed, complex hue. 'What

shit are you talking about? What's love got to do with it? And love for whom…'

Sunflower moved closer to Freckles. 'Love for you, Boss. You think I am not aware the way you look at me. And, as for me? I was aflame with desire when I first saw you. You were the one I knew. Hand on my heart. When they drugged me, tortured me day and night and inflicted punishment on me in Virginia, do you know what kept me going? I dreamt that one day I would be near you. That is what kept me going. That is what keeps me going…'

And then, without permission Sunflower gently caressed Freckle's face and kissed him under the staircase in the waning light of the day.

For a moment, a stillness descended between the two men.

And then, Freckles savagely hit Sunflower in the face and sent him staggering under the staircase.

Bloodied, Sunflower slowly got up and came out of the dark of the staircase, standing in front of Freckles, risking more punishment.

'You have already checked me out, Boss, haven't you? You know every episode of my life, my life's curveball journey. You know I am an abandoned child raised by missionaries in a Bombay orphanage. You know what I am all about, Boss. The kind of man I am.

'Similarly, Boss, I have also checked you out. And surprise of surprises, you are also an orphan, a child abandoned in a dustbin in the Bronx. We share a bond, Boss, an invisible line runs thorough us, joins us, we are…'

Freckles simply exploded, 'Shut the fuck up, you dirty, brown bastard! Shut up, shut up! You and I…'

Freckles choked for words. Anger coursed in him. It maddened him.

'You fuck, evil-smelling, curry-eating bastard, you and I have nothing in common! Nothing, do you hear me! There is only the job and nothing else! Get to work and deliver results, you scum, gutter rat, filth of a man…'

Sunflower looked beyond the man in the fading evening light. He felt a sense of peace irradiate him. For the first time in his life, he felt cared for, a person on someone else's mind and a man who evoked desire in another with an unreal intensity. He could hear a music of the universe, low in pitch, rising in intensity, reaching an apogee of majestic cadences and notes. He was blessed to have found true love, blessed that it was not a one-way street obsession, blessed that perhaps there was light at the end of a very long, interminable tunnel.

He wiped the blood off his face with his coat sleeve and walked out of the quiet, dark corner in the fading light.

★★★

Chapter 44

One Monday afternoon, at 3.30 pm, a small team of scientists supervised by Dr Iyer achieved the aspiration of the Indian Prime Minister in the CIRUS reactor. They assembled a nuclear device with a yield of 12 kiloton. However, only a real test, of course, would prove the efficacy of the yield. But the assemblage certainly achieved one thing. It proved that Indian determination, when put to the test, could be extraordinary, unbeatable and path breaking.

It did something else. It wiped the slate clean of past national disasters, failures and embarrassments. The smudge on national character created by the defeat at the hands of the Chinese in 1962 lessened in density. The past humiliations of one of the richest countries of the world succumbing to the machinations of the invaders, both Mughal and the British, became a smoke-filled memory and not a living ember.

The creation of the device was also an expression of

a new-found Indian confidence and collective effort. It showed that India also mattered in the world.

A feat, a success story, the end of a journey—so many ways to describe what had been achieved. But in the end, the tears of a young scientist on the team described it the best. He had wept when they had armed the bomb. And he gave his reasons, 'However much I might achieve later in life when I grow old, it cannot and never will compare with what we achieved here. It was the end of an era of inferiority. It was the dawn of a new age of "We can, when we want to." We felt like pioneers on top of a summit. We felt like winners looking down on the world. It was a giddy feeling. I felt proud to be an Indian at that moment.'

★★★

Chapter 45

Rhino stepped out of the Prime Minister's residence and walked down the gravelled driveway outside. He badly needed a smoke. Within forty-eight hours, his world had soared to an imaginative stratosphere that boggled the mind. They finally had their nuclear bomb. It was ready to be set off. What an announcement India would make to the world!

And then, in less than another twenty-four hours, the dream crashed. There would be no more talk of a nuclear test. No more talk of the bomb. No more talk of an outrageous move by India to shake up the world and take notice of it. Because dreams die first. Outside the residence, a flower-decked cortège had arrived to take the still body from inside the house to the cremation grounds. A steady stream of mourners, all dressed in white, thronged the estate grounds. Political slogans of immortality were being raised by activists on the street.

Rhino's hand shook as he lit a cigarette. The nicotine cleared his mind, and he absorbed the shocking turn of events. Prahlad's still and lifeless body lay on the floor of the main hall in the house. Priya Kaul, dressed in white, sat beside the body of her son caressing his face, her face stripped of all emotion. Kamini was in a state inside the house. She refused to come out and face the reality of her altered life.

Rhino could not stop trembling as he deeply inhaled the nicotine. He had come a hair-breadth close to death. He could not understand his own feelings and emotions. What was tearing inside him the most? That a gut instinct had made him decline Prahlad's insistence in the morning that Rhino co-pilot the Cessna 140 with him? He remembered the early morning phone call so well. Prahlad had called him up, asking him to accompany him on a joyride in the Cessna over Lutyens' Delhi. Prahlad was gripped with a strange excitement. He wanted to show off to Rhino some recently acquired acrobatic skills in the Cessna. A warning bell had gone off in Rhino. At the best of times, he kept a safe distance from Prahlad. More so, when he was proposing something outrageous.

He also knew Prahlad was not a certified pilot. Not that it would have prevented him from taking over the controls of the plane, if he got that in his head.

Rhino excused himself, and Prahlad, determined to try out his acrobatics, dragged in a flying club instructor as his co-pilot. They had taken off from the Safdarjung air strip.

That fateful morning, Prahlad had resorted to push his piloting skills to its limits. At one stage, he took off almost vertically up in the sky. How high and far up he could go?

It was both a real and a metaphorical test for him. He wanted to break a barrier he had set in his mind. But, like Icarius, he ultimately failed in his quest. The Cessna engine stopped working in the vertical climb up. The plane plunged and dropped like a stone in free fall.

Prahlad saw the face of his own death as he plunged to the ground.

Rhino knew in a sense what lay ahead because of a famous death. Probably, the dream of exploding a nuclear device had all but been killed. All the torturous long hours put in by the scientists, their back-breaking race and efforts against time, their endless personal sacrifices, disturbed personal and family life—all that was down the drain.

And why was his mind taking him to such a dark place? Because he knew the mind of his protégé, the only woman he truly loved in the world with all his heart, Priya Kaul. With Prahlad's passing away, and the end of the Kaul dynasty and its vice-like hold of the Indian body politic, Priya Kaul could never be inspired again. She would drift away into nothingness. End of story. He was convinced.

Dr Iyer joined him outside the residence.

'On a day like this, I wish I had a smoking habit. Just to take my mind off things for a moment. So, what do you think really happened?'

Rhino contemplated a reply. 'We will never know for sure. You know, Venkat, I was supposed to be on that plane. A gut instinct made me refuse the joyride. The president of the flying club, that poor bastard, filled my place. He is also dead. Nobody mourns him.'

Dr Iyer put his hand around his friend's shoulder. His voice dropped a notch, 'Thank someone up there for small mercies. You know, Rhino, I hate to say this, but there are many people in the country celebrating this screwball's death. There's a rumour going around that it was not a mechanical failure that brought down the plane. Mid-air his co-pilot was trying to prevent him from doing those stunts. Some say there was a struggle for the controls. Who knows? All I know is there's more sympathy for that president of the flying club than for him.'

Rhino simply shrugged his shoulders and continued smoking, looking in the horizon. Dr Iyer asked him a relevant question, 'So, it's the end of the project, isn't it? All that hard work…to no end, really…all gone to waste…'

Rhino took his time to answer. He stamped his cigarette butt and told the senior scientist, 'Yes, it's the end of the road for the bomb project. No doubt about it. I guess, you can start preparing the team for the disappointment.'

There was no dignity in Prahlad's death. No one felt remorse, pity or empathy in the passing away of the angry petrel of Indian politics. Many people in the country, especially those who had suffered at his hands, celebrated his death. In some quarters, fireworks went up in the sky in celebration.

Nazir mian, whose member had been rendered useless in a sterilisation camp at Turkman gate many moons ago, broke into a dance when he heard the news of the crash over All India Radio.

In the elite Malcha Marg area of Delhi, the scion of an old, rich, reputed family of Delhi, Seth Tarun Bansal was sipping his morning tea on the balcony of his spacious bungalow that fateful morning. He saw the plane shudder as it passed above his head, spinning out of control, going in for a nosedive. Then he lost sight of the plane. Later, when he came down for his breakfast, he heard the news of the fateful crash on the radio.

Seth Tarun Bansal's reaction to the news was extraordinary. He rushed to the prayer room in the house and barricaded himself within. He prostrated himself before the deity and thanked a higher power. He cried and laughed at the same time. The events of the day told him that the wheel of justice turns for everyone. It had turned for him. The last two years, Prahlad had harassed him no end to sell off his bungalow to him for a pittance. For the simple reason that the bungalow was isolated and not far from the ridge which was a jungle essentially, an ideal location for his *Ayash ghar* or pleasure house. A place where he could throw outrageous parties and cavort pleasures of the flesh. Seth Bansal had resisted the buy over. In return for this resistance, he had been slapped with income tax notices and false charges. His premises was raided and he was threatened with MISA.

Seth Bansal did not know how long he could hold on and face the fury of a vengeful state. And then suddenly, everything changed for him in the morning.

The irony of him watching a man who had tortured him no end hurtling in a steel coffin to his death! What would have been the last thoughts of that man in the plane? Would he have felt remorse, perhaps regret, certainly fear, as he must have known his end was near.

He would never know. And he did not care particularly.

★★★

Chapter 46

The inert body was placed in the hearse, taken to the cremation grounds and consigned to the flames. A ritualistic mourning accompanied the final rites. Men and women who knew him, some who admired him, and many more who despised him, they all came and mourned his passing away. It was ritualistic as they all mourned the same way, they all voiced the same expressions of grief, and even sobbed very much in the same way.

After some time, Priya Kaul could bear it no longer and she locked herself in her room. She shut her mind and closed her ears to what was happening outside her room.

She lay on the bed and her mind began throwing pictures she could almost visibly see.

For some reason, she saw Prahlad not as an adult. Images of young Prahlad filtered through her mind. A young Prahlad, full of beans, always up to mischief, always in the thick of things. He had taken a fancy as a kid to an imported toy car big enough for him to sit in and drive around. His dream was to set up a world-class, small car factory on the outskirts of Delhi. Images of young Prahlad flashed through her mind like stills from a projector. The time when he had injured his toe, and he ran to his mother seeking care and caresses of her affection. Or, the time when he smiled beatifically for the camera, his hair smoothly parted, wearing his Sunday best, holding onto his mother's hand.

And then, that aperture of light in a dark room slowly dimmed and closed. A pithy darkness descended. She could see nothing, hear nothing, an enormous weight pressing down on her. Her tears dried and she felt lonely, completely alone, not even a flicker of hope anywhere to break the darkness of her mind.

And then, the pain of his last moments on earth hit her from nowhere. It was almost as if by a twisted miracle she could see him, feel him desperately fighting the controls of the plane to steady the aircraft. She clearly saw the fear in his eyes, his low screams, and a last picture of him shielding his face and eyes as the ground fast came up. A hope that he would survive the crash and, maybe if he shielded his face, his nose would not break, his eyes would not be bloodied, and his jaw still intact after the impact.

A sliver of hope till the very end. After all, he was the prince of India and his life could not end in such a stupid, outrageous, needless accident. He had to survive this, he must survive it, of course, he would survive it.

That imagery played in Priya Kaul's mind again and again like a stuck reel, till her exhausted mind told her enough.

But even then, sleep would not overtake her exhausted body. She lay in the dark, looking up at the ceiling. Staring at it no end.

***

Chapter 47

Sunflower finally came up with the name he would zero in on. Fauzia Hasan was a middle-aged personal secretary to the ISI Chief, General Ishfaq Khan. Fauzia was the keeper of the General's secrets. She knew about every conversation the General had ever had, the intelligence secrets locked up in a bomb-proof, steel-encased underground facility, all his contacts, his supporters and detractors. She knew more about the General, than he knew about himself. And there was a good reason for that. She was super-efficient, akin to a human computer before the age of computers had dawned. And then, there was also the fact that she serviced the General in a very specific manner that pleased and gratified the General no end.

The General was susceptible to the pleasure of the flesh but of the kinkiest kind. Maybe once a week, the General and his secretary would head to an ISI safe house in the Muree hills. Once there, the middle-aged, plump secretary would transform herself into the General's fantasy. She would do a role-play of a widow, or sometimes a woman in a torn saree fleeing the heartless street chased by bad elements. And, in the fantasy, the General would relish the role of a rapacious, swashbuckling, young buck who would rescue and give shelter to the distressed elder widow, and then take her to bed in the night.

Fauzia knew the fantasy was inspired by a Bollywood film *Victoria no 203*, a film the General was obsessed with.

There were many other varieties of role-plays she would perform. In short, both personally and professionally, she knew the General like no one else.

Stepping away from this lurid chapter of her life, she was the widow of a former intelligence officer in the ISI who, some people believed, had been bumped off by the General no less. All Fauzia had in the world, that special someone she really cared for, was her teenage son studying law at Yale University in the United States. The cost of her son's education was borne by the ISI chief. She did what she did, to support him.

It was this relationship that Sunflower got ready to exploit to deliver the goods for Freckles.

It all started two weeks back when Sunflower infiltrated into Pakistan almost effortlessly. There were routes through thick forest in the Pir Panjal range, desert crossings, tunnels dug up a long time ago, and well known 'donkey routes' smuggling human traffic that made ingress and exit almost risk-free and easy. All this despite the two large armies either side of the line of control.

In Pakistan, Sunflower made tracks to reach Islamabad. He had grown a thick beard and coloured his short cropped hair with a florid shade of henna. He wore thick blue-tinted glasses to completely alter his appearance. Bell bottoms and shirts with floral motifs completed the makeover. The shirts, in the fashion of the times, would almost always be left unbuttoned right down to the trouser belt. Pakistani Punjabi men took to the trend quickly as it gave them an opportunity to show their hairy chests sporting gold chains and silver-studded lockets with peace and cross insignia.

In short, Sunflower deliberately changed appearance to a well-heeled beefy hippie, the kind who studies abroad and returns home to flash an aspirational lifestyle.

Surely this well-heeled hybrid hippie had to be the offspring of wealthy and influential parents. This also meant that the Pakistani police, notorious for harassment of vulnerable sections of society, would leave him alone.

And then there was the matter of a middling staffer of the American Embassy, Alicia Jones. On weekends, the lady would take leisurely walks in the Ayub national park in Rawalpindi which was spread over an enormous acreage. Parks with water-spouting fountains are favourite transactional grounds of intelligence operatives since it is next to impossible to bug and listen in an unregulated environment.

And so, one evening, when the light in the sky was almost gone, Alicia Jones innocently left a sealed packet in the shrubbery. A short while later, Sunflower collected the packet and briskly made his way out of the park.

The packet contained a key to a CIA safe house. The one-room tenement was stacked with modern reconnaissance devices and equipment. There was even a Glock 19 automatic in one of the drawers. More importantly, the safe house was proximate to the ISI headquarters. Seeing is believing. And the safe house was good for that.

The packet left behind by Alicia also contained a Zippo lighter that performed a dual task. It had a tiny storage space, just enough for a microfilm. Whatever was in the microfilm could be seen in the apartment, courtesy a decoding device. The idea was that if future exchanges took place between Alicia and Sunflower, then the Zippo would become the conduit for the two-way exchange of information.

The first piece of microfilm contained names of operational and administrative staff in the ISI with short resumes on them. Fauzia Hasan was an easy pick for Sunflower. Unlike most others in the organisation, she had a level of vulnerability.

Sunflower used all the weapons he had at his disposal to try to crack Fauzia. A long-range telephoto lens, a radio frequency microphone picking up chatter from a distance, psychological pressure mounted through blackmail, coercion and the threat of exposure, the entire arsenal at the disposal of a determined spy was used by Sunflower to get to Fauzia. And even then, it was still touch and go.

★★★

Chapter 48

Fauzia, getting on in her middle years with matronly looks, surprised Sunflower. She had a core of toughness which surfaced up when least expected. She would just not spill out what she knew. Sunflower confined her in her residence and interrogated her for over nine hours. Yet, he almost failed to get what he was looking for.

It all began with another woman sceptical of Sunflower's ability to prise open secrets. Alicia Jones outrightly refused Sunflower's demand to abduct Fauzia's son from the Yale campus, keep him in a safe house, rough him up, and take pictures of the event.

'We don't do that sort of thing in the CIA. No go,' she curtly told him on the phone when he made the request.

Sunflower laughed at the assertion. He softly replied, 'Well, I am a living proof that you do that. You nearly took my nails off, suffocated me with a wet rag on my face, and poured water on it till I nearly copped it. Miss

Jones, you do all of that. Especially to brownies like me. And Fauzia's son is a brownie. So, get on with it, will you.'

She shot back, 'And I am black, you grasshopper! Don't ever talk race with me. What part of "we don't do that" you don't understand? This conversation is over.'

Yet he persisted and finally got to her. And then one night, young Suleiman, Fauzia's son, was abducted from the Yale campus, taken to a safe house, roughed up, and filmed.

Meanwhile, Sunflower mounted an in-depth surveillance of Fauzia at her house. She lived alone, the Pakistani version of the merry and isolated widow. After a week, he knew it was time to bring things to a head. In any case, he had all the material he wanted.

One rainy night, when the heavens had opened above Islamabad, he broke into Fauzia's house. He tied her to a chair and monitored her reaction. She was oddly very composed. That unnerved him, but he quickly came to the point and demanded, 'Answer a simple question, and I will let you go. Why is the ISI dragging its feet with the Americans over the Mujahideen deal? Is someone else calling the shots or putting on the pressure? You need to give me a name.'

She surprised him by laughing in his face. He changed tack. He waved the Glock in front of her face and slapped her.

'Your life is at risk here. And you feel amused by it'?

She laughed some more and pithily replied, 'Do some

more of what you do. I am not afraid. I am a patriot. I don't sell my country down the tube.'

He then finally moved to his next stratagem, a step he was not particularly wild about, but knew deep within that he would have to take. He showed her photos of Suleiman tied to a chair, his face bruised and battered, his masked abductors standing behind him.

The photos got a reaction out of her. She went ballistic. 'You bastard! How dare you touch my son! Who are you? An Indian agent? Free me, and I will show you what a Pathan woman is capable of…'

She struggled against her chair, writhing against the ropes, her face mottled with rage. He whispered in her ear, 'It does not matter who I am, Fauzia. We will never meet again after this. You need to give me a name. Otherwise, your son will die as surely as the sun will rise in the sky in the next two hours. I will then make a phone call…'

She screamed and wept hysterically, struggling against the ropes. She was completely out of control. He moved back and slowly paced the room, waiting for her to reach her breaking point.

Finally, having spent all her energy and passion, she stopped struggling and looked at him in the face. A strange light shone in her face. She whispered, 'Come closer, and I will tell you in your ear.'

Something was not right, and he knew it. But he obliged. She spoke slowly, but clearly, 'We are a family of patriots. If I, or even my son, has to die for this, then so be it.'

And then, she lunged at him and tore at his ear. A spray of blood shot up. He recoiled and controlled his reaction. It would be so easy to repay her with violence. He realised it was not about physically or even psychologically breaking down a person to extract a secret. It was about degrading a human being, blackening the soul of the target, till he or she crumpled from within and complied.

It was a moment of revelation for him, and he knew the next step. He stopped the bleeding with a strip of cloth and dragged a chair up to her. He calmly sat in front of her. He opened a briefcase and took out a cassette recorder. 'I want you to listen to this,' he said.

He switched the tape recorder. The sounds and grunts, the role-play's lines, her impersonation of either a sexually charged dominatrix or of a victim who sells herself sexually for money or security—all that could be heard clearly.

She suddenly went quiet, a pensive look on her face. He moved in.

'I also have pictures to hold up these recordings. So, Fauzia, the question for you is this. You may be courageous to sacrifice your son for your silence, but do you have the courage to look at your son in the eye after he discovers the filth his mother generates in bed to keep her job and fund his studies…?'

She looked at him vacantly. A look of exhaustion

clouded her face. He knew he had won. But it was a bitter victory. He felt the bile come up in him. He had broken down a courageous woman. Whose soul was more blackened and degraded?

He questioned her, and the facts tumbled out.

She told him about the story of Viper and the group of officers within the ISI who were backing him. The constraints holding back the ISI chief from fully co-operating with America's demands. She gave details of the complex Pakistan-India-Afghan Mujahideen equation. She told him the manner Viper had re-organised sleeper cells, especially those located near top Indian army strike units.

His final question to her was also the obvious one, 'So, where can I find this Viper? Give me his present location.'

Fauzia Hasan shook her head.

'He is two steps ahead even of us. He stopped communicating some time back. We are trying to buttonhole him. We will eventually find him. But he has gone dark for the moment.'

★★★

Chapter 49

Freckles could not decide what was more frightening—the face of the Afghani Mujahideen fighter who carefully took out a Stinger missile from the case and adjusted the lethal missile system on his shoulder, or the look on the man's face. Hawk-like eyes that could look right through you, the look of a man easily carrying the weight of centuries-old tribalism and a sense of fierce independence. The man had an air of suppressed violence about him. It would be advisable not to stare back at him.

Or was it foolhardy to be pacing up the terrace of an ISI safe house near Kabul airport, a Soviet-occupied airport in war-torn Afghanistan. They were a small group of people secretly gathered to watch a live demonstration of the Stinger missile's lethality. The American technician who had trained the Mujahideen was in attendance. Standing next to him was the sceptical-looking ISI chief, furtively looking at his watch. And to Freckles right, eerily composed, was the legendary Afghani resistance chief, Ahmed Shah Massoud.

They were all looking at their watches. At precisely 2 pm, a convoy of Soviet Mi17 gunship helicopters took off from the airport for reconnaissance and interdiction mission in the mountains. Soon, the gunships were a blip in the sky.

Freckles nodded to the technician, and he issued rapid fire instructions in Pashto to the Mujahideen fighter. The man pivoted the missile system to the disappearing blips in the sky, locked in, and then fired. There was a lag of a few seconds. And then, one of the choppers in the convoy exploded in the sky. Grunts of quiet satisfaction rippled through the men at the safe house.

Freckles carefully looked at the ISI chief's face. There was a look of incredulity on the man's face. He had never before seen such a precise and deadly demonstration of firepower. Freckles could not help but smile.

'You can say it, General.'

General Khan swallowed some spit, and his pride, and spoke clearly, 'Yes, I have never seen anything like this before.'

'And, it can all be yours if you stop dragging your feet,' rejoined Freckles. 'Surely the mighty General can quickly and efficiently deal with a group of recalcitrant and undisciplined officers within his own organisation?'

The ISI chief looked at him quizzically. 'So, you know all about my constraints. Why am I not surprised? Your moles would have penetrated…'

Ahmed Shah Massoud put a hand on the General's shoulder.

'A word with you, *biradaar*.'

The two men walked some distance away across the terrace. Massoud spoke with some urgency.

'I need you to open the supply routes as of yesterday so that the Americans can come in, and arm and train my men. Biradaar, you know perfectly well the Americans are fickle. If there is too much humming and hawing, they could lose interest in this entire situation. Now that would not be in the best interest of both you and me. If you want, I can handle the dissidents within your organisation quietly, without fuss and no questions asked…'

The General held up his hand. 'That won't be necessary, Massoud *bhai*. I grasp the point you are making. You are right. I have been waffling for too long. It will be done. I will clear the passage for you.'

The technician intervened and spoke to Freckles, 'We need to get going, Sir. The reds will start combing operations soon. And then all exit routes will be blocked. Now we wouldn't want that, would we…'

From the far end of the terrace, General Ishfaq Khan flashed a thumbs up sign to Freckles. The CIA station head knew the General was completely in the loop now. Things were finally beginning to fall in place for him.

★★★

Chapter 50

The US embassy car dropped Freckles at a kerb near avenue 3 in the Diplomatic enclave of Islamabad. It was night. Freckles raced out of the car and melted in the shadows of intersecting streets. He backtracked, crossed and recrossed streets and lanes, all the while keeping in the shadows. He was certain the ISI would be tailing him even though there were no discernible signs of anyone following him. He deployed elaborate shake-the-tail-off manoeuvres to lose anyone who might be tailing him to make his way to his asset in the safe house. He could not risk the exposure of the safe house or of Sunflower to ISI agents. But he had to meet Sunflower urgently. There was always a risk that an intelligence agent could be exposed or compromised in this cat-and-mouse game. He had taken the risk. After elaborate circumnavigation on the streets of Islamabad, he finally reached the safe house where Sunflower was holed up.

The apartment was poorly lit, and both men preferred it that way. Freckles stood behind Sunflower. His reflex tone of being short with Sunflower was missing. He placed his hand on his shoulder and softly asked him, 'Have you eaten?'

'No. There is not much in the fridge. Maybe an egg and the remains of a stale piece of bread. I can rustle up an omelette and we can share it. Care for it?'

A moment's silence and then both men laughed. There was some more awkward silence. Freckles was in a mood to push in a conversation.

'We finally got today what we had been after for a long time. Thanks to you. How's the target doing?'

'She will survive. She's still in my custody. I will release her when I leave the city in a few hours.'

'You do that,' concurred Freckles.

Freckles kept his hand on Sunflower's shoulder. His voice trembled when he spoke, 'Turn around, and look at me. I don't want to see your back.'

Both men faced each other in the dark. Freckles ran his hand across Sunflower's face, tracing its contours.

'You are beautiful, Sunflower. You have a god's gift to open and receive, and give your utmost. You are a man of passion. I am not that, and will never be. There are feelings that run subterraneous in me. They rarely bubble over to the surface. Sometimes, even I am not aware of the extent of my feelings. I can't tell you how sorry I am for the way I treated you at the coffee shop in Delhi…'

Sunflower took Freckles hand and gently kissed it. Freckles frame shook as he took a step closer to Sunflower.

'Tell me honestly, Sunflower. When did you know what I felt for you? Was it at the coffee shop?'

'Does it matter?' answered Sunflower huskily. He took his superior officer in his arms locking him in to stir up a slow, aromatic brew of passion and exploration.

They stripped each other of all clothes; Freckles somehow managed to open the fridge door to see in its light every sinew and muscle of the man on top of him, behind him, next to him. It was a wondrous dance of passion in the dark and contrasting fridge light.

Both men could not have enough of each other. Later when they had spent their passion, Freckles unlocked from Sunflower's embrace and crawled to a corner at the dark end of the room. He curled up in a foetal position and wept.

Sunflower ran to him and took him in his arms. Freckles' dam burst.

'My mother was white trash, and my father black. I have only anecdotal evidence of it, but there is proof the world found me bawling, abandoned in a trash can. Imagine a state of being when you cannot trace why and how you were born. A child desperate to survive and be owned by someone. I was born a genetical absurdity. Leper-white skin, freckles pock marking my face and red hair. The absurdity of it all. Whoever said children of mixed race always have beautiful skin? Is my exterior my only pain point? Or is it the fact that my clinical, analytical exterior masks a deep-rooted column of resentment, one that runs through my being? A realisation that I don't resent anger and violence, but carry within me an alternative self, constantly churning with a quiet malignancy. I am never at rest, Sunflower. I am walking contradictions. I am a cry in the dark, for being born in a trash can.'

Sunflower wiped Freckles tears and said, 'My story is not very different from yours. It can't be a coincidence that we have met. We believe in the planetary conjunction of stars in India. Freckles and Sunflower were waiting to happen.'

Both men swapped stories till the early hours of the morning. A refreshing hue was spreading in the sky, and they knew it was time to leave. They quickly dressed up and Freckles was again business-like.

'There's one more job that remains. You and I are now aware that the cyst in the General's bum is this man, code-named Viper. He has some influence within the ISI rank and file, especially among the younger officers. He is intrinsically opposed to the Pakistan-Afghani Mujahideen deal. His focus is completely on India. It is said he marches to his own drum beat and doesn't care too much for the General. He is also known to be extremely cunning, ruthless and capable of outrageous violence. This man can single-handedly derail the deal we have reached with the Pakistanis. The ISI have been kicked where it hurts, so that they do something about him, but I am not too sure. At present, he is operating somewhere in India. We don't know where. You find him and eliminate him for me. No questions asked. Kosher, my friend?'

Sunflower buckled his belt and looked up.

'Understood, Boss. It will be done.'

Freckles put his hand on Sunflower's shoulder. 'What happens in Islamabad…'

'…stays in Islamabad,' completed Sunflower.

Both men exited the apartment after a time gap and melted away in the early morning chaos of Islamabad.

★★★

Chapter 51

Priya Kaul sat in the garden at the back of her residence, looking at a flower bed. She was wrapped in a Pashmina shawl, a cup of Darjeeling tea lying untouched on a side table beside her. It was still wintry outside, but spring was peeking in with its vibrant colours reflected in the garden. It was ablaze with all kinds of colours and the eternal dance of bees and butterflies. But the world had turned grey for Priya Kaul. She could see only a colour of nothingness. She had lost all interest in her work and spent most of her time in the garden, looking at the colours of nothingness.

A slight step at her back. And Rajan affectionately put his arms around her, kissing her on the cheek. 'Mother, you look so frail.'

A tear rolled down her eye. 'When did you come?'

'Early morning. Christine has also come with me. She is a bit jet-lagged and resting. Thought I would come and have a talk with you.'

She kept quiet and only offered him a hand which he took. The warmth from his hand coursed through her. A sense of life fluttered in her, but it was too soon, too transient. Maybe it was just a smudge in a wintrified window. Still no sight of what lay beyond.

Mother and son stayed in quietude. Then, Rajan spoke with clarity, 'Mother, I am going to ask something from you. Please, look at me.'

She turned to look at him in the face. If he was shocked at her transformation, he did not convey it. She had visibly aged in the weeks following Prahlad's demise. The grief of her son's death hung on her face.

He fished in his jacket and brought out, what was euphemistically called, a Nehru cap. The starch white cap was a symbol of a clean politician of a bygone era. Rajan held the cap in his hands with a sense of reverence.

'Mother,' he said with a sense of finality. 'I want you to crown me with this cap. Please, do it. I want to make sure this cap fits. After all, one must wear something that sits well on the person. It took me a long time to accept that. I know after Prahlad's death your centre of gravity has shifted. Well, so did mine. I now fully accept I cannot escape my legacy. This is what I was born to do. I was escaping it, but no more. I am ready to fill in my brother's shoes. Even Christine's agreed on that. We have moved back to India to stay with you, to be by your side through thick and thin. For a man of few words, I have said enough. Now, mother, I want to know, will this cap fit? Will you crown me with it?'

And just like that the colours of Priya Kaul's garden were restored. The mist of greyness lifted. Priya Kaul, once again, found her purpose in life. Her son was beside her now. The sun also rises.

★★★

Chapter 52

The ashtray was choked with cigarette butts. But that did not prevent Rhino from taking out yet another cigarette from his depleted silver cigarette case and lighting it. Dr Iyer could not be bothered that the room he inhabited with Rhino had become something of a gas chamber. The irony of the two men spending so much time together being that there were more chances of Dr Iyer contracting cancer from Rhino's secondary smoke discharge rather than exposure to a plutonium rod.

Both men nervously eyed the RAX receiver set. They were expecting a call from Narang. A call that could decisively change the course of the country's destiny. Narang had earlier briefed both men that the Prime Minister was out of the woods. The older son's decision to pick up the political gauntlet and step into the shoes of his younger, departed brother had brought a smile to Priya Kaul's face. She had stepped back from the brink.

A buzz grew that she would once again greenlight the nuclear testing mission. She wanted to shake up the world and give a present to her heir apparent. She wanted to send a message that she, and her son in tandem, would henceforth take momentous decisions that would stir the world. Never again would she look back in weakness. Because, her son was by her side now.

Was all the speculation true? They would soon know.

The RAX receiver rang shrilly. Dr Iyer picked it and pressed it against his ear. Narang was at the other end.

Rhino watched the flushed face of his friend as he received the news. Dr Iyer put down the receiver and his body shook. He began to cry like a child.

'It's a go,' he managed to say, as myriad emotions overtook him. Rhino, averse to any show of sentimentalism, took it upon himself to come up to his friend and comfort him.

Dr Iyer spoke between sobs, 'I can't begin to tell you, Rhino, how tired and exhausted I am by the effort that I have put in. My team has put in. We are tired out of our minds by the hard work we have put in. The number of small sacrifices we made each day, which have stacked up to this enormous burden, expectation and uncertainty that we have carried with us. And then to be told last minute the project had been disbanded. You can't even begin to imagine how it tore all of us up. And, why? Because Madam was lost in the woods because of the death of her idiot son. And now, that she has come out of them, it's a go. We are monkeys on a swing, Rhino. Nothing more, nothing less.'

Rhino, the ultimate loyalist of Priya Kaul, did not say a word to contradict or support that. He could only think of what would happen or could happen in the next few days. That was all that mattered to him. The destiny of the country hung in the balance. And, only the man sitting next to him crying his heart out, and his own acumen and foresight to almost see and define the future could tilt the scales in favour of the nation. And nothing could disturb that.

★★★

Chapter 53

In the next three weeks, the finest brains in India went to work to climb the biggest hill of them all. A task group of a select few was set up to realise the nuclear testing mission. It was decided to conduct an underground nuclear test to contain the radiation fallout. The location for the test would be the Pokhran test range in the middle of the desert. The logistics, security and the drilling operation for the test was handed over to the army. The Defence Minister of the country was not taken into confidence for the test, but the army chief was kept in the loop. He, in turn, delegated the drilling operation to a senior army commander.

It was a mission birthed in complete stealth, coated in layers of deception. A core team of mission specialists, working under the overall command of Rhino, was entrusted with the job. The secrecy was such that even the core team members did not know what the other person was working on. They were like worker bees in a hive, where the bees perform their individual roles contributing to the overall potency and efficiency of the hive and strengthening the mother bee. No prizes for guessing who the mother bee was.

Priya Kaul chose to keep her cabinet in the dark on all matters related to the test. In any case, she always reposed her faith in senior bureaucrats, rather than the ministers in her cabinet. It would not be off the mark to say that she was almost contemptuous of them.

Since Rhino headed the overall operation, it was incumbent on him to address the troops as well. After the mission was greenlighted, he met the task force in the task force operations theatre located in an underground bunker, right below the offices in South Block. The location of the warren of offices was South Block's best kept secret. Rhino, in his trademark taciturn, emotionless manner, soon came to the point.

'Make no mistake about it. If the true intent of what we are planning comes to light, the Americans will bomb the project to smithereens either from an aircraft carrier stationed in the Bay of Bengal or from their frontline fighter aircraft taking off from a Pakistani air base in the northern sector.

'That is what is at stake here. They will not tolerate a nuclear armed India.

'Now, here is the challenge. We cannot prepare for the underground nuclear test in the open. Or, at the very least, be seen to be doing so. As all of you know, we have to drill a vertical hole in the desert and insert a shaft that goes 300 feet deep. The nuclear device will be placed at the bottom of the tube and the top will be covered with sand, gravel, gypsum and other materials. What I am trying to say is, the drilling will have to be camouflaged so that American spy satellites do not pick up anything from the air.

'And so, gentlemen we will launch operation "The Buddha is awake" to masquerade our efforts and realise our purpose. It will be the most deceptive, false flag operation that has ever been launched in this country. Ostensibly, we will stage a joint artillery and armoured corps exercise in the same spot we intend to carry out the nuclear test. But, the exercise will not feature real tanks or field guns. Decoy tanks and artillery will be placed in the desert. All this equipment requires massive covering and other paraphernalia. The drilling of the shaft will be held under protection of these covers. Most of the drilling will be carried on in the night. From the air, it will appear as if massive artillery-armoured corps exercises are being planned.

'I repeat myself. We can only succeed if we retain our ability to remain silent and be deceptively unseen. If not, we will lose the game even before we have begun. If that happens, then we will be emasculated by the Americans in ways I shudder to even contemplate.

'This is it, gentlemen. Any questions?'

A junior scientist, looking quite intrigued, raised his hand.

'Why the esoteric name of the operation "The Buddha is awake"?'

Rhino, in his cut and dried tone, answered, 'Because three weeks from now, it will be Buddha Purnima. The Buddha will awaken when we conduct the nuclear blast. Now, the Buddha is resting. Whether the Buddha rests or awakens is the prerogative of the gods. As ordinary men, we will maintain radio silence. Think of yourself as a submarine—silently, stealthily travelling the ocean floor, hunting for an enemy ship. If that protocol is broken by anyone in this room, I will personally eliminate that person. No questions asked. I can assure you of that.'

★★★

Chapter 54

The drilling operation went on without a hitch. Buddha Purnima was fast approaching, and the false flag operation miraculously escaped detection from prying eyes and inquisitive minds. But, it was too good to last. Four days before Buddha Purnima the cover was blown away of the operation. It happened quite by chance. The dreaded American satellite did not blow the cover of the operation. It had indeed picked up preparations for a military exercise in the Thar Desert, and the findings were shared among analysts in the South Asia department of the CIA. The analysts were not too worried about it. Since military exercises in isolated terrain were almost routine in many parts of the world, the Americans thought that the Indians were testing artillery weapon systems and mobility of tank formations. The size and scope of the exercises from the air appeared to be mid-level so there was no threat that Indian armour was amassing to attack

Pakistan. The Americans reviewed the findings and dismissed it as routine.

Beneath the veneer of the exercises, the drilling continued at a frenetic place and even the nuclear device had been inserted in the shaft. The countdown to the blast had begun.

The temperature in Jaisalmer was on the rise. A sleeper agent inserted by Viper in Jaisalmer stepped out of his home to grab a cup of masala *chai* (tea) and to pick up local gossip on city happenings. A popular *dhaba* (makeshift restaurant) down the road was just the place for that. It was a popular rendezvous for many singletons who would land up there to while away their time, play cards, drink tea and gossip.

The sleeper agent arrived at the dhaba, ordered a cup of tea, and picked up a local rag, pretending to read it. All the while keeping his ears sharp for any scrap of information that would come his way. A group of camel racers arrived at the dhaba and occupied the charpoy next to him. They ordered tea and took out their smokes. One of the men in the group loudly complained to the others,'My business is under severe pressure. The army has set up an exclusion zone, and we have been told to stay off it. Tourists have been banned from the area. *Dhanda paani chaupat ho gaya hai* (business has folded up). We are daily wagers. What will we do if the tourist inflow dries up?

'I have seen many army exercises before this. But

this one happening right now takes the cake. They keep working throughout the night. The place is floodlit in the night and strange drilling noises can be heard for miles around. Wonder what they are up to?'

The sleeper agent folded the rag and quietly left the dhaba. Soon, the same information was relayed to Viper's second in command, Mushtaq who, in turn, quickly apprised Viper of the new development.

Viper decided to personally check out what was going in the Thar Desert. He arrived early evening and took charge of the situation. Viper was not travelling light. He had brought with him a large trunk, securely locked. Mushtaq suspected the trunk was crammed with automatic weapons. Something was up in the air, he could not put his finger on it, though.

Viper instructed the sleeper agent that his home would be used as a base camp of sorts. The three-storey house was in an isolated part of the city. It was contiguous with the desert so it was a strategic location. In case of an emergency, a man could disappear in the folds of the desert without a moment's delay.

The sleeper agent, being a bachelor and a local, solved many problems for Viper. He was instructed to be the logistics man for the three-man group. He would cater for the food, keep a look out and, since he was familiar with every inch of the tough terrain, guide Viper to the best spots in the desert to mount surveillance on the ongoing military exercises without fearing detection.

Mushtaq was instructed by Viper to manage the base camp at home. This meant he had to quickly familiarise himself with every nook and corner, room and staircase in the house, every vantage point and even the vulnerable corners. In case of detection of their hideout, Mushtaq would quickly and efficiently lead their exit out of the house and into the desert. And if the situation turned ugly, then they would have to fight their way out.

Mushtaq had a question for Viper, 'Fight with what? I just have a Glock automatic with me.'

'Open the trunk,' commanded Viper, tossing a key his way. The second in command opened the trunk and its contents took his breath way.

There were six Sten guns in the trunk and dozens of magazines to keep them going. A metalled box was stuffed with grenades. Plus, a cache of Glocks and knives completed the arsenal. A machine was tucked along with the ammunition.

'What's that?' asked Mushtaq.

'That's a latest model telex machine to transmit data to Islamabad. We can even send a wire photo, if the need arises. I noticed, there is a telephone connection in the house. Plug in the telex machine to the telephone wire.'

Mushtaq noticed that was not all what was contained in the large lead trunk. There was a locked compartment at the bottom of the trunk. He pressed on.

'And, what's in that compartment?'

'Whatever is in that, is none of your business, Mushtaq. I will handle that. You have the firepower for an unforeseen exigency. Once you set up the telex, we are in business. Now, get moving.'

Later, when the sun set, the sleeper agent led Viper through the desert to a vantage point behind a sand dune. This was just outside the exclusion zone from where he could see the bright lights of the military encampment in the Thar Desert.

Viper and the scout dug a foxhole in which Viper burrowed himself along with the necessary equipment needed for the surveillance. He set up a tripod and inserted a top of the line 35 mm Canon SLR camera on it, embellished with a 400 mm prime lens. He looked through the view finder. He could spot some movement of men and equipment, but not much. And then, eerie sounds of drilling rent the still desert air.

It was no use taking pictures in the night. He would have to do that early morning, at the crack of dawn when the light was good. But looking at the buzz of activity in the far distance, he felt something was amiss. He had a feeling in his guts, a show within a show was going on.

He reached for his rucksack which contained chocolates, dry fruits, a canteen of water and even a Glock automatic, if the need arose. He had everything he wanted.

He turned and looked at the scout in the eye.

'Go back, and wait for me. I have no idea how long this will take. I have infinite patience and tremendous stamina to survive the desert. Keep a look out, and tell Mushtaq to hold the fort and trust no one. Now, off you go.'

Viper settled in to wait out the night. Something was completely off. There were so many civilians mingling with army personnel in the far distance. He had to find out what was going on.

★★★

Chapter 55

Early morning, when the light improved, Viper went to work with the camera. He took rapid fire snapshots of the test range. Through the viewfinder, he could see the turret of a tank with men milling around it. But there was something odd about the tank when viewed from the viewfinder. Was it a case of desert optical illusion, or was it something else? A strange dissonance unsettled him.

Two events unfolded in quick succession. The sky had started darkening rapidly, spreading a giant shadow above the undulating sand dunes. The wind had considerably picked up speed and a wall of dust was quickly building up in the distance. An *andhi* or a desert storm, common in the Thar, was fast approaching across the horizon. Viper burrowed deep in his foxhole, prepared to ride it out. He put the cap on the camera lens to protect it from the intense wind heading directly his way. It was then he heard a rustling sound. He found a saw-scaled snake, the dreaded Viper of the Thar, staring back at him.

He felt no fear staring at the venomous snake. He was not in the mood for ironical humour that his reptilian namesake had appeared just when the entire place would be submerged in tonnes of sand. The prospect of the snake sharing his foxhole with him and the storm blowing around him was not a pleasing prospect. In fact, Viper felt anger stir in him.

It was a question of who struck first. The reptile attempted a strike in the space between Viper's eyebrows. If it had been successful, it would have surely blinded Viper. It came very close to achieving that. Missed, perhaps, by a millimetre. But the human Viper was faster, with more deadly intent. He caught the snake just below its head, its fangs writhing uselessly and, in the inverse case of man attacking a reptile, Viper savagely tore at the snake below the head with his teeth and spat away the decapitated body and its head in two different directions.

The andhi struck with full force at that time. Hot, burning sand swept into Viper, scalding him, inundating him, tearing into every pore and crevice in his body. In a matter of seconds, Viper was submerged in a column of sand. He quite simply could not breathe.

Was it the end for him? The world went dark and quiet for him. He was entombed in sand. His brain told him that it was for less than one and a half minutes that he could hold his breath. That was the outer limit.

He could perish even before that.

His mind was a factory of images. He clearly saw his Apa. He saw her lying in the field with men on top of her. She looked at him, silently speaking something he could not hear, as if imploring him to run away. Rage suffused him. He could not see his wife or his daughter. He could only see Apa, and what they did to her. And he knew he had to survive this thing.

He went still and willed his racing mind to calmness and moved his hands looking for his way out. His hands closed in on the camera tripod. Working feverishly, he burrowed his way out of the sand using the tripod as a shovel. His lungs were bursting when he emerged from the tomb of sand. The desert storm had blown away, the skies were blue once again, and the military camp was shimmering in the distance.

Though he was unsure, an object lying on the ground in the far distance caught his eye. He frantically dug through the sand and his hands closed on the camera case. Miraculously, the camera had not been damaged in the sandstorm. He mounted it on the tripod and brought up the magnification. He looked through the viewfinder and his blood ran cold. The turret of the tank he had taken snaps of earlier was lying on the ground.

★★★

Chapter 56

Viper half-walked, half-ran his way back to the base camp house. Dusk was falling and the house was shrouded in semi-darkness. The sleeper agent opened the door for Viper and in the dim light of the inner courtyard, Viper could make out Mushtaq pacing the floor, a Sten gun slung behind his back.

The sleeper agent had an air about him as if he had followed Viper's instructions to his best ability.

The man smiled at Viper, welcoming him.

There was a whistling sound behind Viper's ear and a large circular hole erupted on the sleeper agent's forehead. He went down.

Viper dived to his left, and Mushtaq, in the inner courtyard, brought up his Sten gun. A burst of gunfire erupted from two ends. Mushtaq trained the Sten from behind a cover in the courtyard. The assassin outside the house let loose a fusillade. In the crossfire, the assassin momentarily lost track of Viper's movements.

Dusk gave way to an inky blanket in the sky. Viper circled back behind scrap machine objects deliberately kept outside the house to provide cover. Ghost-like, he weaved his way through a rusted thresher, a worn-out, Standard car and even a row of junked up, agricultural tools strewn all over the place.

Viper silently came up behind the assassin perched up on a Khejri tree. He broke the assassin's arm, relieving him of his weapon. With the other arm, he pinioned the assassin in a vice-like grip. He could have easily broken the neck of the assassin but chose not to. He whistled to Mushtaq, to give the all clear signal, and both men tied up the assassin and dragged him to the house. Something was going on that he was unaware of. He was determined to find out what it was all about.

The sleeper agent was buried at the back of the house and Viper then returned to work on the assassin in a manner that redefined brutality. The man was hung up between two poles and Viper made incisions on the assassin's stomach. Then, very carefully, he plucked out the man's intestines bit by bit. The room was drowned in horrific screaming and guttural cries for help and mercy. But Viper was not moved. The assassin passed out many times, only to wake up covered in blood, his lower abdomen on fire. It was agony in hell.

After a while, the man pleaded to his tormentor to end

his life. But Viper was strangely silent. He just went on doing what pleased him the most. The walls of the room were sprayed with blood. The man had been reduced to a stinking vegetable, still alive, but only just.

After a while, Viper put his tools on a nearby table and wiped his hands with a rag cloth. He dragged a chair near the man and began his interrogation.

'Okay, Indian agent, I will give you a reprieve before you die. This is the only reprieve you will get. If you tell me the truth, I will cut your throat with a single slicing and end all this. But, if you lie to me, I will keep this up all night. Choose wisely and well. How did you track me down, and who gave you the orders to assassinate me?'

For a moment, the only sounds emanating from the tortured man was pitiful groaning. Then, silence gripped the room. Suddenly, the dying man started laughing maniacally. He groaned again from the wracking pain but then again it seemed he was possessed with a desire to laugh like a madman.

Once again, Viper's blood ran cold. He knew he had made a fatal miscalculation. But, he had to know. To be sure of it. He got up and came up to the tortured man.

'What's so funny?'

The dying man looked at Viper in the eye and whispered softly to drive home the knife.

'Are you really worthy of A-wing of the service, Viper? The great Viper, who cannot distinguish a fellow

Pakistani from an Indian, who is so blinded with hatred that he has no clue that he has put to stake a man from the same service he comes from, taken out the guts of a man who works in the same section as he does? Viper, are you for real? Were you once a noteworthy agent, but now no better than an apprentice in a butcher's shop, cutting meat? Do you not know why I came after you? Do you not know who gave the order?'

An iciness claimed Viper. He was utterly calm, collected and yet spread thin. He knew the sinking truth which the blabbermouth would soon tell him. But it still did not add up. Something was still missing.

Viper's tone softened with a hint of pleading.

'So, the boss sent you?'

The dying man contemplated his response. Suddenly, he felt kindred connect for the man who had put him on death's skid row. He wanted to help the man and not leave him in protracted, unsure hell. After all, Viper was a legend of the service. So many younger officers like him had joined the service, inspired by Viper's feats.

The dying man began to babble.

'Yes, our common boss sent me. To end you. Because you have become the single biggest hindrance to the Pakistani-American deal to arm the Afghan Mujahideen against the Soviets. Know this, Viper. If you were to go back to Pakistan, they will seal your fate with an ordeal worse than mine. All doors are closed for you in Pakistan.'

Viper absorbed the knowledge of his being declared persona non grata. He gently asked a last question.

'You know well, as I do, there is always a man behind a man. Who has been feathering their nest? Who is the one man playing the boss?'

By now, the dying man was breathing like a stuck pig. His eyes were bulging out. But he still felt empathy for his tormentor.

'Again, you know the answer, but pretend not to. Only the Americans can squeeze our balls. And the American who has been rattling our cage is a CIA case officer, nicknamed Freckles. He is their station chief based out of Delhi. He holds the key.'

The dying man went silent and slumped. Viper stood still for a moment and then caressed the dying man's face a last time. He took out his knife and placed the sharp edge against the man's heart.

'I have done you wrong, my friend. I deeply regret it. But it is time to end this. Travel well, my friend.'

Viper pushed in the knife and the man groaned a last time before going still. Viper knew everything around him had changed completely. So much to do, so little time.

★★★

Chapter 57

Viper allowed himself a moment of reflection before he began the endgame. He could not help but think of Salma and Dua waiting his return home. However, that door was shut for him forever. A dying man never lies. He knew the junior officer from his service had spoken the truth. He could not go back. Next steps? He had to start the endgame. He had to try one last time.

He made the call he had never imagined he would end up doing. He was unsure who he hated the most in the world. Would it be his eternal enemy India, or was it the Americans? Yet, here he was, calling up the CIA station chief in New Delhi, Freckles.

Freckles picked up at the first ring. He knew how the call had been routed to him, and it could have only been the work of an intelligence agent. He had a pretty good idea who it might be. The man against whom he had given a kill order. It was a stunning development. What could have led to it?

The two men, separated by hundreds of miles, had their ear to the receiver. Neither made the first move to talk. Finally, Viper relented because he was on a timeline.

'You know who I am, don't you?' Freckles tossed the answer couched in a question in his mind. He quietly responded,

'I might know. Why are you calling me? There is nothing of interest we share with each other.'

'You are so wrong, Mr CIA man,' replied Viper. 'By a quirk of fate, we now share a commonality of purpose. You don't want to see a nuclear armed India. We also certainly don't want that to happen. But that is the path they have chosen. Thanks to you, I have been declared persona non grata in my own country. And so, no one will listen to me in my own country. And certainly, not my own service colleagues. So, I have no choice but to turn to you.'

Freckles cut in.

'You are beginning to bore me. I don't have time for wild talk…'

'Don't cut the call, or you will regret it forever!' barked Viper. 'Listen to me carefully. What if I tell you that anytime now, and certainly in the next twenty-four hours, the Indians will test an underground atomic device in a place called Pokhran in the Thar Desert? You better believe it!'

Freckles felt lifted off his feet. What the hell was this man talking about? Was he completely insane as it was rumoured about him. Or the dangerous entity that he was, he wanted to trigger something cataclysmic? But what if, by remote possibility, he was correct?

There were no easy options for Freckles when he absorbed the shocking news. He was only sure of one thing. He could not show his incredulity to this potently dangerous character.

'I don't know what you are talking about. I know the lengths you went through to route this call to me. And I did you the courtesy of listening to you…your bullshit, I mean. Your conspiracy theories are of no interest to me. So, I am…'

Viper spoke with menace, 'Shut up, Freckles, and listen to me very carefully. This morning a sandstorm hit the Thar Desert. You can confirm that. There is an ostensibly Indian military armoured corps exercise going on in the Thar Desert even as we speak. I know, your spy satellites would have picked up the activity. And I am dead certain, your lot would have dismissed those army exercises as routine.

'What if I told you your analysts have been completely fooled? What if the Indians are conducting a false flag operation under cover of this exercise? And, what if I told you they would be very soon conducting an underground nuclear explosion? Will you then simply accept this Indian fait accompli? Will you not launch a strike from the American armada in the Bay of Bengal against this country that plans to go nuclear? Will you, or will you not?'

Freckles ran out of patience.

'Listen, you fucking nutjob! Not everyone is crazy like you. Where is the proof of this so-called test? If something was going on, our satellites would have picked it up!'

Viper chilled Freckles with what he said next.

'I have the proof, Mr Freckles. I have photographs which shows the turret of a tank lying on the ground after a sandstorm raged across the desert this morning. A sandstorm however powerful cannot blow away the turret of a tank. Unless, of course, if the turret was made of flimsy wood. This means all the tanks and the artillery packing the test range are flimsy plywood painted over to look like the real thing, much like your sets in those western cowboy movies, all the buildings, saloons, and bars made of flimsy plywood.

'And so, the question you should really be asking, Mr Freckles, is why would the Indians do that? Why would they mount this deception? Unless, of course, they have something to hide. Maybe, they are drilling a shaft in the ground to conduct an underground nuclear test.

'I have also heard drilling noises. Maybe now, you will ask me for proof, a sound recording of those drilling noises? Is that what you are thinking, CIA man?'

Freckles ignored the sarcasm. He could feel a shivering possess him. He tried to sound casual about what he felt.

'There is something known as a wire photo. Send those

photos to me. I will take a call on what needs to be done next.'

'That is out of the question.'

'And why would that be? Are you not sure of your work, or is it one of your deceiving games? Or, quite simply, such photos don't really exist? What is it, Viper?'

'I am not sharing my intelligence with you because I don't trust you, Freckles. Probably, you are behind my kill order. Why would I trust you? More relevant, this intelligence is the only leverage I possess in the world. I am a man without a country. But still, a man passionate about my belief that I cannot allow India to win. I know, it is difficult for you, but see it from my point of view.'

Freckles thought about it for a moment. Then he proposed, 'Maybe you have a point of view. So, how do you want to do it?'

Viper was quick to answer.

'There is only one way to resolve this. Send in your man to me so he can verify what I am saying. That man will come to me on my terms. If he has intelligence contrary to mine, then both sets of evidence will be compared and shown to your superior officer for him to take a decision. I don't trust you to take the right decision. We will then have a three-way conversation, you, me, and your superior officer in Virginia. That's it, then. This is the only deal on the table. And remember, the clock is ticking. The Indians could initiate a nuclear test any moment. If I were you, I would hurry up.'

'What guarantee do I have that you won't kill my agent?'

Viper knew he had got the CIA officer where he wanted him. He replied firmly, 'There will be no guarantees, there never are in this game. You know that. Stop wasting your and my time. If you keep on waffling, time will run out for you. Is that what you want, Mr Freckles? And then, will you be able to live with the infamy that you saw the writing on the wall, yet chose to do nothing about it? To be the man who stopped the Indians in their tracks when you had the opportunity, or not to be the man who betrayed his country which had resolved never to allow India to be nuclear armed—that is the only choice, Mr Freckles. Surely, you know that.'

★★★

Chapter 58

The two men met in a room in the American Embassy one last time. It was the same room where Freckles had met Sunflower many moons ago. Talk about life coming full circle. It was early morning and the manicured lawns outside the room were ablaze with colour and the song of spring. Freckles stopped pacing in the room and looked up. Silhouetted against French windows in the room, Sunflower saw only worried lines on the man's face instead of the disarming freckles. Freckles put the proposition on the table.

'How do I say it? I have no choice, but to send you on this mission. There is too much at stake here. In all probability, Viper is deceiving us, but if even a grain of what he has said is true, we will have no choice but to launch a strike against the Indians. So, I need a man out there who will tell me the truth about what is going on in the Thar Desert, someone who is competent, fearless and thinking on his feet, a man who can get the job done.'

'I am honoured you chose me for the mission, Boss.'

Freckles voice choked, 'You might not come alive out of this. Viper is a dangerous animal, an assassin. And then, you will be asked to choose against the country of your birth. You understand my dilemma, don't you, Sunflower?'

'There is no dilemma here, Boss, I assure you. If I may, maybe one more time?'

Freckles nodded and Sunflower came up to him, taking him in his arms. Both men gently kissed, entwined in each other, shutting out the cares of the world. Then, Sunflower broke away.

'It has been a privilege to know you, Boss, just in case, we don't meet again.'

Freckles held back his tears and words. He tried to sound business-like.

'I trust you completely, Sunflower. But the assassin is right about one thing, though. We will have to compare two sets of reality. He has photos with him. You will also take photos. Since you are on the clock and there will be no time to process your set of photos, a little device here will help you. This, Sunflower, is what we call a Polaroid camera. It has not yet made appearance in the American market. But it works. We are already using it in operations in Berlin. It processes photos instantly, no need to go to the lab.'

Sunflower accepted the camera, smiled, and saluted.

'Best then I be on my way, Boss. You will know the real

story in a few hours from now. Au revoir, until next time.'

And just like that, the man called Sunflower exited the Embassy, into the beyond.

Sunflower reached Pokhran close to mid-day. He knew what he was looking for. A man from whom he could purchase two fast-running Bikaneri camels. He found him and and paid him more than the market rate. The seller could not hide his surprise.

'What do you need camels for? And, do you know how to ride them?'

'That's my business, my good man. Camel riding? That could be my alternative profession. Don't worry. I will take care of your camels as if they are my own,' replied Sunflower. 'And remember, I am paying you double the market rate to keep your mouth shut and stop your mind from wandering. You have your money. Now, off you go, and leave me to my business.'

As the local man left the scene, Sunflower took charge of the two camels and picked a spot to while away the time till dusk descended on the desert. And as soon as the uncertain light of the day filtered across the sky, Sunflower took charge of the camels. He rode one of them at a fast clip and had the other one trail them. The sun was sinking into the sky and the light was murky and uncertain. He came near the exclusion zone, knowing he would have to hurry before the light went out or else photography would not be possible. However, he also needed the murky light to escape detection from the test site.

Sunflower slung the Polaroid around his neck and pivoted himself between the two camels, resting upside-down, shielded between them. Then, he spurred them to break the exclusion zone and pace as close as possible to the test site. While they plodded on at a fast clip, he took rapid fire pictures, the world turned upside-down for him.

To the outside eye, it appeared as if two camels had strayed near the test site without their riders. As the camels plodded in close proximity to the camp, the military personnel noticed them and fired warning shots in the air to deter them. The two camels quickly reversed and paced away from the exclusion zone to a more friendly territory.

Out of sight of the camp, Sunflower mounted up again, and rode and guided the camels close to where he had purchased them from. The evidence he wanted was in the Polaroid. His job was done. He had been instructed to wait at the gossip dhaba before Viper's man would pick him up. Night had fallen and he had arrived early. He saw a pensive-looking man sitting on a chair, looking out nowhere. He approached him and made his offer.

'My good man, I am in a very charitable mood today. I want to gift these two camels to someone who will look after them well. You look just the man. Take them for free, but look after them as if they are your children.'

With that out of the way, Sunflower settled in to

wait. Close to 10 pm, a beat-up Standard car, driven by Mushtaq, came to a stop near the gossip dhaba, its engine still running. Sunflower braced himself. He walked up to the car and exchanged the password with Mushtaq. Viper's second in command confirmed it and instructed him to sit next to him. As Sunflower eased himself in, Mushtaq tossed a cut-out sack at him.

'Put this on your head. We don't want you to see the way to our place, now do we?'

★★★

Chapter 59

Around midnight, Sunflower entered the lair of the beast. He soon understood why Viper enjoyed a dreaded reputation in the intelligence community. The man might be feral, but his strategic instincts were excellent. His henchman drove the beat-up Standard all over the city of Jaisalmer to shake off anyone who might be in pursuit. Sunflower had no idea where he was being taken to. Finally, they made it to the house at the edge of the desert. Sunflower was taken to the same room where hours ago the junior officer from ISI had been tortured and killed by Viper.

The dead man still hung between two poles. Flies were buzzing all over him, his body in a state of acute decay in the spring heat. The room smelled nauseously of putrid flesh. The walls were caked with splashes of dried blood and gore.

It was a scene out of a B-grade horror film. And yet, it was all real. Viper sat on a chair, feet propped up on a table, a Sten gun in his lap. Mushtaq motioned Sunflower to sit on the chair opposite him. Both his captors were armed with Stens. Mushtaq silently went behind Sunflower to stand guard. Viper eyed the man in no apparent hurry to initiate a conversation.

Sunflower immediately knew it was a chess move. The mise en scène in the room was deliberate. It was designed to intimidate and browbeat him, to make him nauseous, so he could quickly agree to their terms. He noticed the man's eyes staring at him. There was something inhuman in them. But even the eyes of a beast reflect contrarian emotions at times. He was sure there was just a hint of vulnerability in those eyes. He would have to trigger that vulnerability and exploit it.

He opened a conversation.

'Nice place you have here, Viper. It's smelling of roses. And the hygiene is laudatory. So, how do you want to do it? Shall we talk business?'

Viper shrugged playing the game. Sunflower waited for the next move. Both men went silent. Finally, Viper relented.

'You are in no hurry it seems, and then, come to think of it, why should you be? Your fellow Indians will soon explode an atomic device, so you can strut and crow in front of the world. You are a fucking Indian, are you not, despite your deceptive skin colour? I can smell the likes of you a mile off. How did a man like you become a confidant of a CIA bureau chief?'

'Well, you would know something about smells would you not?' retorted Sunflower. 'Growing up around butchers cutting meat would be garden variety for you. So, if we have dispensed with the insults, you want to show me some proof. That's what I came for, remember?'

'You first, you Indian fuck. What kind of photos have you taken in that fancy camera of yours?'

Sunflower shrugged and opened the Polaroid. The photos instantly developed in the camera came out. Sunflower held them in the palm of his hand. He chipped in, 'We show the snaps in our possession simultaneously. Okay?'

Both men held their photos up. Sunflower, in a flippant mood, held them up against his forehead carefully watching his antagonist's face all the while. He made out that Viper was good, but not that good. The colour of his eyes briefly conveyed shock and disappointment when he saw the snaps. They showed tank turrets, several of them, completely intact idling in the sand.

'There is something wrong. A turret was blown off. How can they be intact? Maybe they fixed them quickly. After all, they are made of flimsy material?'

Sunflower leaned forward.

'All I know is, our photos are showing two different sets of reality. Obviously, one of us is wrong and the other one is right. So, shall we show these photos to my boss? Let him take a call? You have a provision to wire these photos?'

Viper thought about the suggestion, then nodded at Mushtaq. He wheeled in a mobile tray containing a connected telex machine. Both sets of photos were taken by Mushtaq and wire photos were sent to Freckles, who was standing by for developments.

In response, the telex phone line rang shrilly. Viper picked it up. Freckles snapped at him.

'I will have a conversation with you, later. First, I must speak to my man. And I am warning you, Viper, if something happens to him, all bets are off.'

Viper held the receiver in his hand and thought over his next move. Standing behind Sunflower, Mushtaq involuntarily tightened his grip over the Sten. All three men in the room felt the weight of unbearable tension. It was the moment of reckoning, a moment of truth. They were a hair's breadth away from the room exploding in bursts of gunfire. Or maybe the possibility of a nation attacked for defying the mightiest superpower in the world. Or perhaps even the grim prospect of two arch-enemy nations going to war. All three options suddenly became real in the room. One badly taken step could lead to a terrifying catastrophe.

Viper took a call, and tossed the receiver to Sunflower.

'Make it short, whatever you have to say. One wrong move, and I will blow your head to bits.'

Sunflower took the receiver and pressed to his ear.

He was breathing irregularly. Freckles, at the other end, asked him, 'What has happened? How is all this even possible? How can a reality change so quickly? What is the truth, Sunflower?'

Sunflower closed his eyes and spoke, 'This is the last time I will be speaking with you, Boss. Because, I know, I will not survive this. So, listen to me very, very carefully. Viper is sitting in front of me, holding a gun to my face. He took the photographs from a distance. The tank turret in his pictures is somewhat blurry. Probably, it was another object on the ground that he mistook for a tank turret. Sometimes, you look at something and want to believe in that desperately. He wants a military strike on this place at all costs. Or maybe his endgame is to ignite a conflict between India and Pakistan. Maybe he is delirious, conniving, or just opportunistic. I say that because I took pictures very close to the test site. I saw those tanks for real.

'Considering the time I have spent with you, know that I will never lie to you. But even then, you must finally judge whose reality is real…'

And then, in a flash, Sunflower ripped the receiver from the telex machine and threw it away. Viper, stunned at the turn of events, was just a little slow to react. His brain told him he should have blown off the man's face even before he had reached his conclusion. A sinking feeling inside told him that his enemy had sacrificed himself to sow doubt in the mind of the CIA officer. Freckles would never listen to him now. The Indian had closed all his paths leading to the American. He could not match the Indian's duplicitous and cunning ways at a time when it mattered the most.

An inhuman rage built up in him like a vortex. He would tear this man to bits. But even then, he would be left insatiated. He had to inflict the pain of a lifetime on this man. He brought up his Sten gun to blow the Indian to bits.

★★★

Chapter 60

A few hours ago...

While Mushtaq was driving Sunflower all over the Jaisalmer city, the Indian Prime Minister, along with her son and Christine, sat down at the dining table to indulge in some pasta prepared by Christine. Rajan had opened a bottle of red wine, and Priya Kaul, already two drinks down, was basking in the afterglow of filial affection they had once again discovered for each other. The uneasy relationships, strained and broken earlier, appeared as an anomaly of the past.

The happy turn of events would, of course, reach its apogee tomorrow, on the day of Buddha Purnima. Priya Kaul was scheduled to fly out to Pokhran early morning. The underground nuclear test would be conducted at the first light of dawn of a new day. There was excited chatter at the dining table, and all of them forgot that another Kaul was in the house, brooding in her room. Kamini, for reasons best known to her, had come to stay in the house of her late husband for a few days. Did her visit bridge the gap that existed between her and her mother-in-law? Not in the least. It yawned bigger with each passing day.

The Kauls raised their wine glasses to a toast, and Kamini walked to the dining table unannounced. She was swaying from drink which she had in her room. She clapped loudly and walked boldly to the dining table, taking a seat uninvited. She took the bottle of red wine and drank straight from it. She sat facing her mother-in-law, the resentment dripping off her.

'At least somebody at this table should have had the courtesy of inviting a house guest for dinner. But then, who cares for normal behaviour in this house, right, mother-in-law? Dysfunctionality rules this family. I should know a thing or two about it, should I not?'

Kamini drank some more from the bottle and continued, 'Look at this family! Dear mother-in-law, in case you have forgotten, your son has been snatched away from you in the prime of his youth. And what do you do? You sit at the table drinking red wine, making merry conversation, waiting for your pasta cooked by a white trash waitress. A waitress who, in record time, has learnt the art of the deal. Chummy up to future mom-in-law and all the goodies in life will flow to you! Well, I have news for you, sister. I will certainly not bend or scrape in front of anyone, especially the likes of my mother-in-law!'

Priya Kaul cut in sharply with authority, 'Kamini, you are drunk, and you disgrace yourself. This is not how we behave at the dining table. Leave the table immediately, and go to your room.'

In response, Kamini drank some more from the bottle, and a laughing fit seized her.

'Look at all of you, so hoity-toity! So serious! You make me laugh, mother-in-law. Well, never mind that. Here's the deal, then. I couldn't care less for the pasta cooked by this waitress. I have come to claim what is mine. I believe, you are off to some jaunt tomorrow in Rajasthan. After you are back, I want you to publicly announce that I, Kamini Singh, widow of Prahlad Kaul, will officially be taking charge of the youth wing of the party! I know all about your devious plans to declare this older, duffer son of yours, as your heir apparent!

'Imagine that! He does not even know or understand the first alphabet of politics! Prahlad and I built the youth wing of the party together. We sacrificed so much...he sacrificed his life...and now it is only right his widow gets her due. That's the long and short of it. Right, mother-in-law?'

Rajan could have sworn at that moment that his mother resembled something excavated from centuries old tomb, cold, lifeless, yet menacing.

Priya Kaul slowly got up and came up to Kamini. A mocking smile was beginning to grow across Kamini's face. It was out of place compared to what would happen next. A binyeo pin held Kamini's long hair in a kind of knot, euphemistically called, a chignon. In quicksilver movement, Priya took out the binyeo pin from Kamini's hair and threw it away. It made a loud clattering sound as it fell on the marble floor. Kamini was too shocked to even understand what was happening to her. Her long hair, as if in slow motion, danced through the air like a dervish. Priya caught her hair with extraordinary strength; Priya Kaul stood transformed. She was a spitting image of an angry goddess, her eyes lit with fierceness. She looked murderous. She jerked at Kamini's mane lifting her off her seat at the table. She spun the mane and crashed Kamini on the floor. She spat it out. 'You don't deserve a seat at the table. Not now, not ever.'

Kamini shrieked and struggled uselessly as Priya Kaul dragged her across the floor, out of the drawing area, and past the main door with extraordinary energy. The security staff outside stood in shocked silence, unable to say or do anything, as Priya dragged Kamini across the driveway all the way out of the main gate.

She deposited a kicking, screaming, and howling Kamini outside the gate and shut it. She looked over the gate, her voice followed like a whiplash, 'You are out of our lives. Never again have the temerity to look at my house and my political party ever again! Never again will you step in this house. You were trash that Prahlad picked from outside the house, and that is where you go back. If you ever look in again…'

Kamini suddenly looked at the woman transformed in front of her. Her eyes blazed with anger; her hand a fist ready to strike. Kamini shivered as fear coursed through her. She could not look into the woman's eyes. It was not her mother-in-law who stood at the other side of the gate. It was some unearthly entity that was vindictive, revengeful, and ready to strike.

***

Chapter 61

Present day

In his moment of crisis, Freckles found his way out. He resisted the impulse to immediately call up the central command in Virginia to report the developments at Pokhran. He wanted to toss over the issue of conflicting realities in his mind. He wanted to look at the issue from all angles before making the call. The real question, he knew, was not whether India was deceiving the world about its intentions behind its nuclear programme. The real issue was that, despite a stuttering, almost comatose, economy and a near-authoritarian leadership, India was neither a country in Africa, nor a small island in the Pacific. It was a nation of a multitude of people proud of their civilisational heritage. It was too huge to be treated like an errant child who had to be punished.

And assuming India had crossed the line, what then? Would flattening of a test range and a nuclear reactor in

Trombay stop the Indians from trying again?

What then made America different from Britain that had colonised India not so long back?

Part of the issue was also American exceptionalism, was it not? The overriding belief in keeping things simple, in trusting the old dictum—'either you are with us, or against us'. The world, he knew, did not particularly run on a diet of Coke, John Wayne and a trigger-happy belief in 'Hang them high!'

And then, there was the personal aspect of the altered reality. Why should he believe a man like Viper, who was paranoid in his hatred for India? Why should he not put his trust in Sunflower, who had put his life at stake for him to achieve the mission? A man who, he knew, loved him passionately.

Was the issue then not of geo-politics, but a question of the intensity of love and hatred? And, why should he not choose love over hatred?

And finally, what was the coda, the real, hidden meaning of reality? Was it limited to only national reality and interests? If so, then the issue would not be that America destroyed an Indian test site or a nuclear reactor. Rather, it would be whether India could ever forgive America for their action over the next hundred years.

Reality was not two sets of conflicting and confusing photos. Neither was it a state obligation. Reality was the imprint of a man based on a lifetime of varied experiences.

It would be different from person-to-person. It was shaped by passion, not simply cold logic.

Sunflower, he knew, was passionate about him. He was a man in love with him. He would go to the ends of the earth for him. The photos were his imprint, borne out of passion and love for him.

★★★

Chapter 62

How do you escape a bullet coming towards you? How do you hold off the grim reaper urgently knocking at your door? A visitation of death, not even a foot away, looking at your face. Viper fired the Sten gun aiming it at Sunflower's face. Sunflower escaped, not because he was an acrobat, but because he was a child of the Bombay docks. Ever since he had learnt early to fend for himself, he had been dodging bullets—sometimes from rival smuggling gang members, sometimes from the police.

And so, Sunflower dodged Viper's furious salvo. It took a chunk out of his ear, but still found its mark in another body. Mushtaq went down, a part of the salvo ripping into his abdomen. More than the pain, it was the look of shock and surprise on Mushtaq's face. The man he had come to idolise in such a short period, had shot him.

The misappropriation of firepower did not, in the least, stop the two combatants from trying to rip each other apart. Viper fired again but the Sten jammed, a common occurrence with the Sten gun of the seventies. Viper threw it away and, in a flash, he took out a blade and slashed at Sunflower. The boy from the Bombay docks responded by unsheathing his own knife from his belt and lunging at Viper.

Thrust, cut, serrate, slice. In the blink of an eye, both men had opened hundreds of cuts in each other in a wordless fierce duel. A fine mist of blood particles hung in the air. Small geysers of blood erupted. But no question of a respite for both. They parried, cut, and opened each other's body parts with venomous ferocity.

Even in a state of intense excitement and overflowing adrenalin, the brain processes reality. Viper could not but be impressed with his opponent. This was not an ordinary antagonist he was facing. He more than matched him in hand-to-hand combat, in the art of survival when facing death. His brain also told him that uncontrollable anger would eventually finish him off. In the end, all fights ought to be strategic and not visceral. Only fools made it a do-or-die issue of honour and anger. He had to survive the fight to complete one final objective.

Stopping the underground test was out of his control. But he still had some leverage left. That would be his final legacy, his ultimate imprint on this world.

This meant he had to withdraw and race up to the top floor to realise his objective. His opponent could be damned for all he cared. He would, in any case, not survive what he had in mind.

Viper made a deceptive movement pretending as if he was lunging forward, but in reality, he pivoted himself to escape through the door at the back. His next move deceived Sunflower of his true intent. He went out, slammed the door after him, and bolted it from the outside.

He breathed easily and realised it was the best decision he had taken. The game was still on for him.

★★★

Chapter 63

Early next morning on Buddha Purnima day, Sunflower betrayed his friend, lover, and boss Freckles of his true intent. India successfully conducted an underground nuclear test in the wastes of Pokhran in the Thar Desert. Perhaps Sunflower's role in the entire affair will remain a footnote of history, but it is an important one nonetheless. He led the Americans up the garden path, deceiving them of his real intentions.

He used Freckles to paralyse and confuse the American thinking and intent. It was not a sense of duty that made him do that. He played a high stakes game of deceit and deception, out of love and passion.

To understand the man and what he stood for, it is essential to carefully look at the snapshot of the man called Sunflower. There is so much there in the snapshot which was all true, but there is much else in his background which had never surfaced.

In the end, an illegitimate child, who grew up in the docks of Bombay, rose to rescue the country from a deadly fate, from the vengeful long arm of the Americans.

A snapshot of the man called Sunflower…

★★★

Chapter 64

8 years ago

Twenty-two-years-old Flight Lieutenant Vikramaditya Singh aligned the single-seater Sea Hawk fighter aircraft with the short runway of the aircraft carrier *Vikrant*. He could see the catapult lying in wait, and even the tail hook. He steadied the aircraft, swaying in the stiff breeze. He was fast approaching the deck, the sun in his eyes.

Easy-peasy he thought. 'Done it a thousand times.'

And yet, deep down, he knew despite the number of flying hours he had clocked and the scores of missions he had undertaken, landing the aircraft on the carrier with just a tail hook to snag the holding wire, has always been an adrenalin-busting, fearful, yet joyful moment.

Vikram landed the Sea Hawk with a hop and a skip on the carrier deck. The tail hook snagged the wire cutting the descent of the aircraft at speeds close to 150 km per hour to instant zero.

Vikram emerged from the cockpit and took in deep breaths. He would always compare the freshness of the salty ocean air with the regulated air and claustrophobia of the cockpit. That might be the case, but even a day spent without a flying mission would induce severe withdrawal in him. He quite simply lived to fly. Soaring in the sky above helped him forget his past, sordid life. He walked the deck, flight helmet in hand, looking forward to the evening. The aircraft carrier *Vikrant* would soon be docking at Goa for a few days, which meant nights out in town with the boys. That was always something to look forward to.

Later that night, the entire strength of the Sea Hawk squadron, ten navy pilots, landed at a nightclub in Panaji and were soon smashed with drink. It wasn't hard to imagine that if the drinking and yelling continued, then, as sure as rain, some of them would end up in beds of the desirable ladies of the night, some of whom were already in the bar, eyeing and admiring the brawn and verve of the young pilots.

Vikram downed a last drink, killed his cigarette and announced walking back to his quarters. His teammates groaned and rebuked him for spoiling the party, urging him to stay on, promising him a night of unchecked fun. Vikram knew what exactly that meant and he wanted to stay clear of all that. He said his goodbyes and walked out of the bar to the sound of his mate's yelling 'Spoilsport!' He had no desire to foray in late night wild adventures.

He had had enough of that in another life of his.

As he walked down the street next to the Mandovi river, a shadow fell before him. He looked sideways and was surprised to see the man coming up behind him.

'Father...this is a surprise,' he manged to say.

'Hello, Vikram,' answered Rhino. 'Hope this is a pleasant surprise for you. I was in Goa on work and came to know your ship had docked here. So, I thought...'

'Father, it is always a pleasure to see you. You know that.'

'Indeed. Well, my hotel room is just round the corner. Care for a night cap, even though you look quite sloshed?'

Vikram laughed full-throated, 'I will never refuse a drink with you father.'

Both men went up a hotel room nearby and sat on the room balcony, looking out at the river. It was a pleasant evening; both men smoked cigarettes and drank their whiskies. Rhino swirled ice in his glass.

'It's a pleasure to see you fitting in so well...eh...all settled. I have come to know, you are really good at what you do. Well, no surprises there...'

'How do you know, father? You know someone in the navy?'

Rhino laughed an enigmatic smile flitting his face.

Vikram got up and leaned against the balcony, looking at Rhino.

'The past still troubles me, though. It usually comes up at night when I go to sleep. Sometimes, I can't sleep.'

'Best let it go, son. Bury your demons. You have a life ahead of you.'

'Easier said than done, father. You promised to tell me the truth one day. Why not today? I am no longer the kid you took charge of. There are still so many gaping holes in my life story. Maybe I can find my peace if they fill up…'

'Maybe another day, son…'

Vikram went down on his knees and implored Rhino.

'Why not today? Let's not make it a special occasion. I am old enough to absorb anything you tell me. Tell me all the fine, little details that even I am unaware of in my life story.'

Rhino thought about it long and hard, and decided it was time to prise open the seal covering Vikram's life. He spoke matter of fact, keeping the emotions out.

'I first met you at St Ignatius School in Colaba. You were in high school then, and you would have been 15 years old. Something about you struck me even then. You had shifty eyes and a face that had seen a slice of life even at that age. Your fingertips were yellowed, which meant you were a chain-smoker. The occasion was a quiz competition at school. The principal had called me to give away prizes since I was an old boy of the school. I am a Delhi person, but I was on deputation to Bombay at that time.

'What struck me then, was not that you had won the quiz getting all the answers right. It was the way you answered. You had a look of disdain and contempt about you. An air of meanness about you, I distinctly remember. It unsettled me.

'I inquired about you from the school principal. He told me you were a bundle of contradictions. You were razor-sharp, intelligent, but also the most violent boy in school. He then told me of your background. Your Italian mother abandoned you at Colaba church, leaving a note explaining her story. She lacked the courage to take care of you. The church did try to find out your Sikh father. But they were unsuccessful.

'The church gave you to an orphanage which was an extension of the church. They raised you at the orphanage. You must understand how kids turn out in the best of such places. They are on their own and grow up tough, many of them falling prey to the vices of life. You were not an exception. You would eat meals at the orphanage and even attend school, but in your spare time you had started to do odd jobs at the docks. You excelled in your studies and yet you were working for the underworld.

'I still remember clearly, you could wield the knife and a gun with dexterity. You were so good at conning people. I also came to know you had become part of a particularly debauched group where everyone was sleeping with everyone. In short, at an early age, you had become the poster boy of all vices in life.

'I was strangely not repelled when I came to know what kind of a person you used to be then. The question that must be answered is, why was I drawn to you? We had nothing in common. Maybe an early divorce in my life had left me unsettled. Maybe, in you I saw the child I never had. In any case, I frequently visited you and inquired about your progress. You did respond to me, though on your terms. You would take my help, but emotionally you were closed and unapproachable. I remember I tried so hard to reach to you. Strangely, you had become a challenge to me. It was as if my own kid had gone off the rails. I so desperately wanted to restore the balance in your life.'

'Yes, father, I remember those days clearly. I was a different entity then. A terrible person. I am ashamed to think what I was then…'

'No, Vikram, you were not consciously at fault. My empathy and respect for you only increased when I could see you were struggling and trying to break free from your own background.'

'I am relieved to hear all this, father. We should have had this talk earlier. But it's okay. Now is as good a time for this. And then that incident happened…'

Rhino was lost in thought. He then knew the time had come to reveal it all. He would have to address the issue. He could not escape it.

'Yes, son. That incident. You stabbed a person in a Colaba bar and killed him. The inquiry established that you were drunk and raging and maybe a neutral observer would argue that your rage was justified. A so-called friend of yours, also completely drunk, was making fun of your parentage. He went on and on. You told him to stop. He would not listen. In rage, you smashed a beer bottle and stabbed him with the serrated edges. He died instantly on the spot.'

Rhino paused as he approached the truth. He could almost predict what Vikram would ask him next.

'The police saw it differently. They blamed you completely. Since you were a minor, they were all prepared to send you to the juvenile prison, which meant, if that would have happened, your life would be over. You would in all probability have come out a hardened criminal…'

Both men kept quiet. Rhino dreaded the next question coming his way. It was the moment of truth, both for Vikram and Rhino.

'And yet, father, mysteriously, I never went to juvie prison. I was given a reprieve. That incident shook me. I realised the monster I had become. I was given a second chance in life. It brought me closer to you. But the question remains. How did I escape my fate? We can't evade this question any longer. I have constantly thought about it. You must give me an answer.'

Rhino got up and went to the balcony. The city spread all around the Mandovi was ablaze with lights. What was the value of a singular human experience in the larger scheme of things? Rhino was looking for an emotional lifeline. There was none in his consciousness. He told

Vikram what he had to, at one shot.

'You escaped your fate because I am a man of influence. All the policing agencies in the country report to me. They cannot act autonomous to what I tell them to do. I once told you a long time back I was a mid-level bureaucrat in the government. That statement is not completely true. I oversee all the different intelligence agencies in the country. Their bosses report to me and I, in turn, report only to the Prime Minister. My name does not appear on the books anywhere. Think of me as a super adviser to the Prime Minister. You call me father and, for mc, you are the son I never had. That is true. But it is also true that I cannot acknowledge you in public. Your background will come up in the spotlight. I cannot go around explaining to everyone what I feel for you and why I have forged this relationship with you. Maybe someday I will gather the courage for that. But not today.'

Vikram felt strangely relieved when he heard the confession. For some strange reason, he felt like crying. He had never cried as a child. He had grown up in tough street. But he could no longer hold back his tears. Rhino hugged him passionately and kept on repeating, 'I know I have hurt you deeply, Vikram. I will make it up to you one day. That's a promise. But don't abandon me. I need you in my life, son. Nothing will ever change what I feel for you.'

And yet, something did change after that. An ill wind blew and challenged the relationship between father and son. An unthinkable turn of events happened soon after.

Three days later, Vikram took off in his Sea Hawk for a routine flight from the technical strip at Goa airport. He completed his sortie and piloted his aircraft back to base. As he approached the landing strip, the unthinkable happened. Both engines of the aircraft experienced bird hits. The impact was so severe that not only both engines failed, but even the landing gear could not be deployed properly. In a matter of seconds, the plane became a metal, flying coffin.

Vikram urgently radioed back to control tower. Fortunately, his Squadron Leader was in the vicinity. When apprised him of the situation, the Squadron Leader gave a direct order.

'Vikram, you will crash in less than two minutes if you don't eject. Your life is more valuable to us than the plane. Eject, eject, eject…'

Vikram ejected, and felt as if a sledgehammer had hit him at the base of his spine. He felt his spine crumple up. He lost consciousness and parachuted down near the runway.

He was rushed to hospital and taken to surgery. He woke up after two days, confined to a hospital bed. His teammates visited him to boost his morale. They made jokes about him becoming an honourable member of the Martin Baker ejection club. When the jokes died down, and his teammates went back to the *Vikrant* reporting for duty, anxiety gnawed at him. He was left alone. He had received word that Rhino was rushing back from a foreign location to be with him. His mind was taken up by the inevitable medical test that would be conducted after he had fully recovered. If he flunked that test, his career as an ace navy pilot would all but be over.

Rhino dropped everything to be with him when Vikram needed him the most. He helped him in his rehabilitation process. Finally, the time came for his medical report review. He walked in one afternoon, saluted smartly to the medical board and took his seat.

The senior doctor reviewing the report, his Squadron Leader, and a Vice Admiral in the navy sat in the review meeting.

His Squadron Leader asked him.

'How do you feel, Vikram?'

'Absolutely fine, Sir. I am raring to join duty immediately.'

The Squadron Leader looked expressionlessly at the senior doctor, who took it up from him, 'Flight Lieutenant Vikramaditya Singh, I am delighted to know that you have made such quick recovery. Besides the excellent work of the surgeon, your recovery is also a tribute to your extraordinary fitness levels and faith in yourself. As you are aware, in such cases the recommendation of the senior doctor is final. Even the Navy Chief cannot overrule him.

'I am afraid I have some bad news for you. Your examination shows that the lower discs in your spine have severe contusions and at least a couple of them have suffered irreversible damage. It's all there in this report. You do not experience pain because overall you are extraordinarily fit. But over a period, you will be plagued by back pain. You cannot escape that. As you know, the Navy pilot is one of the finest species of human being. You are supposed to be the best of the best—in terms of skill sets, motor functions, cognitive skills, overall physical fitness and, not to forget, in terms of crisis management.

'In short, what I am saying is, now that we are aware of your disabling injuries, we cannot risk another fighter aircraft under your command. These aircraft are hugely expensive national assets.

'Keeping in view the contradictions in your case and the severity of your injuries, it is the unanimous opinion of this board that you be given an honourable discharge from the navy.

'I am sorry, I wish I had better news for you, son. There will be no further review of these medical findings. If you wish though, we can consider a desk job for you in the services…'

And just like that, the board shut the door for Vikram. The job he loved the most in the world, the passion that made him soar to the skies, was denied to him. The prospect of doing a desk job like a clerk, while his mates flew to glory, enraged him. He would have none of that.

Vikram was inconsolable after that. He was in despair. Rhino tried to pull him out of it. And one day, it appeared Vikram had reverted to his old-self of high school.

He shouted at Rhino.

'I ask you, father; I beg of you to use your influence once again and get me my job back. You did it once for me, did you not? You say that you love me. Well, this is the time to show your love, to show you really care for me. You will do it, won't you, father?'

Rhino answered with heavy-handed finality, 'Even if I could do it, I won't go down that path, son. The armed forces are the most sacred institutions left in this country. I won't besmirch their reputation by this outrageous demand. Their order is final.'

Vikram, like the boy of old, raved, ranted, cursed and begged and wept before Rhino, but it was of no use. Rhino left him to find his peace.

Rhino returned a few days later to meet Vikram, who appeared more collected and composed in his passions. Rhino urged him to accompany him to his old school at St Ignatius.

Both men pensively walked the grounds of the school and, on Rhino's insistence, sat down in the shade on a school bench, licking orange popsicles.

'Vikram, I brought you here because I have a job offer for you in mind.'

'I don't want to be a desk clerk, if that is what

you are thinking.'

'Will you hear me out, son?'

'Sure, fire away. What do I have to lose? I have all the time in the world to listen to you.'

'Don't be despondent, son. Hear me out. What I am going to tell you will shock you, but that's the requirement of the job. Ready?'

'Don't keep me waiting, father. You have certainly piqued my interest.'

'Well, Vikram in this job you report to only one person. And that person is me. Your name will be kept off all official records. Your salary will be paid out of a special discretionary fund I control. In a sense, this job require talents and skills that are perhaps even a notch higher than that of a navy fighter pilot. The primary requirement of this job will be to complete it, any which way. There will be none of your military code and honour in this job. You will deceive, lie, cheat, impersonate, fornicate, and even kill to complete your mission. You will venture into enemy territory more often than you sleep on your bed at home. You will have a non-existent family life. You will live only for the mission.

'You will have to be charitable, with both your body and mind. What do I mean by that? You might be asked to sleep with unsavoury entities, both female and male, to get the job done. You might be asked to disappear for months altogether, sometimes even years, to alien lands, or enemy territory. The end goal will be that, like a navy pilot, you will be asked to vanquish the enemy. The only difference being that, unlike a pilot who engages and shoots valiantly, you will kill and destroy by stealth. Stealth and deception will be your coda.

'Now, does the job profile interest you?'

The orange popsicle fell from Vikram's hand. It took him a moment to absorb all this. Then, he got up and faced his father.

'Who are you really? Seriously, should I even call you father?'

Rhino also got up to face his son.

'I am still your father. And I am also the finest and the deadliest spymaster this country has ever seen. Unless, of course, I am surpassed by my own son one day. Which happens to be you.'

Vikram cautiously came up to Rhino and embraced him with passion. He whispered in his father's ear, 'I will do the job, father. I will be the finest ever. I will make you proud of me.'

Rhino replied, 'I know that, son. I have no doubts about that. Just for the record, you will cease to be Vikramaditya Singh from today. Your code name will be Sunflower. And one last advice. You fought for the country in a previous life. In your new life, you will do what you will be called to do out of love and passion. Love and passion for me, your father.'

For the second time in his life, the man called

Sunflower underwent a metamorphosis. He became a ruthless agent beyond compare. He assumed a cover of a low-life, borderline-criminal, a debauched man living off the streets of Colaba. That is how he built a reputation for himself. If anyone checked him out, it would tally with what he really was like at St Ignatius School. By an act of special permission, his identity was wiped off from the records of Indian Navy. His Sea Hawk squadron teammates were sworn to secrecy never to open their mouths about him under the official secrets act.

Rhino and Sunflower agreed that Sunflower's debauched and criminal reputation should travel. That was the reason a real and not a fake FIR (first information report) was filed against him in the Colaba police station.

It was the same reputation that attracted the American Ambassador's wife to Sunflower. Sunflower trapped both the Ambassador's wife and Freckles in a honey trap because the stakes had gone up too high. Rhino was aware that Freckles was greasing some Opposition entities in India with the power of dollar to topple the Priya Kaul regime. But it was not just that. Freckles was the key man who would be sending a report about India's true nuclear intent to Virginia. Based on that, America would decide whether to thwart the test or not. If India's plans were exposed, then nothing was off the table, even a missile strike on the test range and its reactor was a possibility.

But if the test went undetected, then sure hell would

be raised, and India would be sanctioned but the fight would go out of the game. Washington would eventually leave New Delhi alone to its devices.

For all this to happen, Freckles would have to be compromised. And the only man who could do that was Sunflower. He had to play the ultimate game of passion, love and betrayal.

The complicating entry of Viper in the game, and the intelligence picked up by Rhino, courtesy Sunflower, that the Americans had struck a deal with the Afghan resistance, with the Pakistanis acting as broker, queered the pitch somewhat.

But again, Sunflower was the man for the moment.

He played his adversaries out of the game once again. He was still at it when India conducted the nuclear test in the waste of the Thar Desert. In a house in Jaisalmer at the edge of the desert an Indian and a Pakistani were battling it out.

★★★

Chapter 65

Present day

The earth shook as Sunflower found himself locked in the butcher's room along with Mushtaq. Sunflower closed his eyes in relief. He knew immediately that India had successfully completed the underground nuclear test. In the end, it had all finally gone to plan. All the sacrifices he had made, the web of deception he had spun, the game of love and passion he had played—the sum of a man's effort was just the earth shaking for a few seconds and a large crater appearing in the arid waste of the Thar Desert.

Sunflower opened his eyes and steeled himself that the job was still to be done. Outside the room, probably from an upper floor, he clearly heard Viper howling like a wounded animal, screaming guttural obscenities knowing that India had won and its detractors like him had lost.

In a corner of the butcher's room below, another man was dying pitifully and making appropriate noises. Sunflower recovered Mushtaq's Sten and spare magazines from his jacket; the dying man painfully grasped his hand, wishing to speak.

Sunflower decided to hear him out before he went after Viper.

'Say what you must, and make it quick,' he told the dying man.

Mushtaq's mouth was filled with blood, he clutched his stomach till the whites of his hand showed, yet he said his piece, 'I made a mistake trusting that snake. I betrayed my country for him. You might not know, but this is my country also. I converted to please the snake, and look how he has bitten me.'

'So?' shot back Sunflower.

'Please, hear me. Last words of a dying man. Perhaps my redemption in front of Lord Rama will be if I tell the truth. A dying man never lies. The snake has lost, but he is not done yet.'

'What do you mean?'

'He brought a large lead box with him. It is on the top floor. Besides the ammunition and the guns he smuggled in, he also brought with him a chemical bomb with a timer. I discovered it quite by chance. He wants nothing better than to send India and Pakistan at war against each other. If his best bet, that America would launch a missile strike on India, failed, then his plan B is ready.

'He will explode that chemical bomb to wipe out the

city of Jaisalmer. He is sick in the head. Everyone in this city will either be wiped out or will suffer chemical burns for the rest of their miserable lives.

'Go, now, stop him…'

Sunflower nodded acknowledging the revelation. Mushtaq spoke one last time, 'One last thing. I arranged the weapons on the top two floors. You will have to fight your way up to the top. On the first floor, to the room on the right, there is a hidden closet. It is behind a full-length mirror. I have hidden spare ammunition and handguns in there. Go now.'

Sunflower brought up the Sten and fired at the bolts of the locked door. It swung open. In battle mode, Sunflower was once again an ace navy fighter pilot in his mind. The words of the flying instructor at the academy reverberated in his mind.

'The Indian navy pilot is chosen for reflexes and decision-making abilities which are the best in the world. He will be called upon to take split-second decisions against all odds at 50,000 feet altitude. In a crisis, hundreds of options cross his mind. Even faster than a computer, he must choose the right option, exercise it and win! There is no more deadly piece of work than this man!'

Sunflower came out in the courtyard of the house. In less than a couple of seconds, he had devised his strategy. He had to delay arming of the bomb by Viper. He had to draw him out from the top floor. He had to rile him, humiliate him, make him lose control, and then mercilessly eliminate him.

The very next moment, Sunflower was at it. He fired a salvo in the open space above to announce he was out of the room and coming after Viper.

On the top floor, Viper, furiously working to arm the bomb, looked up. His adversary was challenging him. Best to ignore him. His objective was to explode the bomb and not confront him. He smiled and continued to arm the bomb.

Below, Sunflower was only getting started. He bellowed from below.

'You sick, Pakistani turd, I know all about you. Nobody wants you; nobody desires to have anything to do with you, even in your own service. You are an outcast, a misfit, a failed officer who blunders and botches up missions, who sets his country back every time he ventures out. Oh, yes Viper! You are just a scumbag, misogynist, serial-killer who preys on innocents. You hide in the shadows. You lack the guts to fight in the open. Any ordinary soldier can take you down in no time. Your rightful place is in a lunatic asylum, you sick fuck, strapped on a hospital bed with a doctor performing lobotomy on your brain to remove the deranged sections from it…'

Viper's good mood vanished. His forehead furrowed and sweat beads appeared. His hands shook as he feverishly tried to join the wires of the bomb.

Sunflower let loose another salvo from below.

'You hear me loud and clear, don't you, you sick fuck? Well, there's more. I captured and interrogated the personal assistant to your ISI boss. She gave me access to your file. I know all about you. I know about your wife Salma and your kid Dua. I am aware of what happened to your Apa.'

Viper's mouth tightened and he tried to compose himself to finish the job. His face was swimming in sweat. He was having difficulty in fixing the circuit. His training and instinct told him that the Indian was distracting him from arming the bomb. He had to shut out the white noise and focus on the job at hand.

Below, Sunflower was relentless.

'When you die, which will be soon, they create a non-descript grave in your memory in your hometown. And your junior officers, all those you had mentored, they will all go to your grave and take turns to piss on it. Know why? Because you are not a leader of men. You are a selfish, bigoted bastard who has sacrificed so many lives of your protégés to satisfy your pet obsessions. But wait, it won't end there. More hell will chase you. Shall I tell you what will follow next?'

Viper's teeth had begun to clatter, and a fury was slowly building up in him.

Sunflower then struck home with his most deadly cut.

'These juniors will go to your home and take turns to satisfy Salma in bed. You know why? Because Salma wants it. She wants a man's touch. You never satisfied her, impotent bastard, because you were always chasing ghosts in India. You satisfied your pet obsessions in India. She will satisfy herself in another way.'

A guttural scream was building up in Viper and his eyes were bloodshot. He was shaking uncontrollably.

Sunflower delivered the coup de grâce.

'And, here's the best part. Salma will try all positions with them. Can you blame her, the poor thing? She has been deprived for so long. She will have her fill...'

Viper lost it then. He screamed like a gutted animal, stuffed the Sten magazines in his belt and raced out from the room on the top floor. He straddled the Sten in an arc above his head and let loose a full magazine of hot lead below.

The column next to Sunflower instantly exploded with tracer and became pockmarked with the fury of the Sten discharge. Sunflower dived to his left, brought up his Sten and slapped a fresh magazine in it. Responding to fire with fire.

The house at the edge of the desert exploded to the whine of hot lead being exchanged from the two floors. In an instant, the walls were pockmarked with shells and hot tracers flying up and down.

And all the while, Sunflower kept dodging between columns to make his way to the staircase leading to the first floor. He kept firing as he made his way to the upper floor, one step at a time.

And then, a moment of stillness. Both men reloaded and considered their situation. Sunflower was down to his last magazine. Some of Viper's passion had cooled down. He realised he had been manipulated by Sunflower.

He came up to the edge of the staircase on the top floor, going down. He knew there was no other way. A final showdown was unavoidable. It would take place on the floor below him. Viper looked through the vacant space between the intersections of both staircases. And that was when Sunflower made a mistake. He came up to the upper floor, looking at the vacant space, just as Viper, looking down on him from the floor above, fired at close range through the vacant space.

Sunflower tried to dodge the fusillade, but succeeded only partly. Part of the burst from the top ripped into him and hot lead went through his leg and lower abdomen. He grimaced in pain and fired in retaliation, but Viper had taken cover and was out of harm's way. Suddenly, the equation changed once again.

From below, Viper heard the click of the firing pin's empty chamber. He knew Sunflower was empty. Out of ammunition. Time to collar the Indian, and make him pay.

'You are empty, Indian, and wounded. Run while you can. I am coming to get you.'

Sunflower, laser-focused on survival, looked at the only exit available to him. The room at the turn of the skirting, Mushtaq had talked about. He had to get to the room irrespective of his injured leg and his back. He could hear the pounding of feet as Viper raced down from the staircase to the floor below.

Sunflower dragged himself and partly lunged and leapt at the door to the room as Viper appeared on the floor with his Sten. He fired a full magazine, but Sunflower was already on the other side of the door, having bolted it from inside. Made of flimsy wood, the door was pockmarked with gunfire and the bolts at the other end came loose. Sunflower knew the door would not survive another burst of gunfire.

He looked at the full-length mirror in the room and knew this was the moment that would decide his fate. Had Mushtaq send him to his death, lying in his final moments? Or, had he redeemed himself one last time? Sunflower slid the full-length mirror to a side and looked at the closet compartment in front.

Sunflower escaped certain death by a quirk of fate. Viper fired from his Sten gun a couple of seconds before Sunflower discovered a Glock and some magazines in the closet. Viper aimed at the centre of the door knowing well that behind the door Sunflower would catch the full blast of the Sten.

The moment Viper fired, Sunflower, down on knees, was retrieving the Glock from a lower compartment. The fusillade from the Sten ripped open the wooden cover of the door and the blast went above Sunflower's head, pockmarking the wall.

In one quick motion, Sunflower turned and brought the Glock with both hands, before Viper could reload. He fired, and bullet after bullet ripped into Viper, hurling him backward.

Sunflower kicked open the door. Viper lay across the floor railing spouting blood from the holes in his chest. He was holding a small detonator switch case in his hand. Oddly, he was smiling even as death loomed over him.

'You win, Indian, but not quite. You got me back there, just for a moment. My Salma would cut her throat before she would look at another man. I completed the circuit, Indian. The bombs are on the terrace. You cannot reach them in time. See you in *dozakh* (hell), Indian. We will continue our duel there…'

The eye of an Indian navy pilot. There is nothing like it in the world. In Sunflower's consciousness, the roar of the aircraft he was piloting grew tremendously as he aligned it with the snagging wire and tail hook on the deck of the aircraft carrier *Vikrant*. One shot. No room for mess-ups. He would land at one go. No second chances.

Sunflower stood there, his legs akimbo, the Glock in both his hands, looking at Viper sprawled at the railing with the switch in hand, a gallows smile growing on his wasted face. Viper's thumb reached for a toggle switch on the detonator board.

The aircraft was speeding down towards the deck completely aligned with the holding wire.

Viper's hand touched the toggle switch. The aircraft landed instantly, and the snagging wire stretched taut to decelerate the speeding aircraft.

Sunflower fired, and his bullet travelled faster than the time it took for Viper's thumb to push down the toggle switch.

The bullet broke the toggle switch into two and went through the centre of Viper's throat, an expression of shocked surprise on his face.

★★★

Chapter 66

Priya Kaul, Dr Iyer, and Rhino, along with Narang and a top team of senior scientists of the BARC, watched the underground nuclear test from a radioactivity proof trailer-box stationed not far away from the blast site. The earth shook after the blast and a crater appeared, with the Richter scale recording the authenticity of the blast. Other instruments measured its true yield in line with the expectations set for the blast.

By all accounts, the underground nuclear test was a complete success. The scientific talent in that box broke up in loud cheering and clapping once the news of the success of the blast was confirmed. Priya Kaul also cheered along with the scientists, and it is said, only that one time in her life, she stood up and opened her arms and requested Dr Iyer and Rhino to embrace her.

'Both of you made this day possible in so many ways. Thank you, from the bottom of my heart, my friends.

History will never forget your contribution to this valiant effort to uphold the pride and aura of Mother India. Thank you, thank you, dear friends.'

But soon, after emotions subsided, a piquant situation developed. Priya Kaul insisted that she be photographed at the blast site. The scientists would have none of that.

'That is out of the question, Ma'am. Even though radiation levels should be under control, we cannot risk you venturing near the blast site.'

The back and forth continued with the scientists till Priya Kaul snapped.

'Now, all of you listen to me very carefully, I am touched by your concern for me. But ask yourself, why do you think I did all this? Was it simply to make us nuclear enabled? Truth be told, I did it for this one photograph which will be taken, come what may. This photograph will define who I am, what I stand for, and what I am capable of doing. It will send a message to the whole world. Now, out of my way, everyone!'

Priya Kaul strode to the door of the box with a senior photographer from films division in tow. She turned at the door and looked at Dr Iyer.

'Are you too chickenshit, Dr Iyer, to accompany to the blast site?'

The next day, newspaper headlines screamed all over the world,

'Goddess incarnate Priya Kaul conducts India's first

nuclear test in a desert'.

The screaming headlines and the body of the lead story was accompanied by an iconic photograph which has been cherished by a generation of Indians.

The photo depicted Priya Kaul at the blast site, inspecting it, accompanied by an army man and Dr Iyer. Priya Kaul, with her dark oversized glasses, saree *pallu* pulled tightly around her head, the never to be forgotten image of a woman who in her lifetime became 'Priya Kaul is India and India is Priya Kaul.'

★★★

Chapter 67

In the end, when the dust settles down, and the passion and the verve cools down, then the reality bites. Priya Kaul made world headlines with the underground nuclear test. India's standing in the world did go up a notch after the test. But, the political contradictions in India were so severe, its economic situation at that time so fragile, that the euphoria and the outpouring of national pride and goodwill did not last for long. Priya Kaul soon lost the general elections called in the wake of the nuclear test. Strangely, her fate was not unlike Winston Churchill's who led his country with exemplary leadership in World War II but soon lost the general elections held after that.

The day the underground nuclear test was conducted, Freckles realised his career in the CIA was over. He had failed, and he had been betrayed by the one man who, in such a short span of time, had flooded his senses and touched his heart. But, he was not bitter about the whole experience. There had been a growing up for him. He realised he was not cut out for spy craft but for a higher purpose in life. It was time he stepped out of the shadows and emerged in the clear light of the day. Soon after these developments, Freckles resigned from the CIA and left for the United States. He openly emerged as a gay activist and joined the gay pride struggle and movement led by the pioneer gay activist Harvey Milk. He was by Milk's side when Milk was assassinated in San Francisco in 1978.

The man called Sunflower vanished from sight after such momentous events. His invaluable contribution in the staging of the underground nuclear test was never acknowledged. Years later, especially in the ranks of the devout and the faithful, the reputation of one Pahari baba gained huge traction. Pahari baba resided in the foothills of the Himalayas. He led a Spartan life spreading simple and effective message, drawing people towards him from all over to listen to his kind words.

Pahari baba was enigmatically ivory-skinned. He was not mobile, having lost the use of his legs, and moved around in a wheelchair. It was said he was never forthcoming about his past, or how he had lost the use of his legs.

His devout followers, especially those who knew him well, swore that Pahari baba had perhaps loved someone intensely a long time back. It was perhaps a very deep and a moving relationship. The same followers said that often, at nights, Pahari baba would toss and turn in his sleep muttering.

'Know that, Freckles, my love for you was real. But, I followed a higher passion and ideal in my life. I hope you can bring it in your heart to forgive me one day.'

★★★